Claire looked around the tiny, windowless room and felt her forehead prickling with sweat. She concentrated on breathing, angry at her irrational claustrophobia, her fear of entrapment.

Meredith, on the other hand, seemed not only at ease, but in her element. She leaned forward and questioned Detective Jackson as though she were the detective and he a tricky suspect.

"How did you say Ms. DuBois died?" she said suspiciously.

Jackson regarded her with the expression of a tolerant uncle. Claire thought he might even be suppressing a smile.

"I didn't. She was poisoned."

"Cyanide?" said Meredith thoughtfully. There was a pause. Sergeant Barker attempted to catch Jackson's eye, but he was looking straight at Meredith.

"Yes," said Jackson calmly, hiding whatever surprise he may have felt.

"Just a guess," said Meredith, "albeit an educated one."

Praise for *Who Killed Blanche DuBois?*

"[A] wonderful blend of gracious writing, vivid characters, and deft plotting . . ."—Marvin N. Kaye, author of *Bullets for Macbeth*

MORE MYSTERIES FROM THE
BERKLEY PUBLISHING GROUP . . .

CAT CALIBAN MYSTERIES: She was married for thirty-eight years. Raised three kids. Compared to that, tracking down killers is easy . . .

By D. B. Borton

ONE FOR THE MONEY	TWO POINTS FOR MURDER
THREE IS A CROWD	FOUR ELEMENTS OF MURDER
FIVE ALARM FIRE	SIX FEET UNDER

ELENA JARVIS MYSTERIES: There are some pretty bizarre crimes deep in the heart of Texas— and a pretty gutsy police detective who rounds up the unusual suspects . . .

by Nancy Herndon

ACID BATH	WIDOWS' WATCH
LETHAL STATUES	HUNTING GAME
TIME BOMBS	C.O.P. OUT
CASANOVA CRIMES	

FREDDIE O'NEAL, P.J., MYSTERIES: You can bet that this appealing Reno private investigator will get her man . . . "A winner."—Linda Grant

by Catherine Dain

LAY IT ON THE LINE	SING A SONG OF DEATH
WALK A CROOKED MILE	LAMENT FOR A DEAD COWBOY
BET AGAINST THE HOUSE	THE LUCK OF THE DRAW
DEAD MAN'S HAND	

BENNI HARPER MYSTERIES: Meet Benni Harper—a quilter and folk-art expert with an eye for murderous designs . . .

by Earlene Fowler

FOOL'S PUZZLE	GOOSE IN THE POND
KANSAS TROUBLES	DOVE IN THE WINDOW
IRISH CHAIN	MARINER'S COMPASS
	(Available in hardcover
	from Berkley Prime Crime)

HANNAH BARLOW MYSTERIES: For ex-cop and law student Hannah Barlow, justice isn't just a word in a textbook. Sometimes, it's a matter of life and death . . .

by Carroll Lachnit

MURDER IN BRIEF	A BLESSED DEATH
AKIN TO DEATH	JANIE'S LAW

PEACHES DANN MYSTERIES: Peaches has never had a very good memory. But she's learned to cope with it over the years . . . Fortunately, though, when it comes to murder, this absentminded amateur sleuth doesn't forgive and forget!

by Elizabeth Daniels Squire

WHO KILLED WHAT'S-HER-NAME?	WHOSE DEATH IS IT ANYWAY?
MEMORY CAN BE MURDER	IS THERE A DEAD MAN IN THE HOUSE?
REMEMBER THE ALIBI	WHERE THERE'S A WILL.

Who Killed Blanche DuBois?

CAROLE BUGGÉ

BERKLEY PRIME CRIME, NEW YORK

WHO KILLED BLANCHE DUBOIS?

A Berkley Prime Crime Book / published by arrangement with the author

PRINTING HISTORY
Berkley Prime Crime edition / November 1999

The Penguin Putnam Inc. World Wide Web site address is http://www.penguinputnam.com

ISBN: 0-425-17195-7

Berkley Prime Crime Books are published by The Berkley Publishing Group, a division of Penguin Putnam Inc., 375 Hudson Street, New York, New York 10014 The name BERKLEY PRIME CRIME and the BERKLEY PRIME CRIME design are trademarks belonging to Penguin Putnam Inc.

PRINTED IN THE UNITED STATES OF AMERICA

10 9 8 7 6 5 4 3 2 1

For Paul and Katharine

Acknowledgments

First I would like to thank my friend and colleague, Jeff Clinkenbeard, for helping give birth to (and name) Meredith Lawrence. Thanks also to Bruce Edward Hall for the weekends in his wonderful house in Hudson; to Marvin Kaye for his friendship, encouragement, and support; to my editor Hillary Cige and my agent Susan Ginsburg for believing in this book; to Anthony Moore for his companionship on our many upstate rambles; to my siblings for putting up with me all those years; to Chris Buggé, for the steady supply of medical textbooks; to Fritz Capria for his help with fact-checking; to Leona and Cora for their companionship on the trail—and finally, to my parents, for creating an environment that fostered and nurtured creativity.

Erlkönig

Wer reitet so spät durch Nacht und Wind?
Es ist der Vater mit seinem Kind.
Er hat den Knaben wohl in dem Arm
Er fasst ihn sicher, er hält ihn warm
"Mein Sohn, was birgst du so bang dein Gesicht?"
"Siehst, Vater, du den Erlkönig nicht?
Den Erlenkönig mit Kron' und Schweif?"
"Mein Sohn, es ist ein Nebelstreif."
"Du liebes Kind, komm, geh' mit mir!
Gar schöne Spiele spiel' ich mit dir;
manch' bunte Blumen sind an dem Strand,
meine Mutter hat manch' gülden Gewand."
"Mein Vater, mein Vater und hörest du nicht,
was Erlenkönig mir leise verspricht?"
"Sei ruhig, bleibe ruhig, mein Kind,
in dürren Blättern säuselt der Wind."
"Willst, feiner Knabe, du mit mir geh'n?
Meine Töchter sollen dich warten schön,
meine Töchter führen den nächtlichen Reih'n
und wiegen und tanzen und singen dich ein."
"Mein Vater, mein Vater und siehst du nicht dort
Erlkönig's Töchter am dustern Ort?"
"Mein Sohn, mein Sohn, ich seh' es genau,
es scheinen die alten Weiden so grau."
"Ich liebe dich, mich reizt deine schöne Gestalt;
und bist du nicht willig, so brauch' ich Gewalt!"
"Mein Vater, mein Vater, jezt fasst er mich an!
Erlkönig hat mir ein Leids getan!"
Dem Vater grausets; er reitet geschwind,
er hält in den Armen das ächzende Kind.
Erreicht den Hof mit Müh und Noth;
In seinen Armen das Kind war tot.

THE ERL KING

Who rides there so late, through night so wild?
It is a father with his child
He carries the boy close in his arms
He holds him tightly to keep him warm
"My son, why is your face so white?"
"See, Father; the Erl King is in sight!
He stands there in his crown and shroud!"
"My son, it's just a misty cloud."
"Oh, dearest child, come go with me;
many games I'll play with thee;
many lovely blossoms you will behold;
my mother will give you robes of gold."
"My father, my father—why can't you hear
the Erl King whispering softly in my ear?"
"Be calm and tranquil, my child;
it's the wind in the branches blowing so wild."
"Will you come, fine boy, and go with me?
My daughters wait even now for thee;
my daughters will keep you throughout the nights
with singing and dancing and other delights."
"My father, my father, don't you see that face?
It's the Erl King's daughter waiting in the dark place!"
"My son, my son, the face that you see
is just the hollow old willow tree."
"I love you, fine boy; come ride with me on my black
horse;
and if you're not willing, I'll take you by force!"
"My father, my father, hold me tightly to your breast!
The Erl King's icy fingers have me possessed!"
The father shuddered and spurred his horse to run
He held to his bosom his poor fainting son
As he reached his house he was filled with dread:
In his arms the child lay dead.

Chapter 1

The wheels of the train sang like birds. Claire Rawlings gave up on the manuscript she was reading and stared out the window at the river. She had two other manuscripts to read by the end of the weekend, but the Hudson was irresistible, with grey-shaded cliffs giving way to sun-splattered grasslands under a sky full of wispy, violet-tipped clouds. It swelled and curved in front of Claire's eyes, taking her breath away, like a lover who suddenly and unexpectedly reveals himself.

The conductor passed in his shiny blue suit, and the walkie-talkie in his back pocket brushed against Claire's hair. She pulled herself upright in the seat and looked around at the other passengers. It was midweek, and the train was not very crowded. Claire wasn't sure if she felt guilty or not about taking a couple of days off in the middle of the week, but Robert was working all weekend, and this was her only chance to see him. And of course she carried with her the ubiquitous manuscripts—as an editor, she always carried her work with her. Like all editors, she was always backed up with more reading than she could get done during office hours—with phone calls, staff meetings, and lunches with agents and authors taking up most of her work day.

Across the aisle, a small red-haired child with a round, determined face sat on her father's lap eating raisins from a red cardboard box. The man was reading an article about the O. J. Simpson trial in the *New York Times*. In these weeks immediately following the acquittal, it was hard to read about anything else; even the *Times* knew it was good copy and that it wouldn't last forever. The father was thin and gentle looking, ascetic in his gold wire-rim glasses and thinning sandy hair; Claire thought that in a few years he would be no match for his daughter. "*My father always told me to watch out for redheaded women,*" Claire's father had teased her mother. Her mother always rolled her eyes in the same way, but even as a child Claire knew it was a kind of compliment, and knew also that her mother was secretly proud of her abundant auburn hair. Claire looked at her reflection in the train window, saw her own rust-colored curls, and allowed herself a moment of satisfaction. It was like belonging to a club; even Arthur Conan Doyle—himself a redhead—had enjoyed the joke in "The Red-Headed League."

Claire looked back over at the girl and her father. The man was gently trying to wrest a packet of cookies from her, but she held on fiercely.

"You'll get a tummy ache if you eat any more sweets," he was saying in a low voice. "You know you will."

The girl's face grew more set and her plump rosy hands tightened their grip on the cookies.

"Nooooo," she bleated, and a shrill, siren-like wail began to emanate from her throat.

The father looked around in desperation, and his eyes caught Claire's. He smiled miserably, shrugging his shoulders in a gesture of parental despair. Claire smiled back as sympathetically as she could, remembering her own rumpled father, looking after Claire and her brother the fall their mother attended night school. Claire's mother had made parenting look easy, but with her father, even as a child she could see the strain. She felt now that she had never appreciated sufficiently how difficult parenting was, and, seeing the struggle across the aisle, wished she could go back in time and erase any difficulties she or her brother caused her parents. She remembered her temper tantrums, when she would cry so hard she thought her face was going to explode; remembered slamming her bedroom door so violently that the mirror on it broke—remembered, too, the flowered poster which finally replaced the second shattered mirror. *Mirror, mirror on the wall . . .*

Claire stared out her window again, leaving the father on his own. *Why do people do it; if they knew what they were in for, no one would have children . . .*

Half an hour later, looking again across the aisle at the father and child, both asleep, the girl's curly head resting in the crook of her father's arm, Claire thought she had never seen a sweeter sight. The disputed cookies lay on the seat, discarded and forgotten.

The Hudson was awash with the October sun reflecting off the white sails of a couple of sailboats. A breeze whipped around the corners of the river, filling out the sails and making the boats lean out at a sharp angle over the rippling water. The trees swirled and swayed in the wind, their remaining leaves curling and showing their white undersides. The mountains of the Hudson Highlands rose up at uneven, oblique angles all around—grey humpbacked hills, eternally mysterious and beckoning.

Now the sun was hitting the river in full force, creating little points of sparkling light that twitched and danced on the water, and Claire could feel a wave of sunlight euphoria coming on. She settled back in her seat to wait for it—it was like sleep, and couldn't be forced. But then a cloud passed over the sun and the river was once again thrown into shadow. The train rounded a bend and across the river Claire could see the stern stone fortresses of West Point, stark and forbidding on its promontory amid the luscious landscape of the Hudson River Valley. Claire had visited the academy once, and the smooth, blunt-faced cadets reminded her of obedient children, patiently awaiting the orders of grown-ups. They were all so polite, and it amazed her to hear those young men with their cropped hair "yes, ma'aming" her this and "no, ma'aming" her that. It was like traveling through a time warp.

The train rounded a bend in the river just north of the academy, and Claire looked back at the expanse of water. Why was it so thrilling, all of this open water; why did it both invigorate and soothe? Claire felt her breathing relax as she settled back into the Amtrak Custom Coach seat. She sighed and picked up the manuscript on her lap: *The Ku Klux Klan Since the Civil Rights Movement,* by Blanche DuBois. This book was a departure for Blanche, who up until now had written only murder mysteries—very successful ones—and Claire had doubts about her ability to tackle such a subject. But Blanche had worked hard on it, researching for four months before she even started to write. Claire hoped the book was good and that Ardor House would want to buy it. Now she wasn't sure if she was going to have time to finish it before she saw Blanche. She was going straight from Robert's house in Hudson to a party in Manhattan in honor of Blanche's last book, *The Persian Cat Murders,* which had just sold a million copies.

Some loose pages fell out of the manuscript and onto the floor. The thin, ascetic-looking father was awake now, and he leaned down to pick them up. He handed them to Claire with a sheepish smile, holding her eyes just a moment longer than necessary, a vaguely imploring look in his mild grey eyes. *He's shopping,* Claire thought. *Watch out for redheaded women. You'd think he'd know that by now.* She looked at the loose papers in her hand. It was a magazine article about her that had appeared in *New Woman;* she had brought it along to show to Robert. Claire opened the shiny folded pages. EDITOR OF DEATH, proclaimed the title in large Gothic lettering. She read the opening paragraph:

> *Claire Rawlings is no stranger to death—in fact, it's how she makes her living. The deaths we speak of are literary, and they come between the pages of the mystery books she edits in her job as fiction editor at Ardor House Publications. Recognized by many in the field as perhaps the foremost mystery editor, Ms. Rawlings . . .*

Claire put down the article and looked out the window. She had never gotten over the little thrill of seeing her name in print, and although she liked to think of herself as intensely private, she was pleased by the modest sort of fame this article represented. She folded the pages and slipped them into her bag, and as she did she saw the letter she had brought to show Robert. She took it out and read once again the sprawling, untidy scrawl.

> *Dear Ms. Rawlings:*
>
> *I have just finished reading the article about you in the recent issue of* New Woman—*though I must confess such semiliterate pulp came into my hands through my stepmother, who is an arid [sic] consumer of such trash.*
>
> *The sordidness of this "magazine" notwithstanding, the article convinced me that you are an exceedingly interesting person, and I feel we may be able to discuss topics of mutual concern. I may be of some service to you in your profession, as I am something of an amateur sleuth; I have made a study of criminal modus operandi, and have the solution of several school mysteries—mostly petty thefts—to my credit. I can modestly say that in my town I am even something of a minor celebrity.*
>
> *At any rate, I am contemplating a trip to New York and would welcome the opportunity to meet with you. I look forward to hearing from you.*
>
> *Sincerely Yours,*
> *Meredith Lawrence*
>
> *P.S. Since you could not possibly guess it from my writing style, I should mention that I am thirteen years old.*
>
> *P.P.S. The article says you went to Duke. I wonder if you knew my mother there—her maiden name was Katherine Bowers. She has unfortunately left this*

world, which is why I am forced now to live with the
Wicked Witch of Greenwich (d.b.a. my stepmother).

Claire folded the letter and put it back in her bag. She had
brought it along to show Robert, thinking it would amuse
him. She had answered it a week ago—surprisingly, she *had*
known Meredith's mother at school. They sang together in
the Duke Chorale, and both lived in Wilson House, on East
Campus, the smaller of the college's two campuses. This—
plus the fact that both women were redheads—had led to a
casual friendship between them. Claire liked Katherine
Bowers but was intimidated by her; Katherine was a dy-
namo—fierce, competitive, and driven—and Claire could
never match her energy level. She looked at Meredith's vig-
orous handwriting, sprawling all over the page as if about to
jump right off the paper, and decided that the girl took after
her mother.

Claire's palm was itching. Whenever she felt tense, there
was a spot on her left palm that itched. She scratched it absently as she pondered Meredith's letter, then she remembered the beer she had brought with her. She rustled around
in her bag until she found it—Coronas, a good, clear beer
she had come to like during a stay in Mexico. She foraged
around in her bag some more and found the bottle opener.
The beer was not very cold, but it was crisp and clean.

Claire drank it too quickly. Her head felt elevated from
her body, and her brain was full of cotton wool. She leaned
back in her seat and looked out the window. Tall blond
grasses and marshlands swept by. The Hudson swirled on
the other side of them, moody and dark now as the pale autumn sun was hidden by a low grey cloud cover. Moody.
How could a river be moody, really? Claire smiled at the
human need for personification, to turn the forces of nature
into something we can understand . . . She let her mind wander to Robert . . . certainly *he* could be moody. His moods
did descend on him like a cloud cover, opaque and forbidding. It was like a shade being pulled down in a room, shut-
ting out the sunlight, and it made her feel needy and off
balance. She had to remind herself that this was the same

Robert whose skin was so warm under the fabric of his shirt, whose hands were so firm, so graceful on a piano keyboard or on her body.

Claire looked out the window again. She enjoyed the sensation traveling gave her of being cut off, of belonging neither to the past nor the future, but in transit, in between the place you have left and the place you are going. Outside, the sun was setting over the river—the clouds had parted just long enough for her to see a pale pink glow over the western October sky. The wind had picked up and the tree branches along the riverbank swayed to its rhythm.

> *Wer reitet so spät*
> *Durch Nacht und Wind?*
> *Es ist der Vater mit seinem Kind*

Claire shivered. Schiller's poem had always thrilled and frightened her. She had fallen in love with Schubert's musical setting of it in college, but she wasn't sure why it popped into her head at this moment.

> *Er hat den Knabe*
> *Wohl in dem Arm,*
> *Er fasst ihn sicher,*
> *Er hält ihn warm.*

Claire looked across the aisle at the little red-headed girl, still asleep on her father's lap, her stubby hand stubbornly clutching the box of raisins. She was not a beautiful child, and she slept carelessly sprawled on her back, mouth open, but she had the grace of childhood. *Youth is beauty; beauty, youth.* Maybe that's what Plato really meant to say, after all—those Greeks worshiped youth, didn't they? Claire looked down at her own hands, her skin already showing the crisscross hatching of aging. She forced her eyes back to the window; this was an unfulfilling train of thought she refused to sink into, this pointless contemplation of bodily decay.

Claire could see the lighthouse at the bend in the river and knew they were almost in Hudson. The river stretched

out ahead, lit by the afternoon sun. Gulls drifted lazily overhead, wailing their high screeches. The train gave a couple
of long, low whistles and pulled into the station. Claire
looked around for Robert. He had been hired to photograph
a wedding and would probably be out late. She sighed. Publishing and photography—why couldn't at least one of them
be in a nine-to-five profession?

When Claire got off the train she saw Star Taxi's green-
and-red neon sign across the street, but as soon as she had the
thought of hiring a cab she felt a pang of Calvinistic guilt; it
was, after all, less than half a mile to Robert's house, albeit an
uphill half mile. Claire trudged up the hill to Warren Street,
passing the Savoy Bar and Grill, where five or six beer-
bellied patrons sat watching the TV that hung over the bar.
One of them looked out at her as she passed, and the blank-
ness of his stare was startling. She continued up the steep hill
and turned onto Warren Street.

Hudson had been a thriving whaling port in the nineteenth century, and later a fashionable resort, but had fallen
on hard times in the latter part of this century. The last five
or ten years had brought the town the kind of rebirth Claire
had seen in so many neighborhoods in New York City: first
the artists and writers, attracted by the run-down charm and
cheap real estate, then the antique dealers, and then the inevitable yuppies. Claire wasn't sure what category Robert
fell into; neither artist nor yuppie, he was one of the earlier
settlers and therefore looked upon latecomers with the contempt which is the right of any true pioneer. Also, Robert
was English, so condescension came naturally to him. In
spite of its renaissance, the town still retained a worn,
shabby working-class appearance, and as Claire walked up
Warren Street she passed the archetypal Hudson family: a
fat, stringy-haired mother with three dingy, pasty-faced children. All the joy seemed to have drained from the woman's
face years ago, and the children looked as worn as their
mother. The sight of them depressed Claire, and she quick-
ened her steps. The architecture of Warren Street was actually of great interest, as Robert had pointed out to her.

Today, however, the street looked bleak and lonely. She was glad when she reached number 465.

Robert lived in a large, heavy, late-nineteenth-century brick town house. He had painted it a light, creamy green, with forest-green trim. It loomed over her, its shutters closed and locked; Robert did not like the noise from the street during the day, preferring to spend his time in the back garden, which faced a quiet alley. Claire knocked just to be sure Robert was not in, and then, hearing no answer, slipped her key in the lock and entered.

The house was dark and quiet. Only the Tiffany hall light was on, casting a green glow over the dark woodwork. Claire walked through the long narrow hall into the kitchen, with its blue willow china stacked neatly in the glass cupboards, the knife rack full of perfectly sharpened knives, the antique iron stove beautifully polished. Robert did everything so well, so meticulously, that next to him Claire felt sloppy and undisciplined. She looked out the door to the back porch, almost expecting to see Robert out there, sitting on his chaise reading or puttering about in the garden, digging up forgotten bulbs. But the only sound that came from the garden was the dry rattle of dead leaves as the wind ruffled through them.

Claire went back inside the house and put the kettle on for tea. It was a habit she had acquired from Robert. Since they had been together she had switched from coffee to afternoon tea with an ease that surprised her. Coffee had always signified the urban existence to her, but now she took tea in the afternoon, just like any English woman.

She wandered through the house while the water was heating, into the long back living room with its deep red velvet couch and faded Persian carpets, then into Robert's study, with the fabulous sliding mahogany doors closing it off from the back parlor. There was no doubt that this house had "character," and Robert's careful decorating had enhanced its quirky charm. Robert hated anything done badly. He tackled everything with a grim determination until he had mastered it. Claire's own strivings toward excellence often took second place to her desire for comfort, but Robert was different, and she respected him for that. She sometimes found his constant need for achievement tiresome, but she would never have admitted it.

Things had moved so quickly with Robert that she didn't really feel like she knew him very well yet—he had just sort of swept her off her feet with his attention. There was so much that she appreciated about him: for instance, he didn't mind if she brought work up with her when she visited; in fact, he encouraged it.

"It's interesting, what you do," he said, and then he would ask her things about her job. Claire had been with some men who only wanted to talk about themselves, and she found Robert's attentive interest in her life flattering. He liked mysteries, and had read several of her authors.

The teakettle in the kitchen began its slow ascending whistle and Claire walked through the front hall toward the kitchen. A riding crop leaned up against a brass-handled walking stick in the corner by the front door; above them an intricately carved hat rack hung from the wall. Claire had once teased Robert about having taste as good as a gay man's, but he did not find her comment particularly amusing. Not that there was anything latently homosexual about Robert, as far as she could tell; with his even, sure strokes and deft hands, he seemed totally at ease with heterosexual coupling. Claire poured the tea and sat down in a deep red velvet armchair. She leaned back and closed her eyes, letting the steam from the tea envelop her face. She drank a little and put the cup on the floor, then closed her eyes again.

As the sun sank over the Hudson Claire dreamed she was walking through a winter landscape, under a low slate-colored sky. Bare tree branches whipped back and forth in the wind, and there was no sign of life anywhere. Claire didn't know where she was headed, only that she must get there before nightfall.

Wer reitet so spät durch Nacht und Wind?

She was alone, and yet she had the feeling she was being followed. She stumbled across the frozen ground, tripping and catching her coat on brambles, afraid to turn around and look. She walked faster, but the faster she walked the more she felt the unknown pursuer closing in on her. She began to run. An unseen vine wrapped around her leg, pulling her down to her knees. In terror, she turned to look back—

"Claire, darling, wake up."

She opened her eyes to see Robert bending over her. A lock of his light brown hair fell over one eye. He was handsome, she thought, so handsome: strong Celtic jaw, high cheekbones, and blue, blue eyes.

"Oh, Robert."

"What is it, darling?"

Claire stretched and looked around the room. The lamps were lit and Robert's photography equipment lay on the couch.

"Are you all right? You look upset."

"Oh, it was nothing—just a bad dream."

"Well, it's all right now—I'm here to protect you." Robert turned and picked Claire's coat up from the couch where she had left it. "Come on, I'll make you a nice cup of tea, then, shall I?"

"Yes, thank you."

As Robert picked up the coat, the article from *New Woman* fell out. He bent over and picked it up.

"What's this?"

"Oh, I brought that for you to see—it seems I'm getting my fifteen minutes of fame after all."

"Well, then, we must celebrate. How about dinner at Antoine's?"

"Oh, that would be lovely!"

"Right. I'll just see about tea, then."

Robert went into the kitchen. *Lovely.* A few months ago Claire never would have used that word, but she had absorbed some of Robert's Englishness by osmosis. She went into the kitchen, where Robert was preparing the tea tray with his efficient, smooth gestures.

"Mind if I check my machine for messages?"

"Help yourself," he said, indicating the phone.

Claire dialed her number, and the machine picked up

after two rings, indicating that there were messages. Robert wrapped his long arms around her, resting his head on her shoulder.

"How about a little hors d'oeuvre?" he whispered into her ear.

She pressed the "2" button on the phone to access her messages and listened to a long harangue from Willard Hughes, one of her authors, about how Ardor House really had to work harder to sell his books.

"Oh, God—Willard!" she said as she hung up.

"Never mind; you just go into the parlor and I'll bring the tea in there," Robert said.

Claire went back to the parlor, sat down, and leaned back in the chair, listening to the comforting sounds of rattling china.

> *"Mein Sohn, was birgst du so bang dein Gesicht?"*
> *"Siehst, Vater, du den Erlkönig nicht?*
> *Den Erlenkönig mit Kron und Schweif?"*
> *"Mein Sohn, es ist ein Nebelstreif."*

Chapter 2

Claire stood in the middle of Amelia Moore's crowded Upper West Side living room, hoping Willard Hughes would not see her. Willard Hughes was an extremely unpleasant person. His voice had a plaintive, whining quality, subtle but insistent. He also had a disquieting nervous habit: when he was feeling anxious or pressured, his shoulders would twitch upward in a kind of involuntary shrug. This mannerism had the effect of undermining whatever he was saying at the time, as if he were qualifying it with this gesture of ineffectuality. Actually, Willard was not ineffectual at all; he was energetic, insistent, and demanding. He called her up more often than any of her other authors, to cajole advances or complain about publication deadlines, and he was in need of frequent hand-holding during the time period in which he churned out his books. Claire had to admit he could write, though there was an essential nastiness underlying all of his work; he seemed to revel in the most sordid aspects of crime. He was Claire's best-selling author until Blanche's latest book outsold all of his.

Claire moved over to the punch bowl to avoid encountering Willard. She knew Amelia had invited him so that Claire would have more people to talk to. Amelia Moore was so sweet, so oblivious to malice of any kind, and she had no idea that Claire felt distaste for Willard. Claire had considered telling Amelia in confidence, but she could imagine how Amelia would deal with the news: there would be phone calls to Willard, invitations to tea to "talk things over" and "iron out this misunderstanding." Amelia just didn't understand that it was possible to simply dislike someone. She opened her heart and her home to anyone and everyone, with a largesse that made Claire worry about her.

Amelia Moore's parties were legendary. Her father had been chairman of the music department at Columbia, and when he died her mother moved back to eastern Long Island. The spacious nine-room apartment on West 116th Street had gone to Amelia, and she celebrated her good fortune by entertaining lavishly. Amelia knew an amazing assortment of interesting people. She knew everyone on the Columbia music faculty, and gave occasional voice lessons herself, so there was always an abundance of musical types at her parties. At the last one Claire was proposed to by an eighty-three-year-old Irish concertina player, a courtly man whose disappointment at her rejection was swiftly dispelled by a rollicking rendition of "Haul Away Joe."

Amelia moved through the room, greeting people and keeping an eye on the food supply. She was in her element; her eyes shone and dimples appeared on her plump cheeks whenever she smiled. She wore a billowy blue flowered dress which concealed her *avoirdupois,* as Blanche called it. Claire wandered through the room, past two separate groups of people talking about the Simpson verdict.

"You can't even begin to understand," an elegant black woman was saying to her companions, two white women. One of the white women listened intently, forehead furrowed; the other, who was short with frizzy grey hair, interrupted impatiently.

"But it was another case of a *man* murdering a *woman*," she said. "Don't you *care* about that?"

Claire didn't stick around to hear the black woman's response; she found the whole subject depressing. Until the Simpson verdict, like a lot of white people, she was unaware of the depth of racial enmity within the country. The verdict hit her hard, more because of what it revealed about racial division than anything else. She was in an exercise class at the gym when the verdict was read, and was startled and horrified by the whoops of joy from the black women in her class.

At the punch bowl, Claire pretended to refill her glass, fishing at a strawberry that floated and bobbed between ice cubes. She glanced in Willard's direction, but to her relief he was busy with other quarry. He had cornered Blanche DuBois and was digging in, lighting a cigarette without taking his eyes off her. Even in the dimly lit corner of the room, his balding head shone like a beacon through the pathetically thin strands of black hair he insisted on combing over it.

Willard had always been jealous of Blanche, and once he even accused Ardor House of promoting her books more than his. Claire could see Blanche's discomfort; as she shifted her punch glass from hand to hand, her eyes moved around the room. Willard was speaking so loudly Claire could hear him.

"What do you *mean* you don't decide the means of murder until it happens?" His left shoulder was beginning to twitch spasmodically.

Blanche answered in the deliberate, calm tone of a parent trying to quiet an unruly child in public. Claire couldn't quite make out the words. She thought about rescuing Blanche, then decided she really didn't have the emotional energy. Besides, Blanche could take care of herself. Claire smiled. Could Blanche's parents have known how much she would resemble Tennessee Williams's heroine when they named her, or had Blanche deliberately set out to live up to her name? Actually, Blanche's appearance was misleading: her fluffy, dyed blond hair and frilly pastel dresses camouflaged a determined, iron will; like many other Southern women, she had merely learned to hide her strength.

Willard looked really angry now. He was hunched over, jabbing at Blanche with his index finger. Claire could hear his voice, hoarse with emotion, but the din from the party was getting louder and all she could make out was "no—imagination—need—interesting methods . . ." Blanche was staring rather rudely into space, just past Willard's head, but evidently he didn't notice. Her fingers played with a loose strand of hair, and she looked meditative, thoughtful.

Across the room Claire could see Blanche's sister Sarah, dressed as usual in somber colors: a trim rust jacket over a formal black skirt, her short brown hair lying smooth against her head. Sarah DuBois was older than Blanche, and though neither sister would reveal her age, it was rumored Sarah was quite a bit older, maybe even the child of another father. That certainly seemed possible—the qualities which in Blanche resulted in trim girlishness had, in Sarah, produced a thin ascetic. Taller than her sister, Sarah was long and lean and given to boniness. Her high cheekbones and thin patrician features would have been striking if it weren't for the sour, disgruntled expression stamped on her face. She always wore her dark hair straight and unadorned—for all anyone knew, Blanche's hair was naturally the same, but Sarah disdained bleaching and curling, just as she disdained other "coquettish affectations." It was as though Sarah had taken every personality trait of her sister's and flipped it over; she was the exact opposite of Blanche in so many ways it was sometimes hard to believe they were sisters.

Claire inched her way toward the food table. As usual, it was filled with a staggering quantity of rich and interesting delicacies: three kinds of pâté, salmon mousse in a fish mold, puff pastry stuffed with *bruxelles*, an amazing mushroom soufflé, an almond vol-au-vent, fresh fruit tarts. In the center of the table was a large basket with baguettes and round loaves of *pain de campagne*. Amelia had spent her junior year of college in France, and had been a passionate cook ever since.

"Claire!"

Claire turned and saw Amelia bustling toward her.

"Oh, Claire, don't forget to try the *bruxelles*—I made them with some morels I dried last spring!"

Amelia leaned over the table, straightening napkins and brushing away crumbs. She lived for these parties, in which she was both the hostess and, in her own modest way, the star. She spooned up some of the steaming mixture from the silver chafing dish.

"Do you know, Claire, I found these morels in North Carolina this spring when I went down for the Duke reunion. I was so excited—it made the trip worthwhile!"

Amelia loved to cook, but mushrooms were her passion. She had learned to hunt them while in France and now went out to Westchester regularly on weekends, wearing a large sun hat, a flat wicker basket over her arm. With her floppy straw hat and round little body, Amelia herself resembled a ripening mushroom, its cap already beginning to droop and brown. She had probably always been a little plump, but looked even more so next to Sarah's angular asceticism and Blanche's trim girlishness. The three of them together reminded Claire of the fairies in Walt Disney's *Sleeping Beauty*—a sort of comic trio. Claire sometimes wondered what Amelia saw in Sarah, but knew they had been roommates at Duke and that Sarah was fiercely devoted to her.

"How was the reunion?" Claire said.

"Oh, it was very nice—I'm only sorry that Sarah didn't go."

"Sarah's not really the college-reunion type."

"No," Amelia said sadly, "I guess she isn't."

Amelia was exactly the reunion type, though—and it was just like her to give a party for Blanche. Amelia and Sarah had been roommates during their last year together at Duke, while Blanche was a freshman at nearby UNC in Chapel Hill. Amelia and Claire met in a poetry course taught by the imperious Grover Smith, a leading expert in the poetry of T. S. Eliot. A tall bullet of a man with a sloping belly, thick white hair and skin as pink as a baby's, he was one of the campus characters Duke's English department was famous for. He charged around the campus in full regalia: crisp bow ties, suspenders and white linen boating jackets. Amelia and Claire hit it off in his class, and though Amelia was a music major while Claire was majoring in English, they remained friends. Claire had even stayed with Amelia for a few weeks when she first moved to the city.

Now Amelia was tugging at Claire's arm.

"Here, Claire, open up."

Claire opened her mouth to receive the spoonful of hot *bruxelles*. The flavor exploded in her mouth in stages, each more subtle than the last. She closed her eyes. Amelia was right: here were gastronomical fireworks, stages of ecstasy, and her taste glands trembled with delight.

"This is how food used to taste before people started breeding out all the flavor," Amelia said, stirring the steaming mixture.

Claire envied Amelia her rich life of the senses, her ability to throw herself into life with a childlike fervor. Claire often felt herself pulling away from intensity of experience. Even the strength of the *bruxelles* put her off a little bit; it was too much, too strong. All her life she had distrusted her senses, resisting the pull of her bodily urges—a legacy of her family's Calvinism.

Just then the front door was flung open: Anthony Sciorra was Making His Entrance. Accordion slung across his broad shoulders, his thick black hair shining in the light, he lustily sang the drinking song from *La Traviata:*

> *Libiamo, libiamo ne'lieti calici*
> *Che la bellezza infiora*

People smiled, some of them uncomfortably, some enjoying the show. Claire looked at Amelia. She had dropped the serving spoon and held her hands out to Anthony, singing in a ripe, quavering mezzo:

> *E la fuggevol, fuggevol ora*
> *S'innebrili a volutta.*

She and Anthony advanced toward each other across the room, singing. Anthony's fine accordion playing supported their singing, so that even with their imperfect voices the overall effect was pleasing. People stepped aside for them as they advanced, in mock *opera seriosa* fashion, enjoying this public attention. Amelia's cheeks were hot and flushed and her eyes glittered, just like the consumptive Violetta.

Poor Amelia. She adored Anthony with all the selfless passion of an operatic heroine, but she didn't really exist for him. Nobody really existed for him except Blanche, Blanche of the bleached and processed hair, Blanche the well groomed, so carefully put together, every ounce of fat trimmed from her lean bones as though she were an expensive cut of veal. Amelia was so full of life, and Blanche had life so under control.

Blanche knew about Anthony's devotion, of course; sometimes she encouraged it by flirting with him and sometimes she ignored him. This made him pursue her with a frantic, jealous ardor. Anthony was a handsome man with beautiful black eyes and flawless olive skin, but he was only a research chemist, an occupation not nearly glamorous enough for Blanche, who probably saw herself in an English country house, surrounded by servants. Now she was leaning against the wall, enjoying this spectacle, a superior smile on her peach-frosted lips.

I hope to God I never smile like that at a man who loves me, Claire thought.

Anthony and Amelia concluded their duet on bravely pursued if not quite captured high notes, and everyone applauded enthusiastically. Anthony smiled and bowed, and Amelia's round cheeks were moist with happiness. Was it possible Anthony was unaware of Amelia's loyal, unwavering passion? From his lapel he took a white carnation. Claire held her breath, thinking he was about to give it to Amelia, but his eyes searched the room. Seeing Blanche, alone now in the corner, cool and fresh as a spring lily, he pushed his way over to her and presented the flower with a little bow.

"Un di felice, eterera," he said ardently, looking into her eyes.

"Why, thank you, sir, I am honored," she replied. Claire could swear she was actually batting her eyelids, heavy with mascara, her Southern accent exaggerated, thick as molasses.

Claire looked over at Amelia. She looked deflated and

sad, her eyes searching for a place to focus. Several of the
guests, aware of the situation, looked away quickly, pretending not to see her discomfort. Claire felt her own cheeks
flush for Amelia's sake. Inwardly she cursed Anthony's
blithe thoughtlessness. Did he have no idea what Amelia
felt, how she suffered for him? Claire had suffered once like
that for a man, and had vowed never again to. She kept
Robert at arm's length on purpose, to maintain control, and
it felt better that way.

Anthony was now making his way through the guests.
Anthony was a toucher. He advanced slowly toward the bar,
shaking hands, laughing, slapping people on the back. Claire
looked over at Blanche, still leaning against the wall, a little
smile on her face. She hadn't spoken to Blanche yet and
knew she had to or it would look odd. Blanche wasn't one
for making overtures, so Claire would have to make the first
move. Claire started pushing through the inevitable cluster
of people around the food table. Before Claire could reach
her, though, she saw Sarah DuBois step abruptly in front of
her sister, a scowl on her thin face.

"What on earth is the matter with you?" she said in a
loud, angry whisper. "Why do you lead on that poor, mis-
guided man?"

Blanche rolled her eyes like a teenager about to receive a
boring, familiar lecture. She played with her swizzle stick.

"You know damn well Amelia loves him and you don't
have any interest in him beyond seeing how far you can lead
him by the nose, so why don't you just let him off the
hook?" Sarah hissed.

Blanche regarded her sister languidly.

"This is none of your business, Sarabelle," she said
sweetly, "so why don't you just go off and find a nice quiet
mountaintop to meditate on?"

Sarah leaned in closer to Blanche's face, her eyes spitting
sparks.

"Listen to me, you overdone cupcake. You leave off flirting with men you don't care a hoot about, or I swear—"

But she was interrupted by the arrival of Anthony, all
smiles, holding two drinks. He handed one to Blanche and

smiled cheerfully at Sarah, who gave a last sharp glance at Blanche and walked away. Claire wondered if Anthony was really as dense as he sometimes seemed, or if his obliviousness was a screen, a sort of camouflage.

Claire wandered around the room for a while, then finished her drink and went over to pay her respects to the guest of honor. Sarah had disappeared, having skulked off somewhere. Claire suspected that some of Sarah's anger at her sister was jealousy over Blanche's success as a writer. Claire herself still couldn't understand how such an essentially hollow person as Blanche could be such a good writer—within the limits of the genre, perhaps, but a good writer nonetheless.

When Claire approached her, Blanche gave a wry little smile.

"It seems we had a little mise-en-scène," she said. Blanche had acted in college and was always misusing theatrical terms.

"I must apologize for my sister's behavior—she has a crusader impulse which often vents itself on me."

Claire smiled absently. She knew Blanche was making a play for her sympathy, but she sided with Sarah on this one.

"You know," Blanche continued, "that little *contretemps* was not about Amelia at all—Sarah's still mad at me for stealing her beau back in school."

Claire vaguely remembered a story about a medical student at Duke who had pursued Sarah for a semester, only to be lured off by the flashier charms of her sister.

Just then Anthony reappeared, having scurried off to greet one of his fans. He beamed at Claire.

"Mi' amore," he said in an extravagant accent. He kissed Claire's hand. "Blanche doesn't appreciate me; why don't you run off with me?" he continued cheerfully.

"Claire already has a boyfriend," said Blanche. "At least, that's the rumor, but no one's actually seen him. Perhaps he doesn't exist—maybe Claire's using him as an excuse not to socialize more." She looked at Anthony with a conspiratorial smile, knowing that he would follow any lead she set like an obedient dog.

"Well, maybe she does have some proof of his existence—a picture, perhaps?" he suggested, looking to Blanche for approval.

Blanche bobbed up and down like a puppet, as though she were suspended by a string on top of her head.

"Oh, yes, Claire—let's see a picture of him, please?"

Claire fidgeted uncomfortably. She was embarrassed to admit that she did have a picture of Robert in her wallet, taken in front of the Croton Reservoir; he was squinting into the overcast glare, not exactly frowning, but not smiling either.

"Oh, look, she's shy," said Anthony.

"Please, Claire, let's see," begged Blanche in an eager, childlike voice. At times like this Claire could see how she managed to charm people—men, women. Claire pulled the picture out of her battered red wallet and handed it to Blanche. Just then she felt a hand on her shoulder and turned to see Marshall Bassett.

Marshall was Blanche and Sarah's cousin. Like them, he was extremely thin. He had dark oily hair and was fond of wearing black; he always reminded Claire of Snidely Whiplash. He was gay, but loved to flirt with women, and his hand did not move from Claire's shoulder. His palms were always unpleasantly damp, and Claire could feel the moisture through her thin silk shirt.

"Is it show-and-tell time?" Marshall said. He was an oral surgeon, working out of an office in his sprawling house in New Jersey, but his real passion was the Civil War. He owned no fewer than three rifles and two uniforms from the period—one Union and one Confederate. Marshall was always hunting down Civil War treasures, traveling all over the country to find them.

"Claire was just showing us the picture of her boyfriend," said Anthony.

"Oh, and is he a handsome sward?" said Marshall.

"Yes, very handsome—here, judge for yourself." Anthony took the picture from Blanche and handed it to Marshall, who looked at it and then smiled at Blanche.

"What do you think, Miss DuBois?" he said. "You're something of an expert on men. Is he handsome?"

Blanche did not respond. In fact, she looked distracted, as though she had suddenly remembered some very important errand.

"Uh, will you all excuse me for a moment? I—just remembered something." Avoiding their questioning looks, she turned quickly and went into one of the bedrooms, closing the door after her.

"Well," said Marshall after she had gone, "I'm used to having an effect on women, but it's usually not that dramatic."

Anthony looked worried.

"I better find out what's the matter," he said, looking after her. "It's not good when she broods about things. It gets her upset."

"Maybe you should leave her alone for a few minutes," Claire suggested gently. "She looked like she wanted to be alone."

"Well, maybe after a little while . . ." Anthony said vaguely, and then he wandered off into the party, which was in full swing. No one else seemed to have noticed Blanche leave; they were all having a wonderful time without the guest of honor.

Marshall turned to Claire.

"Alone at last!" he said.

Claire was amused in spite of herself. Marshall was fun because he did not ask to be taken seriously; in fact, he seemed to invite dismissal. This made Claire relax in his presence—everything was a game with Marshall, and he was a relief after all the earnest people in her life. She turned to him and smiled.

"Take me to the Casbah," she said.

Chapter 3

Claire spent most of Saturday reading manuscripts, and then, feeling restless, went for a long walk in Riverside Park. A bitter wind was blowing in off the Hudson, and except for a couple of heavily bundled joggers, she had the park mostly to herself. She walked down to the boat basin and watched the boats, swaying in the swelling waves, their rigging pullies clanking plaintively against empty masts. A few of the house boats had lights on inside, the lamps shining yellow in the gathering grey sky. A couple of cyclists rode by on mountain bikes, heads bent against the northerly wind. Even the seagulls who strutted on the boardwalk looked cold, their grey and white feathers ruffled by the gathering gale. Claire looked up the river, at the rising cliffs of the Palisades—the Indian's called them "rocks that look like trees"—at the Hudson which swelled and twisted as it moved north into the Highlands. *Land of dreams, land of eternal mystery and delight.* Those cliffs, with their majestic spread of water below, could move Claire like few other sights: every time she saw them she felt pulled into the landscape as though she were a part of it and always had been. She thought of Robert, alone in his house in Hudson, and had a sudden urge to talk to him. She pulled her coat around her neck and headed back toward her apartment, her eyes watering from the stiffness of the wind. When she called Robert's number his machine picked up and she hung up without leaving a message. Claire didn't want to appear clingy, even though she was sure she valued her time alone as much as Robert did his. She sat on the edge of the bed and looked around the room, trying to decide whether she should read another manuscript or give up for the day. Just then she heard her fat white cat, Ralph, under the bed, batting something around on the floor. She bent down to see what he was up to, and saw that his toy was the tape from her answering machine. He had somehow managed to pry it out of the machine and sent it clattering across the hardwood floor, ricocheting against the floorboards. She realized at that moment she had forgotten to feed him this morning; this was his revenge. Whenever she neglected him, he let her know by very pointedly attacking some object she used: one night he sent the entire contents on top of her dresser crashing to the floor and another night he tipped her bedside glass of water over onto her face as she slept.

Claire picked up the tape and put it back in the machine while Ralph sat calmly licking himself.

"All right, come on," she said, and he followed her into the kitchen, his eyes wide with innocence.

She opened a can of Liver 'n Onions and spooned half of it into his dish. As soon as he heard the sound of the can opener, he wound around her legs, purring sweetly. Then Claire remembered she hadn't picked up her mail yet and went downstairs to the mailbox. Besides an offer from TWA to go to Europe at the lowest possible fare, there was a plain white business envelope addressed to her in a disorderly scrawl. Before she opened it, she knew it was another letter from Meredith Lawrence. Claire opened it in the elevator, and when she was back in the apartment she settled in her favorite spot, the red leather armchair by the window, to read it.

Dear Ms. Rawlings,

I am delighted to be in receipt of your missive and feel certain that in you I have finally found a long-

awaited soul mate. You can imagine what this means to my young impressionable mind, as my father is a dull, pale creature of habit who could not possibly interest a child of my gifts. He is a physician, and is hopelessly trapped in left-brain cognitive reasoning.

But on to more cheerful matters: our burgeoning relationship! The warmth and understanding evidenced in your letter to me quite took my breath away, and so I make bold here to quote Goethe (but not Robin Williams, God forbid), who said (among other things) "Seize the day! Whatever you can do, or think you can, begin it!" (Of course, the phrase is more charming in the original German, but even in translation I think the gist is there.)

And so, my dear Ms. Rawlings, I am going to Seize the Day. I shall be arriving at Penn Station Sunday on the 9:45 A.M. train from Hartford. I am sorry to get you up so early, but I want to slip out of the house before my parents awaken.

What an adventure! What a grand time we shall have together! Thank you, my dear, dear Ms. Rawlings, for giving me this opportunity—I promise you won't regret it!

> *Warmest Regards,*
> *Meredith Rawlings*

P.S. I don't know how long I shall stay—that will depend in part upon you, of course. I am buying a one-way ticket.

P.P.S. Don't try to call me and change my mind—you can't anyway, as my father's phone number is unlisted. (My stepmother is afraid of obscene calls from lunatics, although to my mind anyone who would make an obscene call to her is barking up the wrong tree.)

P.P.P.S. I will be wearing a red carnation.

Claire put down the letter and looked out the window. A strong wind whipped the branches of the tree in front of her apartment, causing them to strike the window. *Rat-a-tat-tat*. The window rattled with each gust, and Claire could hear the faint, high-pitched howl of the approaching gale.

> *Willst, feiner Knabe, du mit mir geh'n?*
> *Meine Töchter sollen dich warten schön . . .*

An egotistical thirteen-year-old prodigy who quoted Goethe was arriving by train tomorrow morning and there was nothing Claire could do about it.

Claire looked at her watch, then picked up the phone and dialed the number of her police precinct. It rang twice, then she hung up suddenly. Maybe it would be best to meet the girl first and see how persuadable she was before involving the police. Maybe she wouldn't even show up; maybe the whole thing was an elaborate hoax.

Claire leaned back in the leather chair. Ralph entered the room, jumped up onto her lap, and began licking his whiskers. Claire frowned. Who did this girl think she was, Snow White? Outside the storm gathered in fury. The tapping of the tree branches was accompanied now by a pelting rain which drove at the window in sheets. Ralph looked up with a panicky expression and then jumped off Claire's lap and bounded out of the room, headed for the bedroom closet, his favorite hiding place.

"Coward!" Claire called after him, but he was gone already, to curl up between the mohair sweaters and wool jackets, white cat hairs thickening the dark closet air.

Claire folded Meredith's letter and laid it on the coffee table. She picked up the remote control and switched on the television. *The Honeymooners* was on, the episode in which Ralph appears on *The $99,000 Answer*, having learned everything about his category—popular songs—except for "Swanee River," which Norton keeps playing over and over again on the piano. When Claire tuned in, Ralph had just missed his big chance and was being pulled offstage by a young woman dressed like Barbie at a debutante ball. Ralph was sputtering and sweating, refusing to believe he had just blown his big chance. Comedy was so cruel, Claire thought.

Poor Ralph—what was the moral of this episode, leave no stone unturned? Don't ignore what's staring you in the face? Claire switched off the television and went into the bedroom. When she turned on the closet light, Ralph looked up at her with a stricken expression. White cat hairs floated all around, gently airborne. Claire laughed, remembering something Marshall Bassett once said: "Who in their right mind gets a white cat?" Ralph looked at her reproachfully.

Claire slept restlessly that night, and dreamed she was being chased through deserted city streets by Meredith's stepmother, who resembled Margaret Hamilton and kept shouting "I'll get you, my pretty—and your mangy little cat, too!"

Claire awoke shivering at eight-thirty, the alarm clock bleating in her ear. The rain had stopped during the night, but the temperature had dropped drastically and the parquet floor was like ice under her bare feet. She pulled on a turtleneck sweater and wool socks, gulped down half a cup of tea, and dashed out to meet Meredith's train. When Ralph heard the bolt on the front door, he sauntered into the living room, but he arrived just in time to see the door shut in his face.

At Penn Station, Claire peered up at the arrivals board. The 9:45 train from Hartford was on the board but the track number was blank. Finally the sign clicked over to read TRACK 17, and Claire's heart jumped a little. She maneuvered herself into the line of people headed down the stairs, most of them passengers. Afraid of missing Meredith on the platform, she pulled away from the pressing throng as it began to descend the stairway to Track 17. After a few minutes several arriving passengers began straggling up the same staircase. Claire searched them anxiously. Maybe Meredith had been discovered by her parents, or better yet, given up her mad plan.

Behind a fat man in a tan raincoat, struggling with an impossibly big, battered suitcase, was a tall, thin, red-haired girl. In the lapel of her winter coat drooped a sad-looking red carnation. Claire stepped forward.

"Meredith?"

The girl smiled broadly and let the suitcase drop with a

thud. She extended her hand, and when Claire offered hers in return she shook it energetically.

"Thank you for coming to meet me! I was prepared to make my own way to your apartment, but this makes things so much simpler. I've been to New York before, you know," she said breezily. "Several times, actually. I find the intellectual climate so stimulating."

She paused, then picked up her heavy suitcase again. "Well, shall we go?" She looked up at Claire cheerfully.

There was no denying she was an odd-looking child. Her hair was—well, orange, and so kinky that it stood up thickly in all directions. Deep-set blue eyes peered out from her pale face. She was almost as tall as Claire; all arms and legs, she reminded Claire of a headstrong roan colt. Claire took a deep breath.

"Uh, Meredith—we really need to talk, you know."

Meredith put down her suitcase.

"All right, I was hoping to avoid this. No, I'm not going to get back on a train to Connecticut, though if you insist, I will call my father when we get to your apartment. However, under no circumstances are you to give him your number. Agreed?"

She spoke as if Claire were the troublesome child instead of herself. Claire suddenly felt exhausted, oppressed by the squalor of Penn Station. She thought of the long wait they would have if they went to the police station.

"All right. Let's get a cab and go to my apartment."

In the cab Meredith said, "I'm a big fan of Blanche DuBois. What's she like?"

"Oh, she's sort of odd . . ." Claire laughed. "She has an admirer who goes around singing opera arias to her."

Thirty minutes later Meredith was seated on the red leather chair with a cup of tea in her hand and Ralph on her lap.

"Animals take to me," she said in a confiding tone. "They know I understand them." She took a bite of a Mint Milano. The large suitcase, it turned out, had been stuffed with bags of Pepperidge Farm cookies, crammed in between her clothes.

"All right," said Meredith, putting her teacup down on the coffee table, "I'm ready to call my father. Where is your phone?"

"In the hall."

Meredith brushed cookie crumbs from her lap.

"Don't worry, I'll call collect."

Ralph, irritated at losing his lap perch, followed Meredith into the hall, stiff-legged, shaking his feet as though he had just stepped in a puddle. Claire listened from the living room.

"Hello, Father. Yes, I'm fine, drinking tea and eating cookies—no, Father, it was all my idea. Ms. Rawlings has never met me and she's not a pervert. She happens to be a highly respected editor. I *told* you, she knew Mother at Duke! Father, listen to me. I'd like to stay here for a few days . . . yes, I *know* it's almost the holiday season, Father. I promise I'll be there for Thanksgiving Day, all right? . . . Well, no, she hasn't said for sure—very well, I'll let you talk to her."

Meredith's head poked around the corner.

"He wants to talk to you."

Claire rose and took the phone.

"Hello?"

"Ms. Rawlings, this is Ted Lawrence. I must apologize for my daughter's outrageous behavior."

The voice was smooth and cultivated, a real New England WASP. Claire imagined the man's house: understated, tasteful, potted philodendrons and unstained wood floors.

"There's no need to apologize; I know she acted behind your back."

Meredith, standing in the doorway, rolled her eyes extravagantly.

"Do you—oh, this is awful, but—" The man was struggling with his Yankee pride.

"Yes?"

"Well, of course we would pay for everything, including a governess, if you like—" The man's voice broke.

"Yes?"

"Well, it's her stepmother . . . she's having a rough time

of it right now. The doctors have diagnosed a nervous condition of some sort, and they're advising total peace and quiet for a while. We could send Meredith to my sister's in North Carolina, but she already has two children, and . . . I mean, I just thought, since you knew Katherine . . ." There was a pause. Claire could hear the man's anxious breathing over the phone. "I'm afraid things are rather busy for me right now with my practice and everything . . ." He sighed, a great heaving of air, and when he spoke again his voice sounded weary and defeated. "Of course, it's quite impossible. Forgive me, please; I don't know what I could have been thinking."

Claire looked over at Meredith, who was threading Ralph's tail through the handle of her teacup. Her thin white fingers touched the flickering tail delicately, experimentally. Claire experienced a sudden, animal craving to have a child in her life.

"Mr. Lawrence?"

"Yes?"

"Uh, I would like to have Meredith stay with me for a few days—that is, if you trust me. I realize you don't know much about me—"

The voice on the other end of the line hesitated.

"I would be forever grateful. Actually, Katherine spoke of you—"

"She did?"

"Oh, yes. She—she admired you . . ."

He paused, and then Claire heard a woman's voice in the background but couldn't make out the words. She heard Mr. Lawrence say something like "Of course not, don't be paranoid," to the woman, and then he spoke again into the receiver.

"I'm sorry, my wife was saying something to me. I'll send you a check by express mail, if that will be suitable."

"That's fine. We'll call you every day to let you know how Meredith is. Don't worry, Mr. Lawrence; I'm sure she'll be fine. I'll speak to you again tomorrow evening."

"Will you tell Meredith—tell her I love her."

"Of course. Good-bye."

Claire hung up and turned to Meredith.

"Your father wants me to tell you he loves you."

Meredith rolled her eyes and released Ralph from a half nelson.

"Oh, that's so *nineties,* isn't it? Have you noticed how lately everyone goes around saying that constantly? 'I love you, I love you, I love you.' It loses its meaning after a while, don't you think?"

Claire sat down on the couch next to Meredith.

"I'm sure he does love you."

"Oh, I'm sure he does, too. It just gets on my nerves to hear about it all the time. Too much sentiment dulls the intellect, you know."

"Your father is a doctor."

"A *gastro*enterologist," Meredith replied, her voice dripping with disdain. She popped the last cookie into her mouth. "He looks at people's colons all day long," she muttered through the crumbs. Then she hopped off the couch and took her cup and saucer out to the kitchen.

Claire looked out the window. The sun glinted on the windows of the apartments across the street, turning the glass into opaque mirrors. She tried to imagine herself inspiring admiration in someone like Katherine Bowers, who gave off such sparks, who was always the star of any group. *Well, the grass is always greener . . .*

The phone rang sharply, making Claire's nerves quiver. Some author in the throes of creative torment, no doubt, needing a security call. She should have turned off the phone after Mr. Lawrence's call. She picked up the receiver reluctantly.

"Hello?"

"Ms. Rawlings?"

"Yes?"

"This is Detective Jackson, Homicide, Ninth Precinct. Do you know a Ms. Blanche DuBois?"

Claire felt her stomach contract on the word "homicide."

"Yes, I do. I'm her—her editor." *Her editor.* Claire almost said "friend," but the word stuck in her throat.

"Could you possibly come down to the station for questioning?" The voice sounded weary, almost bored.

"Why?"

"Ms. DuBois was found dead in her apartment this morning. We suspect it may have been a homicide."

Claire felt as though a metal band were contracting around her head. She sat on the edge of the couch; the room had shrunk to the size of the portable receiver in her hand. The only sound in the world was the voice on the other end of the phone line.

"Homicide? What happened? How—" Her own voice sounded faint, distant.

"I really can't say anything at this time. If you'd come down to the station—"

"Uh, when?"

"Now, if you don't mind." The voice was patient, gently insistent.

"Well, I—"

"We can send a car up for you if you like."

Claire turned to look at Meredith. She was sitting on the floor looking up at Claire intently, her bony white arms clasped around her knees.

"Just a moment," Claire said to the weary voice, then turned to speak to Meredith. Before she could open her mouth, Meredith jumped up from the floor.

"Someone's been killed, haven't they?" she said quietly.

Claire nodded dully. She felt as though everyone in the world was one step ahead of her.

"Who's on the phone, the police? They want to question you?" Meredith didn't even wait for Claire to nod this time.

"Let me come with you, please, please! I'll be quiet, I won't get in the way! Oh, please!" Her voice was tight with excitement.

Claire didn't see that she had a choice. She could leave Meredith in the apartment, but that didn't seem safe under the circumstances. Besides, she certainly couldn't trust the girl to stay there. Claire returned to the weary voice on the phone.

"I'll be there, but I have to bring my"—what *was* she?—"niece," she lied.

"Fine. I'm at the Ninth Precinct, on Fifth Street between First and Second Avenue. Ask for Detective Jackson."

"Right."

Claire hung up and leaned back on the couch. Meredith sat in the red leather chair.

"They think it was murder, don't they?"

Claire nodded. Meredith's eyes widened.

"Are you a suspect?"

The word was like a splash of cold water in Claire's face. She stiffened.

"No, I don't think—I mean, he didn't say anything about—why would they suspect me?"

Meredith nodded seriously. Then her face relaxed.

"No, you're right—if you were a suspect they would have come up here to get you."

Meredith jumped up from her chair. She seemed to be given to abrupt movements.

"Come on, let's get down to the station. I'll get your coat."

Minutes later Claire was seated in a cab next to this odd child, this sprite who had appeared like an undine, uninvited, into her life.

Chapter 4

The Ninth Precinct station house was an imposing grey stone building with heavy wooden doors. The grubbiness of the interior, however, seemed to mock the solemn majesty of the exterior. Cigarette butts littered the cracked tile floor, and the dingy blue paint on the walls was dirty and chipped. Old wooden filing cabinets sat in corners; plastic chairs were scattered randomly around the floor, and Claire smelled the close odor of stale cigarette smoke. Plaques lined the walls behind the sergeant's desk, and a large glass case titled COMMUNITY APPRECIATION AWARDS contained pictures of smiling officers. Behind the docket stood two young policemen. One had cropped blond hair, the other brown; both sported little mustaches on their pale, bland faces. A thick, middle-aged blond woman sat at a small desk near the door, smoking a cigarette and eating a ham sandwich.

"Can I help you?" she said in an accent distinctly of the boroughs. Meredith stepped forward and began to answer her, but Claire interrupted.

"We're here to see Detective Jackson."

"Oh, just have a seat—he'll be back in a minute." The woman indicated one of the stained plastic chairs. Claire thanked her and motioned Meredith over to a couple of chairs against the far wall. Above them hung a bulletin board with letters of commendation; sections of the letters were highlighted in yellow. The phone on the blond woman's desk rang. She picked it up, tucking the receiver onto her shoulder, smoking and chewing as she talked.

"Where was the car when it was stolen? Can I have the license-plate number?"

A stubby, red-faced officer stubbed out a cigarette in front of Claire and walked over to a thin, dark man with a scraggly goatee and tattered clothing.

"Elijah Cobb?" the policeman said.

"That's right," answered the man.

"You filed a complaint for burglary?"

"That's right."

Claire had mistaken the thin man for a felon, and noted sadly that in this neighborhood the victims often looked a lot like the criminals.

Just then the heavy wooden door swung open and two men in trench coats entered. The younger one was tall and rosy and fresh-cheeked; the other was of medium height, with shaggy grey hair. He walked with a weary air, shoulders slightly stooped. The woman at the desk caught Claire's eye.

"You were waiting for Detective Jackson?"

"Yes, thank you." Claire rose and stepped hesitantly toward the two men. The older one addressed her.

"Ms. Rawlings?"

"Yes."

"I'm Detective Jackson. This is Sergeant Barker." His voice was remote, courteous.

"How do you do?" The younger man smiled widely, showing broad, even teeth. *Caps,* Claire thought. He reminded her of an eager golden retriever.

"I'm Meredith Lawrence, Ms. Rawlings's—ward," said Meredith, extending her hand. Sergeant Barker took it with a captivating smile.

"Very pleased to meet you, Ms. Lawrence."

Detective Jackson motioned them into a small, cluttered office. He took the seat behind the desk. Claire and Meredith sat opposite him on the only two other chairs in the office. Sergeant Barker settled himself on the corner of the desk, pushing aside piles of papers that teetered precariously on the edge of the desk. Claire noticed uncomfortably that the room had no windows, with only the thick smoked glass on the door to let in the outside world.

"I'm sorry to bring you out on a Sunday, but I'm afraid murderers don't restrict themselves to weekdays," said Detective Jackson.

Meredith broke in. "Is Claire a suspect?"

Detective Jackson regarded the girl through heavy-lidded eyes. His grey eyes were large, with deeply creased circles under them. The rest of his features were large, too; he had a wide mouth and long nose. His face was long, with high cheekbones under a headful of shaggy grey hair. His long pale fingers twirled a rubber band. Looking at him, Claire felt a hollow twinge in her stomach.

"No, we have no real suspects at this point," he said to Meredith in the same polite, disinterested voice. Claire decided his faint accent was northeastern, perhaps Boston.

"Are you going to question us?" Meredith asked eagerly.

Sergeant Barker leaned forward from his perch on the desk.

"That's right—just like in the movies."

"There's no need to condescend to me," Meredith replied sharply. Sergeant Barker recoiled with a wounded expression, like a reprimanded puppy.

Detective Jackson leaned back in his chair.

"We are questioning Ms. DuBois's friends as a matter of course, especially those who may have been the last to see her alive."

Claire looked puzzled.

"You were among the people who attended Amelia Moore's party on Friday night?"

"Yes, I was."

"What time did you leave?"

"A few minutes after twelve."

"Was Ms. DuBois still there when you left?"

Claire tried to visualize the party as she had left it: An-

thony was playing his accordion to a small band of listeners
in the kitchen; Marshall was flirting with some blowsy,
overblown blonde, and Amelia was tidying up around the
food as people picked over what was left of her delicacies.
She could not remember Blanche or Sarah as having been
among them.

"I'm not sure, really. I didn't see her as I was leaving."

"Did you see her the next day—Saturday?"

"No. I had just arrived from a trip upstate and I had un-
packing to do. When did she—"

Jackson interrupted her, as if saving her from saying it.

"Sometime Saturday evening, probably after eight P.M.
We're still waiting for the complete PM report."

"Postmortem," Meredith whispered to Claire.

"The body was discovered by her sister this morning. Initial estimates are that she had been dead about twelve
hours."

Claire shuddered. She glanced at Sergeant Barker, who
was looking sulky after Meredith's rebuke. He had risen
from his perch on the desk and stood with his hands in his
pockets, a pouty expression on his face.

Claire looked around the tiny, windowless room and felt
her forehead prickling with sweat. She concentrated on
breathing, angry at her irrational claustrophobia, her fear of
entrapment.

Meredith, on the other hand, seemed not only at ease, but
in her element. She leaned forward and questioned Detective Jackson as though she were the detective and he a tricky
suspect.

"How did you say Ms. DuBois died?" she said suspiciously.

Jackson regarded her with the expression of a tolerant
uncle. Claire thought he might even be suppressing a smile.

"I didn't. She was poisoned."

"Cyanide?" said Meredith thoughtfully. There was a
pause. Sergeant Barker attempted to catch Jackson's eye,
but he was looking straight at Meredith.

"Yes," said Jackson calmly, hiding whatever surprise he
may have felt.

"Just a guess," said Meredith, "albeit an educated one. I've made a small study of the most commonly used poisons in murder cases and cyanide leads the list, along with arsenic, which is somewhat more nineteenth century—Madame Bovary and all that—so I chose cyanide. Also, the odor of bitter almonds which often occurs in a cyanide poisoning would lead you to regard this death as suspicious, which would explain the unusually speedy autopsy."

Detective Jackson nodded gravely. His face in repose looked sad, the heavy eyes drooping. Again Claire felt a tingle in her stomach.

"Cyanide is not difficult to obtain," said Meredith. "It is used more often than you think—for example, in the making of jewelry, and also in the development of photographic images."

Sergeant Barker was looking at his watch and shifting his weight from one foot to the other, like a child waiting for permission to go to the bathroom.

"Uh, sir—" he began.

"Go ahead, Sergeant Barker. Just try to be back in an hour," Jackson said wearily.

Sergeant Barker looked at Claire apologetically.

"Nice to meet you, Ms. Rawlings. I have to go to an audition now." He deliberately avoided looking at Meredith and stumbled out of the room, rattling the thick glass on the door as he closed it behind him.

"An audition?" said Meredith loudly. "What for? Is he an actor or something?"

"He's trying to be," said Jackson. This time Claire was certain his lips curled briefly upward.

"Actually, he's appeared in two films. Strictly extra work; but now he's been bitten and is studying nights at HB Studio. But to return to the matter of Ms. DuBois's murder . . ."

"How did it happen?" said Claire softly.

"The poison was concealed in a piece of fruit—an apple."

"How positively Grimms brothers," said Meredith cheerfully.

"The apples were delivered to Ms. DuBois's building while she was out. It is possible they were poisoned before they arrived; it is also possible they were poisoned while in the building, although that it is somewhat less likely. There is a doorman who swears he was there until Ms. DuBois returned to the building, at which point she took the apples up to her apartment . . . in any event, sometime Saturday night she ate one of the apples and died—"

"Within fifteen minutes," Meredith broke in.

"Yes," said Jackson after a slight pause.

Claire had to admire the way he hid any irritation or amusement he might have felt toward Meredith and just continued on calmly after one of her interruptions. Here was a man in control of himself.

"Did anyone see the apples being delivered?" said Meredith.

"Unfortunately the doorman was away from his post when they arrived. One of the neighbors might have seen something; we haven't interviewed any of them yet. The apples were apparently sent as a gift. The card was addressed to Ms. DuBois, and, as I said, she took them upstairs herself."

"Did the card say anything else?"

" 'From an admirer.' "

Claire felt her stomach tighten. Anthony! Was he capable of . . . she couldn't allow herself to think any further. She noticed with alarm that Jackson was looking at her.

"Did Ms. DuBois have any admirers that you know of?"

Claire felt an urge to protect Anthony.

"No. I mean, yes, many—"

"Anyone in particular?"

"Detective, I wouldn't feel good about implicating anyone—"

Jackson sighed and rubbed his forehead wearily.

"It's all right, Ms. Rawlings; we already know about Mr. Sciorra. I was just wondering if there was someone—a fan, perhaps—that you might know of, since you were Ms. DuBois's editor."

"No—I didn't read Ms. DuBois's fan mail. I'm afraid I

can't help you." Claire suddenly felt irritated at this weary, patient man, with his long fingers and tired shoulders.

Meredith sat up in her chair.

"Mr. Sciorra—was he the guy you told me about, the one who sings the arias?"

"Yes." Claire had forgotten that she discussed Anthony and his accordion-courting techniques with Meredith.

"Well, you can obviously eliminate him from your list of suspects," said Meredith briskly.

"Oh?" Jackson allowed himself a slight smile this time.

"Certainly—that is, unless he wished to be apprehended. If he did it, he made no effort at all to cover his tracks, and it would have been so easy. He could even have shifted the blame onto someone else." Meredith paused, frowning. "Of course there is always the Raskolnikov Factor."

"The what?" asked Jackson.

"Surely you are familiar with *Crime and Punishment*, Detective?"

"Yes."

"Well, one of the conclusions Dostoyevsky draws in his book is that criminals sooner or later yearn to be caught and punished for their deeds, which, undiscovered, weigh too heavily on their conscience. I call it the Raskolnikov Factor, and it can't be discounted in the solution of a crime, especially murder."

Detective Jackson nodded. "I see."

"Have you interro—spoken with Anthony yet?" asked Claire.

"Mr. Sciorra came in to see us earlier today."

"Do you think—is he—?"

"We have no official suspects as yet." Jackson leaned back in his chair, a scratched, scarred old wooden captain's chair.

"Anthony is a chemist, though," Meredith said thoughtfully, "which means he has access to drugs."

"Did Ms. DuBois have many enemies?" said Detective Jackson. The question implied that she must have had some, that it was a matter of numbers.

"No, I don't think so."

"Was Mr. Sciorra in love with her?"

Claire tried to choose her words carefully.

"He . . . he was pursuing her—" Instantly she regretted her choice of words. She made him sound predatory—poor, lovesick Anthony.

"I understand Ms. DuBois and her sister had a fight the night before she was killed."

"Yes, but it wasn't serious."

"What was it about?"

"Sarah thought Blanche was leading Anthony—Mr. Sciorra—on."

"Was she?"

"Oh, I don't know . . . yes, I suppose so."

"Why would Sarah DuBois want to kill her sister?"

"I have no idea . . . I—" Claire felt confused and on trial herself, even though rationally she did not think she was a suspect. Meredith spoke up abruptly.

"Could we continue this questioning later? Ms. Rawlings had to get up early on her day off this morning to meet a train and she's very tired."

Claire looked at Meredith gratefully. She was tired, so tired . . .

Detective Jackson rose.

"By all means; I think I have what I need for the present. Thank you both very much for your time." He extended a hand, which Claire shook. To her relief, his palm was dry. She hated sweaty palms—and then she blushed, embarrassed by her mind's wandering.

Half an hour later Claire was sitting in her living room, drinking tea and watching Meredith, who lay on her stomach reading. Her orange hair fell in unkempt curls around her face. *Some people burn,* Claire thought, *as fierce and bright as comets.* Even Meredith's hair was like a flame, a beacon—even reading, she sizzled with energy. Claire sipped her tea. Her own flame burned lower, with more of a blue-green light. She might never ignite the world like Meredith, but she was drawn to these kinds of people, warming herself in their glow. This fire, this energy, was neither necessarily good nor evil, she felt, but was the seed of great deeds, both good and evil. The thought of so much energy turned to the service of evil frightened her. She wondered if she'd ever known anyone who was capable of real evil. Then she shuddered: in all probability, she knew the person who had killed Blanche DuBois.

Chapter 5

When Claire and Meredith got home there was a message from Sarah DuBois on Claire's answering machine. Claire had always thought of Blanche and Sarah as opposites, but as she listened to the message, she was struck by how similar their voices were in timbre and dialect. But while Blanche's accent had dripped Deep South, Sarah's was all crispness, even in her grief.

"Of course you will have heard the news by now . . . the police are coming over sometime this afternoon to 'ask a few questions,' as they so delicately put it . . . but I wonder if you would consider dropping by. I called Amelia, too, but I think she's gone down to identify the—they asked me to do it, but I couldn't . . . I suppose it's wrong of me, but I asked Amelia if she would. I know it's cowardly, but I don't think I could take it right now . . . please call me when you get in."

The machine clicked, and the tape rewound. Claire thought of Amelia down at the morgue, waiting in the cold, hollow white room for Blanche's body to be wheeled in by a white-jacketed attendant. Poor Amelia; she was always cleaning up the messes left by her friends. Maybe it was her own fault, for letting herself be used, and she never complained, but sometimes she seemed like a servant, and it made Claire angry. Well, this was the last duty she'd be asked to perform for Blanche.

The phone rang and Claire answered it, but as soon as she did the line went dead. She put the phone down and walked into the kitchen, where Meredith was rummaging through the cupboards. Sitting on the shelf was a jar of peanut butter, honey, and some crackers.

"Do you have any cookies?" Meredith asked when she saw Claire.

"We have to go to Greenwich Village; you can have some cookies there," said Claire. "Did you eat all the ones you brought?"

"Yup," Meredith replied, spreading some peanut butter on a cracker and topping it off with a glob of honey. Ralph circled at her feet like a fat shark, hoping for scraps.

"Come on, get your coat," said Claire as she dialed Sarah's number.

Sarah DuBois lived in Greenwich Village, in a nineteenth-century town house on Bethune Street. Claire had always loved that part of the city, over by the river, where tourist activity was more sluggish than in the heart of the Village. The sidewalks over here held a calm on a Sunday morning, interrupted only by the occasional dog-walking or stroller-pushing resident. Claire and Meredith got off the bus and walked through streets that twisted and turned around each other, past French restaurants tucked snugly into the narrow first floors of the three- and four-story brick buildings which made up this old part of the city. A woman with a *New York Times* under her arm was being pulled along the street by a large, smiling black Labrador, which stopped to inspect Meredith's shoes briefly, tail wagging. The woman smiled apologetically and yanked on the leash, and they were off again, the dog towing her as if she were on water skis.

"Dogs are very sweet," mused Meredith as they walked on, "but more emotionally needy than cats. I used to think there were cat people and dog people, but of course life is more complicated than that, isn't it?"

"Uh-huh," Claire murmured. She was getting used to the

idea now that she did not have to meet Meredith's formidable energy head-on, that she could let the girl dance little circles around her while she kept still, conserving her energy.

As they climbed the steep stone steps in front of Sarah's building, Claire tried to imagine the street in the 1820s, when this building was new: horses and carriages, men in tight trousers with cutaway coats, women in floor-length gowns, hair piled high on their heads, bustles supporting their drapery. The street—cobblestone? Mud? Claire wasn't sure. The country entering its fifth decade of nationhood, with another four decades to go before the abolition of slavery.

Meredith pushed the buzzer, and Sarah's dry voice answered over the crackle of the intercom. "Yes?"

"It's Claire and Meredith," Meredith yelled into the speaker. Claire flinched; Sarah hated loud noise. Claire had explained to Sarah on the phone who Meredith was—not in detail, but enough to prepare Sarah for her—or so Claire hoped.

They were buzzed into the foyer and stood in its dim coolness. The hallway had no right angles, and smelled of apples and eucalyptus. A narrow oaken staircase lurched up to the second and third floors; Sarah's apartment occupied the entire first floor. They walked through the hallway, its wide floorboards creaking under the long Persian runner that led to Sarah's door. The door opened and Sarah's thin body leaned out briefly.

"Thank you so much for coming," she said, holding the door open for them. Claire had a brief impulse to hug her, but was put off by the woman's stiff, almost military reserve.

Meredith followed her into the apartment, stepping into the high-ceilinged living room. Sarah's apartment was as spare as Blanche's was cluttered. A huge teal-blue Oriental rug was bordered by a few pieces of simple furniture of Quaker design, austere unstained oak. On the coffee table was a paperback copy of *Zen and the Art of Archery*. Claire and Meredith seated themselves on a stiff-backed couch. Sarah's furniture made you feel like you had to keep your back straight to avoid getting your knuckles rapped. Sarah sat opposite them on an unpadded oak chair.

"It's so good of you to come," she said as warmly as Sarah could say anything. "I—I just don't know what to do with myself. Of course all I can think of is who would *do* such a thing . . . the thing that torments me is that we quarreled right before—before . . ."

Sarah looked down at her tightly clenched hands and rubbed her eyes wearily.

"I'm sorry; I'm ranting," she said dully.

Claire was about to say something comforting when the phone rang. Sarah glanced at it.

"The press," she said. "They've been calling me all day for quotes. My number isn't even listed, but somehow they got hold of it." She reached over to unplug the phone jack. "It's terrible, the kind of scavenging that goes on after something like this—"

Before she could finish, the air was cut by a shrill whistle.

"Oh, that's the teakettle," said Sarah. "I thought you might like something hot to drink on a day like this." She rose and went into the kitchen.

Meredith leaned toward Claire and whispered, "She seems very upset. I wonder if it's an act."

Claire was about to rebuke her when Sarah entered the room with a tray of tea things.

"This is a habit I got into during a brief liaison with an Englishman," she said almost apologetically.

"Quite civilized, if you ask me," Meredith remarked cheerfully.

Sarah poured them all tea out of a surprisingly delicate pink-flowered pot and passed around a plate of petits fours.

"Amelia sent me these cakes—she doesn't think I eat enough." She gave a little laugh, then her face wilted and she began to cry. Claire sat uncomfortably balancing her steaming cup, feeling that it would be rude to drink her tea at this moment. After a minute Sarah spoke, her voice thick with grief.

"Oh, she wasn't the best sister in the world, but then, neither was I." She wiped her eyes with a tea napkin. "Still, for all our differences, you know we've never really been separated. I guess there's a kind of comfort in knowing someone's near, like when you go to bed at night and you think of the other people in the nearby apartment buildings sleeping in their bedrooms . . . the next day you might hate the crowds but at that moment their presence is a comfort. I don't know; maybe I liked the thought of Blanche's presence more than I actually liked her, but now I don't have either . . ." She began to cry again. "I'm sorry; I'm really sorry about this."

Claire looked around Sarah's pristine apartment and thought of her own mother, apologizing for crying after her grandmother's death. She wanted to say something comforting, but even in grief the woman seemed essentially remote, formidable. Sarah guarded her personal life closely, and though Claire had known her for years, she realized that she knew very little about her.

Sarah cleared her throat and picked up her teacup.

"You know, Amelia used to say Blanche was the smart one, because she always got what she wanted." She sighed. "That little backhanded compliment was probably the closest Amelia has ever come to criticizing someone else."

Just then a large, tortoiseshell cat sauntered languidly into the room and rubbed itself against Sarah's shins.

"I knew you were a cat person the minute I saw you," said Meredith, reaching to stroke the long, luxuriant fur.

"This was my sister's cat, actually, and I seem to have inherited her. Amelia brought her over on her way to . . ."

"Did you know that if a cat has more than two colors in its coat it's always a female?" said Meredith eagerly, her mouth full of cake.

"No, I never heard that," Sarah answered. "Cat hairs make my eyes itch, so I never had any, but I'll keep Camille for a while, anyway." She smiled. "Just like Blanche to name her cat Camille, isn't it?"

"So you've seen Amelia?" said Claire. "How is she?"

"Oh, in shock, I suppose; we both are, I think . . ."

"What was your sister like?" asked Meredith. "I mean, apart from naming her cats after doomed heroines?"

Sarah looked at the child with what Claire thought was alarm, and then laughed—a dry, painful sound.

"Pardon me for asking, but do you spend all your time collecting facts?"

"Yes," answered Meredith, so seriously that Claire almost choked on her tea.

"Well, how—studious," said Sarah. "I fancied myself a scholar when I was in school, but I don't know that I ever had quite your determination."

"Oh, I'm very determined," said Meredith, still not smiling. "Ask Claire. You said you were in school—where was that?"

"Duke University."

"Ah, yes, the house that tobacco built."

Claire felt the conversation was taking a dangerous turn.

"Sarah and Amelia were roommates," she said hastily, with a manufactured cheeriness in her voice which she recognized as her mother's.

To Claire's relief, though, Sarah just looked amused.

"You're right about the tobacco money, which of course I knew about, growing up in the South, but which scandalized poor Amelia once she got down there. Amelia has always been easily shocked, I suppose . . . in fact, I'm worried about the effect of Blanche's death on her more than anyone . . ."

Meredith leaned forward and put down her teacup. She reached for Camille, who glided nimbly away.

"What was Blanche like?"

"Oh, she could be childish, petulant, willful—determined, like you. Nobody could tell her what to do if she didn't feel like doing it herself. People said she wasn't a great student at school because she was vain and lazy—which she was—but they were wrong. She could have been Phi Beta but she only studied what really interested her: history and literature."

"I heard what interested her was men," Meredith said

coolly. Sarah laughed again, a sound that threatened to turn into a sob.

"You *do* collect facts, don't you? To tell you the truth, I don't think my sister was so much interested in men as she was in their admiration . . . except maybe once."

Just then the phone rang and Sarah rose to answer it.

"Hello? Oh, hello, Marshall." Sarah's voice expressed unmistakable disdain. "I've already decided where to hold the service . . . Marshall, she was *my* sister and I am having the service in the neighborhood where she lived. Yes, at Grace Church." Sarah sounded irritated. "I'm sure when there's a reading of her will you'll be notified. And now if you'll excuse me, I have some guests here." She hung up and turned to Claire. "One of the more annoying aspects of this horrible affair is that I'll have to see my cousin Marshall on at least two occasions in the near future." A hint of her Southern roots showed in her voice as she said this. Try as she might to suppress it, every once in a while a whiff of the Piedmont crept into Sarah's accent, a cadence that was unmistakably Dixie.

"Why don't you like him?" Meredith mumbled through the sugar cookie she had stuffed into her mouth.

Sarah sat down wearily.

"I don't really care to talk about it right now, if you don't mind. Don't you have any relatives you just don't like?"

Meredith did her best to swallow, but a fine dust of crumbs sprayed from her mouth as she spoke.

"Oh, sure—I hate my stepmother and she hates me."

Claire felt she should object. "Meredith," she said without enthusiasm.

"Well, it's true, isn't it?"

Sarah leaned back on her couch and looked at Meredith.

"Child, I think you are the oddest creature I have ever seen."

Just then Sarah's buzzer sounded loudly, making Claire jump. Sarah rose and spoke into the intercom.

"Yes?"

The speaker crackled and sputtered.

"It's Detective Jackson."

Sarah buzzed him in and came back into the living room.

"I'm sorry about this, but I'm afraid I'll have to see the detective now. He wanted me to come down to the station, but I insisted on his coming here, so if you'll excuse me . . ."

"Not at all," said Claire, standing up quickly. She noticed that whenever she was around Sarah she tended to adopt her formal manner of speech. The thought of seeing Detective Jackson made her feel confused and flustered, and she picked up her teacup with unsteady hands and headed for the kitchen.

"Oh, just leave those—I'll get them later," Sarah said, fetching their coats from the hall closet. As she pulled Claire's coat from its hanger a shawl fell from the upper rack. It was wool with peach-colored flowers, and Claire recognized it immediately as Blanche's. Sarah must have seen her looking at it, because she scooped it up off the floor. "Oh, Blanche lent me this the night of Amelia's party. I was cold, and then I just wore it home . . ." Her voice trailed off sadly.

As Claire and Meredith were putting on their coats, Detective Jackson entered the foyer, and Claire could feel his eyes on her back. The low, weary voice spoke.

"Hello, Ms. Rawlings."

Claire turned to answer. Detective Jackson wore a long, somewhat tattered grey overcoat; the top button was missing and the cuffs were frayed. Claire realized suddenly that there was no woman in his life, and the thought made her flush. To her relief, however, Meredith had taken all social duties upon herself.

"Good evening, Detective Jackson. I think you'll be interested in some of the things Ms. DuBois has to say."

The detective cocked his head to one side like a spaniel and raised his eyebrows politely.

"Oh? Thank you for the tip, Ms. Lawrence."

"Not at all."

The buzzer sounded again.

"That will be Sergeant Barker," Jackson said to Sarah. "He was a couple of steps behind me."

Sergeant Barker came bouncing in the door.

"Oh, boy—I just saw the greatest *character* out there, this old *man*—I just had to stop and watch him for a while! You never know when that kind of thing will come in handy." He looked around, as if expecting applause.

As Claire and Meredith turned to go Detective Jackson spoke.

"Oh—Ms. Rawlings?"

Claire turned around.

"Yes?"

"Could you stay for just a few minutes? I have a couple of questions I'd like to ask you."

"Of course we can stay," said Meredith. "We don't have anywhere we have to be, right?"

Claire looked at Sarah, who shrugged.

"All right, if you want," Claire said, removing her coat.

"Just a couple of things—it'll only take a few minutes," said Jackson, sitting in the chair Sarah offered him as though he'd been on his feet all day. Meredith sat across from him and leaned toward him eagerly.

"What do you want to know?" she said, eyes shining.

Jackson turned to Claire, who stood awkwardly in the doorway, coat in hand.

"Was there anything Ms. DuBois said to you the night before her—the night of the party—that you remember as being unusual in any way?"

"Let me see . . ." said Claire, and then suddenly she remembered the strange mood that had come over Blanche at the party. "There was something odd—not unusual for Blanche, really—but in retrospect, it was strange. We were all standing around, and suddenly she seemed . . ."

"What?"

"Well, distracted or something, and she excused herself and left the room."

"Where did she go?"

"I believe she went into one of the bedrooms. Amelia could confirm that."

"Was it something someone said, do you think?"

"I don't know . . . I don't remember anything in particular. Blanche could be touchy, but she usually hid it."

"Who was there—around her—at the time?"

"Well, besides me, there was Anthony, Amelia, and Marshall—Marshall Bassett, Blanche's cousin."

"Her cousin?"

"Yes. He lives in New Jersey—in Montclair. He's an oral surgeon."

"I see." He turned to Sarah. "He's your cousin, too, then."

Distaste flickered over Sarah's lean face.

"Yes."

"Do *you* have any idea what might have upset her?"

Sarah leaned against the fireplace mantel, resting her thin arm on its pink marble surface.

"Not really . . . but Blanche was like that—"

"Like what?"

"She was always what you might call . . . moody."

Detective Jackson looked directly at Sarah, his grey eyes still and piercing.

"And what would *you* call it, Ms. DuBois?"

Sarah shrugged, as cool as the marble under her arm.

"I would call her spoiled, but then what older sister wouldn't feel that way about a pampered younger one?"

Jackson turned to Claire, and she felt the blood rising to her cheeks.

"What do you think, Ms. Rawlings?"

"Well, I'm not sure . . . Blanche was—temperamental, that's for sure."

Sarah's sharp voice cut in.

"Blanche was more concerned with the effect she was *creating* than with the impact she was really *having* on people."

"Did you like your sister, Ms. DuBois?"

"Like her? I suppose I didn't much like her at times, but I did love her." Although Jackson made no gesture in response, she added, "You *can* have one without the other, you know, Detective."

"Yes, yes; I'm sure you can," Jackson replied thoughtfully.

"And I certainly don't think my sister deserved what happened to her," Sarah continued in a chilly voice. "And now, if you'll excuse me for a moment, I'll go make us some tea." The statement was not an invitation—it was a decree. Sarah could be very brusque with people she did not know; it was one of her protective mechanisms. There was an uncomfortable silence, and Claire could hear the ticking of Sarah's mantel clock, a genuine Seth Thomas, a present from Amelia.

"Do *you* have any sisters, Meredith?" Sergeant Barker suddenly piped up from where he sat on the sofa.

"No, I have no siblings at all," said Meredith, barely looking at him; it was clear she had dismissed Sergeant Barker as beneath contempt.

"Well, if you have further questions for me . . ." said Claire, feeling trapped in Detective Jackson's spell.

"No, thank you very much, Ms. Rawlings—though if you think of anything helpful, please feel free to call me. Here," he said, scribbling on a business card and handing it to Claire. "On the front is my number at the precinct, and on the back is my home number. You can call me there anytime."

Claire took the card and put it in the breast pocket of her jacket. She wondered if he gave everyone his home number.

"Do you have any suspects yet?" Meredith said eagerly.

"No, not officially—"

"But you're keeping your eye on a few people?"

Detective Jackson laughed. The effect was startling: a full-throated musical chuckle, it was odd coming from this solemn, weary man. Claire found herself smiling in response.

"Let me put it this way," said Jackson. "We haven't arrested anyone yet. If we do—"

"I'll be the first to know?" Meredith said. She sat on the edge of an upholstered footstool, leaning toward Jackson.

Claire stood up.

"Come on, Meredith, let's let the detective do his job," she said, putting on her coat.

"I'm not bothering him—am I, Detective?"

"No, you're not," said Jackson, with a glance at Sergeant Barker, who was sulking again.

Claire and Meredith said their good-byes to Sarah and the policemen, then went out into the grey November afternoon.

"I don't see how Sergeant Barker could be pursuing an acting career and be a cop at the same time," Claire said as they walked along.

"Oh, sure—I saw an article in the *Times* magazine a couple of months ago about this cop who had been in a lot of movies," said Meredith. "He even had a small speaking role in *Goodfellas*. There was a picture of him and Joe Pesci. They like to use guys who have their own uniforms; it saves them money."

"Oh."

"Sarah's hiding something, you know," said Meredith.

"Why do you think that?"

Meredith shrugged. "I've see the same behavior in my stepmother. There's something furtive about her . . . she acts like she's undercover or something. My stepmother acts like that because she's on drugs, but Sarah's not on drugs—or at least, I don't think she is."

"What is it, then?"

"I don't know. It may have nothing to do with Blanche's death, or it may . . . I just don't know yet."

They walked along in silence for a while. A garbage truck sloshed along the narrow street, brakes whining, and disappeared around a corner.

"Do you like Detective Jackson?" Meredith asked suddenly.

"He seems like a nice man."

"Yeah," Meredith said slyly, "real nice."

That night Claire called Robert and told him the news. There was a stunned silence, and then he said, "Oh my God. What—how?"

Claire told him the whole thing, and there was another pause. Then he said, "Are *you* all right?" Claire answered that she was, all the while wanting to wrap herself in the gentle warmth of his concern.

"Do you want to come up here for a few days and get away from it all?" he said.

Claire said she had better stay around for the funeral, and then she told him about Meredith. He was puzzled about the connection, but when she explained she had known Meredith's mother at school, he seemed to understand.

"Are you sure you can handle it—her—right now?" he said, his voice full of concern.

"Well, the thing is, she sort of takes my mind off—you know, gives me something else to think about."

"Well, all right, but mind you don't get too run down during all of this."

"Don't worry, I won't."

"All right. I'll call you tomorrow, then, to see how you're doing."

"Okay. Goodbye."

"Good night."

After she hung up, Claire felt like crying. The past few hours—her fatigue, Meredith's arrival, the visit to the police station—everything had seemed a little unreal, as though it were someone else's life. But Robert's kindness released something within her which she had been carefully holding on to, and she felt herself crumple inside.

Just then Meredith called to her from the kitchen, and she decided that at least for the time being she would have to postpone falling apart.

Chapter **6**

Claire put the newspaper down on her office desk and took a sip of coffee. The caption read, *Mystery Writer's Mysterious Death,* and she had to admit that Blanche's death made good copy. The press were literally having a field day, speculating wildly about the nature of the killer, all the while managing to imply that the story's built-in irony was more than just coincidence, that the clue to the identity of the killer lay somewhere in the pages of one of Blanche's books. All of the bookstores were completely sold out of her mysteries, and several titles were already on back order. Claire refused to comment to the press. She had other things to think about—meeting the Lawrences, for example.

Meredith had been with Claire for two days now. Ted and Jean Lawrence had come to New York to meet Claire and take Meredith back to Connecticut with them—although Claire hadn't told Meredith that part yet. Meredith and her father had gone to the Bronx Zoo while Jean did some shopping, then they all arranged to meet at a restaurant. After some thought Claire chose Patzo's, on Eighty-fifth and Broadway. It was fancy enough for people from Connecticut, but relaxed enough that they could wait there without feeling rushed. Also, Claire thought Meredith would like the new wall murals, a sort of trompe l'oeil of the stone wall of a building, with red geraniums blooming in window flower boxes. Claire found it charming; she secretly hoped Jean Lawrence would think it was tacky.

They arranged to meet at six; at five-thirty Peter Schwartz stuck his head in Claire's office and asked if she was busy.

"Uh—not right now."

"Good." He came in and sat down in the armchair across from her desk.

Peter Schwartz was the editor in chief at Ardor House, and was generally well liked around the office. He was a small, plump man, and yet he fancied himself something of a satyr. He had made it clear to Claire early on in her employment that he found her attractive—and did it in a way that was neither obnoxious nor intimidating. Peter Schwartz was a man who responded to women, and in spite of his round little body, women often responded to him. He was on excellent terms with his ex-wife, and Claire had seen trim, clear-skinned women show up at his office after work; some of them looked like former models. "Sexual harassment be damned," Peter said once. "If a woman looks good I'm going to tell her so, and she can bloody sue me if she wants to!"

Peter wasn't English—his family were Polish Jews—but he was a hopeless Anglophile (he had a treasured book about the royal family, autographed by the Queen Mother herself). He loved to sprinkle English phrases in his conversation, which always sounded a little forced; he actually referred to the "boot" and "bonnet" of his red Jaguar. Peter was responsible indirectly for introducing Claire to Robert, whom he hired to photograph a book party Claire attended. When Peter learned they were dating, he nodded approvingly. "Good for you. Ripping good folk, the English. See that you keep him around—you won't regret it."

Now Peter leaned back in the armchair, his little pot belly swelling out over his khakis.

"I was just thinking about Blanche's last book," he said.

"You mean *Persian Cat Murders*?"

"No, no—the Klan book . . . how far along was she?"

"Well, pretty far. I had a manuscript draft that I was reading the night she—died." Claire couldn't force herself to say "murdered."

"Hmm. Have you finished it?"

"No—I was just about to, when . . ."

"Right; right." Peter paused and looked out the window. "Why?"

"Well, the thing is, I'd like to publish it."

"But it's only a draft."

"I know, I know . . . but I was wondering . . ." Peter leaned forward and fixed his eyes on Claire. "Do you—do you think you could finish it for her?"

"But I'm not a writer—"

"No, but you're a bloody good editor, and—well, it's mostly written, isn't it?"

"Well, mostly, I guess . . ."

"I hate to sound mercenary about this, Claire, but Blanche's death got a lot of publicity, and I think this thing would sell, I really do. Of course, if her family agrees, I'll make it worth your while financially."

"Well, I don't know . . ."

"You know, I was humoring her when I gave her the advance for this book in the first place, but she really wanted to do it, and if you're smart, you give the goose who lays the golden egg anything she wants . . . and now it would be a pity to have all her hard work go up in smoke, don't you think?"

"Well, yes, but—"

"Look, just think about it, will you? That's all I'm asking. Ask that sister of hers—Sally, Susan—"

"Sarah."

"Right—Sarah. Ask Sarah what she thinks, whether she would like to see her little sister's last book in print. I'll bet she'll go for it."

Claire didn't say anything; there was no point in elaborating on the jealousy and competition between the sisters. She just nodded.

"Okay, I'll ask her."

"Thanks."

Peter stood up; standing, his posture was stiff, almost military. It was all part of his sexual vanity, Claire supposed, adding what he could to his small stature, but she found it touching. He paused at the door.

"You look good, by the way—this English boyfriend of yours has done wonders for your skin."

Claire laughed and looked away. She could feel the redness creeping up her neck. She looked at her watch; it was five after six.

The goose that laid the golden egg. This goose had not fared so well: now she was dead, and Claire wasn't sure she wanted the job of replacing her.

Claire took a cab to Patzo's and hurried in, feeling guilty and flustered. Though she had never seen Jean Lawrence, she didn't need the red carnation in Jean's lapel—Meredith's idea—to locate her. Jean Lawrence sat stiffly on one of the bar stools. With her tight hairdo and immaculate peach suit, she might as well have written "From Connecticut" on her back in crayon. Claire approached her.

Hello, I'm Claire Rawlings. I'm sorry I'm late."

The woman turned to her and bared her teeth in a sort of grimace.

"That's all right." Her tone suggested that it wasn't.

The maître d' found them a table and beckoned to Claire. Jean Lawrence picked up her drink with a bored air and followed after them. She shrugged when Claire offered her the cushioned seat next to the wall.

Jean Lawrence was small and had tiny white teeth, sharp as a terrier's. She was too well groomed, from her perfectly polished nails to her tinted, sprayed hair: she was a woman approaching middle age tensely, warily, like a boxer sizing up an opponent. She was not a comfortable person; there was an edge to everything she did, whether it was lighting a cigarette with her small gold lighter or sipping her white wine spritzer. Claire felt the woman's anxiety seeping into her, felt her own movements becoming tight and jerky. It seemed absurd that she should have to sit here with this woman, trying to overcome the awkwardness that constrained them both.

The waiter approached their table. As soon as he caught Claire's eye he smiled broadly. He was young and shiny-faced, with very blond hair. Claire thought there was something familiar about him; then she realized it was Sergeant Barker, only he had dyed his hair blond. She opened her mouth to say hello, but he bent down in front of her as if to pick up something off the floor.

As he did he whispered tersely, "Don't say anything. I'm doing research for a role. Pretend you don't know me." He straightened up again, smiling. "Now, what can I get you ladies to drink?"

When they had ordered their drinks and he was gone, Jean Lawrence said, "What did that boy whisper to you just then?"

Claire looked bemused.

"What? Oh, nothing—he just couldn't find his pen."

Jean Lawrence looked at her suspiciously but didn't say anything. She lit a Virginia Slim with her elegant gold lighter.

"You know," she began after their drinks had arrived, "Meredith thinks I hate her, and I don't at all."

No, Claire wanted to say, *Meredith hates you,* but she just sat and sipped her diet Coke. She was beginning to wish she had ordered a red wine—this woman was going to be hard to take cold sober. A light alcohol-induced buzz would have made it easier.

"You know," Jean Lawrence continued, "if that child would just give me half a chance we could be great friends."

Claire doubted if that were true, but she said nothing. Behind her, Sergeant Barker roamed the room, serving drinks, bending over tables, eager as a bird dog. He looked exactly like an actor playing the part of a waiter, and was enjoying himself hugely. Sergeant Barker was the perfect contrast to Detective Jackson. Claire found herself wondering if Detective Jackson's studied air of ennui and indifference was a mask, calculated to put suspects off their guard. She wondered how many women fell for him, drawn to protect and soothe that world-weary soul.

". . . in our days, of course, it was different," Jean Lawrence was saying. Claire realized she hadn't listened to a word the woman had said. She smiled and nodded in a vaguely encouraging way. This seemed to satisfy Jean Lawrence, who nattered on about children and their lack of gratitude, sounding just like a Dickensian villain.

Just then, to her relief, Claire saw Meredith and her father enter the restaurant. Meredith came in first, straggle-haired and grimy-faced, her father following meekly behind, looking totally worn out. Ted Lawrence was a good-looking man—tall, sandy-haired and lean, with aquiline features. His nose was long, with a sort of ridge in it—Meredith had said the Lawrence family all had "mountain noses." It was attractive on him, but Claire doubted if it would look good on a woman. Meredith quickly spotted them and waved. Claire waved back, but she could feel Jean Lawrence tensing and drawing into herself as Meredith and her father approached the table. Meredith greeted her stepmother cheerfully enough, sitting down with a plop on the high-backed chair next to Claire. Her father sat heavily, and Claire could see it had been a long day. When Sergeant Barker came by with water for the table, Ted Lawrence reached for his gratefully and drank it down without pausing.

"Well, you look as if you have been through the mill," his wife said with an attempt at a smile which came off as a smirk. Her long peach-colored nails wrapped around her white-wine spritzer and her face on its thin neck was rigid as a mask.

"The best thing was the snake house," Meredith said, addressing her remark diplomatically to the company in general. Her stepmother shuddered.

"Ugh—snakes are disgusting!"

Meredith looked at her calmly.

"Just because you have Freudian conflicts about snakes doesn't mean other people can't enjoy them."

Jean Lawrence's manicured fingers tightened around her drink glass. Claire could hear her sharp little intake of breath.

"Must you always fling your intelligence around as

though it were a weapon?" she said shrilly, and, getting up from the table, stalked away toward the rest room. There was a pause at the table and then Ted Lawrence spoke.

"That wasn't a very nice thing to say, Meredith."

Meredith snorted.

"Oh, good Lord, Father, you've got to be in pretty bad shape to let a kid get to you like that."

"Don't swear, Meredith," her father said perfunctorily, then inclined his dignified head toward Claire.

"My apologies, Ms. Rawlings; I'm afraid my wife is a rather nervous woman. Lately she has been particularly strained."

"I don't see why," said Meredith sulkily. "*I've* been out of the house." Her father looked at her reproachfully, then turned back to Claire.

"Meredith has this idea her stepmother doesn't like her."

"Oh, come off it, Father! She can't stand me, and we both know it. Don't worry; my young self-esteem is not injured by her rejection of me—I'm not crazy about her either."

Claire felt an impulse to laugh, but the serious expression on Ted Lawrence's face stopped her.

"Meredith, I'm sure Ms. Rawlings doesn't want to hear our family problems."

Meredith shrugged.

"Okay, but I didn't start it." She looked moodily at her ginger ale and poked at the ice cubes with her swizzle stick. Her father turned his attention again to Claire. She felt the man's deliberate self-control a bit chilling but smiled in response to his attempt at diplomacy.

"I was very sorry to hear about the"—he paused, searching for the tasteful word—"tragedy. It must have been a shock to you."

"I figured Meredith would tell you all about the murder," Claire said, emphasizing the word "murder." She felt an evil urge to shake this man out of his restrained dignity.

"Actually, my wife went to school with the—with Blanche DuBois," he said. "She was interested in the article about you in *New Woman* because she had known Blanche at UNC."

"Oh? Did they know each other well?"

"They lived in the same dorm for a while, until Jean transferred to another school."

"I didn't know that," said Meredith.

Just then Jean Lawrence returned to the table and sat down without looking at any of them. Her nose was red; Claire wondered if she had been crying.

"I must apologize for my abrupt behavior; I've been under a lot of strain recently," she said stiffly, addressing her remarks to the salt shaker. Claire noticed that her eyes were bloodshot.

"I understand you were at UNC with Blanche," said Claire.

Jean Lawrence looked startled. "Yes," she said in a tight voice. "I was very sorry to hear of her . . . death."

"Had you kept in touch at all?"

"No, not really . . . not for some years now."

"Claire—Ms. Rawlings—went to *Duke* with Mother," Meredith said.

"I'm sure we all must be starving; I know *I* am," said Ted Lawrence, motioning for the waiter. Sergeant Barker came bouncing over cheerfully, and they turned their attention to the menus. Meredith ordered a turkey burger; Claire and Ted both had pasta. Jean Lawrence ordered a salad with dressing on the side.

While they waited for their food, Meredith played with the bread sticks, scraping all the sesame seeds off and eating them one by one. Claire could see Jean Lawrence tensing as she watched this operation, and wondered if Meredith was doing it especially to get on her nerves.

"So what did you buy today?" Ted Lawrence said to his wife in a hearty voice that didn't even begin to hide the apprehension behind it.

"Oh, nothing much . . . these New York shops are overrated, if you ask me."

"Where did you go?" said Claire politely, ignoring the slight.

"Oh, Madison Avenue mostly. Everything was very trendy and very overpriced."

"Did you buy any drugs?" Meredith murmured under her breath.

"What did you say?" said Jean Lawrence sharply.

"Lots of good rugs," Meredith replied blandly, scooping up a sesame seed and delicately chewing it.

"So, Ms. Rawlings," began Ted, turning to Claire.

"Oh, call me Claire, please."

"Claire, I can't tell you how grateful I—we—are," he added, with a nervous glance at his wife, "for all you've done for Meredith."

"Oh, it's been fun."

"Well, I know she can be a handful—"

"No I'm not; I'm fun, just like Claire said," Meredith said without looking up from her breadstick project. Jean Lawrence snorted softly.

"Well, in any event, you were very kind to take her on like this," said Ted Lawrence.

"Did she tell you I'm helping her solve a murder?" said Meredith.

"What?" Her father looked puzzled.

"What—murder?" said Jean in a startled voice.

"Well, Blanche DuBois's, of course. What else?" Meredith replied disdainfully.

"What—what do you mean, you're 'solving it'?" said Jean.

"I mean Claire and I are helping the police solve it."

Ted Lawrence smiled indulgently at his daughter, and Claire sensed a real tenderness toward her, an affection that coexisted with an equally real lack of understanding. It was as though Meredith were a lovable, eccentric foreigner. Just then Sergeant Barker appeared with their food, and for a few minutes they all had a welcome diversion.

"I'm sure the police appreciate your help, Meredith," said Ted Lawrence as he sprinkled grated cheese on his fettucine prima vera, "but all good things must come to an end. We want to take you back to Connecticut with us."

Meredith looked at her father as though he had slapped her. Claire sensed a scene about to happen.

"I don't want to go back to Connecticut! I want to stay with Claire."

"Don't be ridiculous," snapped Jean Lawrence. "Why should she have to take care of you? *We're* your parents!"

"You're not my mother," Meredith said evenly. "My *mother* is dead."

Jean Lawrence's face tightened and reddened but she said nothing.

"Look, Meredith, you can't stay here forever. You have to go back to school," her father said in a pleading voice.

Meredith sighed deeply and looked at Claire, who couldn't think of anything to say.

"Well," Meredith sighed, "I don't want to be a *burden* to anyone."

Of course Claire realized this was a cue to deny that Meredith was a burden, but she felt that she should support Meredith's father at this moment.

"You can come back and visit soon—how's that?" she offered.

"Can I really?" Meredith said, looking at her father.

"Of course—you can visit, if that's all right with Ms. Ra—Claire."

"Of course it's all right," said Claire. "It'll be fun."

"Can I stay for the funeral at least?" Meredith looked at her father with pleading eyes, soft as a beagle's.

"Well . . ." he said, avoiding looking at his wife, and Claire knew the answer was yes. She was relieved that the crisis was over, at least for now.

"I'll take the train up right afterward," Meredith chirped. "Then when I come back there's still the *murder* to solve."

Just then Jean Lawrence choked on a piece of spinach, and everyone occupied themselves gratefully, slapping her on the back and offering medical advice. After a few violent coughs, she was all right, though her face was red and her eyes watered.

"Excuse me for a moment," she said, rising and heading once again in the direction of the rest room. Meredith gave Claire a meaningful glance, but what the meaning was Claire could not guess.

It was decided that Meredith would go back to Connecticut immediately after the funeral, which was two days away. Ted Lawrence insisted on paying for their meal, and as they all stood outside the restaurant, he pressed some money into Claire's hand.

"This is for your trouble."

Claire tried to give it back, but it was an awkward situation, and she ended up stuffing it into her coat pocket as she and Meredith hopped into a cab. Meredith had wanted to walk home, but Ted Lawrence insisted on hailing a cab for them.

Later on, in the cab to Claire's apartment, Meredith said, "I wondered why Sergeant Barker glared at me when I started to speak to him, but then I figured it out, of course: he's working undercover. He makes a better waiter than policeman, if you ask me."

Later, in the apartment, Meredith was seated in the red leather chair, a bag of Bordeaux cookies open on the coffee table.

"What did you think of my *step*mother?" she asked, helping herself to another cookie.

Claire felt she should play the sage adult.

"I know you don't like her, but you could treat her more gently. She's evidently highly strung—"

"*Highly strung?*" Meredith threw back her head and laughed. "No; *I'm* highly strung; *she's* a drug addict."

"What?"

"Did you notice how red her nose was when she came back from the rest room?"

"Yes. I thought she had been crying."

Meredith snorted again. "Yeah, right—crying. There was something up her nose, but it wasn't tears. And did you see how nervous she was all the time?"

"Yes, but—"

"Well, cocaine does that to you."

"Oh my God—really? She—"

"Comes down every Saturday to get her drugs in the city. She could get them up there, but she's got a supplier here, and no one will recognize her—or so she hopes."

"Oh, God—your poor father."

"My 'poor father' married her—against my wishes. He deserves what he gets," Meredith said bitterly.

"Does he know?"

"Of course he *knows*, but, like most people, he has an endless capacity for self-delusion. That's why I wanted to leave so much—I couldn't stand it anymore. It's bad enough with her, but watching my father . . ." Meredith's face began to soften, and Claire thought she was going to cry, but just then the phone rang. Meredith nearly tripped over Ralph as she rushed to get it.

"Hello? Oh, hello, Sarah. Yes, she's right here. It's Sarah," she said, handing the phone to Claire. Claire took it, and Meredith scooped Ralph up in her arms and carried him from the room, his paws dangling helplessly.

"Hello?"

"Hello, Claire." Sarah's cultivated voice was as dry as corn husks. "I just thought I would let you know about the service for Blanche. We thought we'd have it at Grace Church. I hope you can come."

"Of course I'll be there. Uh, Sarah—at Duke, did you know a Jean—I don't know her maiden name—a friend of Blanche's at UNC?"

"Jean . . . oh, yes, of course: Jean Cummings. Lots of Maybelline. I met her my senior year. What about her?"

"Well, was she a friend of Blanche's?"

"Yes, for a while. They were roommates freshman year. They had a falling out over a scandal involving a plagiarism charge—it seems Jean copied one of Blanche's old papers and submitted it as her own. When she was tried before the disciplinary board, she wanted Blanche to lie for her, but Blanche wouldn't do it." There was a pause, then she continued in a sad voice. "Blanche had her faults, God knows, but lying wasn't one of them."

"What happened?"

"Jean was offered a transfer as an alternative to being expelled. She went to UNC at Greensboro."

"So she wasn't much of a student?"

Sarah laughed softly, a short, bitter puff of air.

"Jean Cummings was not attending college. She was playing Hunt-a-Husband."

Claire imagined Jean, polished nails and high heels, sitting in stuffy classrooms pretending to read Spenser, waiting to be noticed by a premed student. Sarah's voice interrupted her thoughts.

"Uh, Claire, I'm sorry—I have to go. I'm at work and someone needs my attention right now."

"Thank you Sarah, and I'll see you tomorrow."

Sarah was head of marketing at Arlene Lucien, a large cosmetics company. She viewed her position with some irony, but which Claire knew she also took very seriously (Sarah took most things seriously). Sarah cared very much about her job.

Her cousin Marshall Bassett took it upon himself to kid her about it, even though she did not find it amusing.

"So how are things at 'Dyes Are Us'?" he would say with the tone of playful malice which he used so often with his cousin.

Sarah would pretend not to hear him, and usually didn't bother to answer, but Claire could see her body stiffen even more, and there would be a thin whooshing sound, which was the intake of breath through her nostrils, as her thin lips remained firmly clenched in a frown.

As Claire hung up she realized she had not taken her coat off yet. As she shuffled wearily into the foyer to hang up her coat, Meredith's head poked around the corner.

"I cannot tell a lie. I was listening on the extension in the kitchen."

"Meredith, that's eavesdropping, you know."

Meredith tightened her grip on Ralph, whom she still held captive.

"Tell me about it. Under normal circumstances I wouldn't think of it, but may I remind you that we are dealing with murder here."

With a wrench and a hiss, Ralph sprang from her arms and to freedom under the living room couch.

Chapter 7

Grace Church really lived up to its name. It was a stunningly graceful example of Gothic architecture: its many ornate spirals, seen from blocks away, rose majestically over lower Broadway. Claire had not been inside for years, and had forgotten the beauty of the tall stained-glass windows and the burnished wood of the pews. An organist was playing a soft interlude on the pipe organ, and as Claire came through the front antechamber into the church proper, she could smell frisia, Blanche's favorite flower. Though not religious in any conventional sense, Claire loved churches, and Grace Church was surely one of the most beautiful she had seen. Meredith had begged to go to the funeral, but Claire suggested she meet her at the reception afterward and skip the service. She was worried the girl would do or say something inappropriate and spoil the solemnity of the occasion.

Claire walked down the immaculate mosaic tiled floor, her heels clicking too loudly on the polished ceramic, past little huddled groups of seated mourners, until she found Sarah, seated near the front. Sarah sat stiff-backed and dry-eyed, as though she were impatient with the whole process, but Claire knew she was suffering. Claire sat down beside her and studied the stained glass. It was a cloudy day, so the colors were muted, but even so, they were incredibly rich. Claire's eye followed the line of a stone column up to the vaulted ceiling, where a single spotlight shown down on the altar.

Mystery. Mysterioso. Mysterium.

Places like this were man's physical representation of the eternally mysterious, the place where life and death merge and become one. As Claire sat there she became filled with a sense of awe, of the power of the life force, but also of the final mystery, death, which seemed to her now less frightening somehow. It was closer here, but less intimidating, because it was an accepted part of the mystery of life.

At the front of the church stood a heavy mahogany coffin. Claire shuddered.

"I know it's hideous, but my sister stipulated an open coffin in her will," Sarah had said a few days earlier. "I don't know where she got such medieval notions—certainly not from our parents, who believed in cremation. I think it's positively macabre, but . . . well, it's her last wish. I just hope they do a good job on the makeup," she added with a sad little smile. "You know how vain Blanche could be, and she wanted to be beautiful even in death."

Repulsed and fascinated, Claire couldn't help going up to look in the coffin. Blanche did look beautiful; her face in death was serene and beatific, her skin ivory white, a pink blush expertly applied to the cold cheeks. Her thin lips curled upward in a slight smile. A clear plastic lid covered the top of the coffin, and Claire was reminded of Snow White waiting in her glass coffin for the magic kiss of a prince to restore her from a deathlike trance. *No prince could rescue Blanche now,* Claire thought sadly as she returned to her seat, *and fairy tales don't really come true.*

> *Manch' bunte Blumen sind an dem Strand,*
> *meine Mutter hat manch' gülden Gewand.*

Claire's ruminations were interrupted by the minister, a tall, long-jawed man whose deep voice echoed roundly through the stone columns and carved oak pews. He stood not at the high pulpit, but before the altar, his notes resting on the outstretched wings of a fierce brass eagle, its sharp beak open, talons gripping a large brass ball. On the opposite choir pew a carved wooden angel kneeling in prayer faced the eagle, as if begging for mercy.

Sarah had arranged a very simple and traditional service, given entirely by the minister. She did not have any patience with what she called "these New Age funerals," where everyone got up to talk about the departed. "They can do that on their own time," she said peevishly, but Claire knew that what Sarah had most wanted to avoid was the suggestion that she herself might say a few words: she was terrified of speaking in public. So she and Amelia had written a tasteful and moving tribute to Blanche, praising her virtues and making light of her faults.

" . . . she was a woman people paid attention to," Father Thomas was saying, "and she could be many things, but she was never boring."

Claire smiled. That much was true. Blanche was exasperating, self-centered and capricious, but though those traits in others could be tedious, in Blanche they had a certain grace which was pure Blanche. She looked across the aisle and saw Anthony Sciorra, his face heavy with grief, staring at the altar with an expression of utter defeat. *Poor Anthony; poor, deluded Anthony.* He looked as though he were in his own world, not hearing a word of Father Tom's carefully enunciated words. Father Tom was a man who liked the sound of his own voice, and he spun out his phrases with a sense of his own dignity. *All is vanity. Well, why not?* Claire thought. *Better vanity than nothing at all.* Next to Anthony sat Amelia, her small, blunt features crinkled into a mask of worry and concern as she glanced at Anthony from time to time. The thought hit Claire that Amelia was not so much mourning for Blanche as she was worried about Anthony.

Claire called Meredith from the church to say she would pick her up on the way to the reception, but Meredith insisted she could make her own way there.

"It's only fourteen blocks, for God's sake," she said disdainfully.

But Claire felt responsible for the child's safety, and insisted on coming by. When she got there Meredith was in the lobby waiting. She wore an ankle-length forest-green skirt under a black silk blouse. She was so thin that no matter what she wore clothes hung limply on her bony frame.

"How was the service?"

"It was nice, actually."

"Any cops there?"

Claire paused. She thought she had seen someone in a battered trench coat leaving the church. Could it have been the familiar weary, sloped shoulders of Detective Jackson. She wasn't sure.

"I don't think so," she said.

When they arrived at Amelia's the reception was in full swing. It looked much like her other parties, except that it was catered and everyone wore dark colors. Claire was surprised to see so many people she had never seen before. She never dreamed that Blanche knew so many different kinds of people. Upper East Side chic rubbed shoulders with East Village grunge: at the bar, a svelte brunette in a black linen pantsuit stood next to a couple of green-haired, nose-ringed teenagers in black leather.

"Wow, Blanche sure did get around," Meredith said with admiration when one of the teenagers turned toward them. Claire inched toward the food table, which was heavily laden, though without Amelia's artistic touch; it looked like catered food.

"I just couldn't face doing it myself this time," Amelia had said apologetically. Sarah insisted on paying for everything, including the two discreet waiters who served drinks and passed hors d'oeuvres. Claire ordered a red wine for herself and a soda for Meredith, and then turned to greet Amelia, who was making her way through the crowd toward her.

"Oh, Claire," Amelia said, hugging her. Then she turned to Meredith. "You must be Meredith. I'm Amelia Moore. Thank you for coming."

"Thank you for having me," Meredith responded politely, then added, "I would have come to the funeral, but Claire wouldn't let me."

"It's not that I wouldn't let you," Claire began, annoyed.

"Oh, a funeral is no place for a young person," said Amelia. "You should be out enjoying life, not sitting in a stuffy church listening to eulogies."

"Oh, but I'm very interested in death," said Meredith. "After all, it's a big part of life."

Amelia's head gave a little jerk, and she looked at Meredith as though the girl were possessed. "Please help yourselves to food," she said lamely. "I ordered far too much . . ."

Just then the front door opened and Willard Hughes entered the room. Claire had not seen him at the service, and wondered if he had bothered to come, or if he had just shown up here in expectation of a free meal. He was wearing a beige suit, which Claire thought inappropriate, considering the occasion. His thin strands of black hair were combed over his shiny bald crown.

"Excuse me," said Amelia, "I must mingle." She wandered off through the crowd, and Claire wondered if she were trying to avoid Willard. *Not a bad idea,* she thought too late as Willard sauntered over to where she and Meredith were standing.

"Hello, Claire," he said in his most civil snarl.

"Hello, Willard," she replied, taking a large gulp of red wine. *I'll be damned if I'm going to face him sober,* she thought. Her left palm began to itch, and she scratched it with the bottom of her wineglass.

"Who's this?" Willard said, turning his gaze on Meredith.

"I'm Meredith Lawrence."

"Well, hello Meredith Lawrence. I'm Willard Hughes."

"Yes, I know."

"Oh?"

"Yes; your picture is on the jacket cover of all of your books."

"Oh, you read my books?"

"Some of them—but Claire has most of them."

"Well, she'd better—she's my editor!" Willard barked, laughing at his own joke. Meredith did not laugh, but looked at him calmly. Her gaze evidently disconcerted Willard, because his left shoulder began to twitch. Claire had an impulse to laugh, but she stifled it with another gulp of wine. The room was beginning to fuzz nicely now, and, feeling her stomach muscles relax, Claire realized that she had been holding them tightly.

"Terrible thing, Blanche's death, wasn't it?" Willard was saying to Meredith.

"Can you keep a secret?" Meredith leaned toward him.

"Well . . . yes, I guess so," Willard said, leaning down, off balance.

"I'm going to find the murderer," Meredith told him in a half whisper.

Willard's mouth formed a perfect "O," but he did not say anything. He just nodded, and his shoulder twitched more violently.

"I see," he managed finally, looking to Claire for help, but Claire was feeling vindictive, so she just smiled and shrugged.

"Well, I suppose I'd better go greet the other bereaved mourners," he said finally, and then, turning to Meredith: "Can I tell you something from experience? The murderer is often the last person you would suspect. Take it from me; I've created dozens of them."

Meredith rolled her eyes.

"That's fiction. In real life it's different."

Willard smiled. "Is it? I wonder."

With a final smirk at Claire, he wandered off into the crowd.

"He's creepy," said Meredith. "His books are creepy, too. I read them, but I've always thought the person who wrote them must be weird—and I was right."

Just then Claire saw Peter Schwartz coming toward them. He looked natty in a black suit with dark blue pinstripes over a crisp white shirt.

"Claire—I'm so glad you're here. I just narrowly avoided

a 'close encounter of the third kind' with Willard. Hello," he said, seeing Meredith. "I'm Peter Schwartz."

"Hello," said Meredith.

"This is Meredith," Claire said. "She's—"

"I'm her ward," Meredith interrupted, holding out her hand.

"Well, well—why you didn't tell me, Claire?" said Peter, shaking Meredith's hand.

"The papers haven't all been signed yet," Meredith continued, "but it's just a matter of time."

"Well, congratulations to both of you," Peter replied amiably, raising his glass.

Claire raised her glass and drank. She did not have the energy or the gumption to explain anything right now. She would tell Peter the whole story at the office on Monday.

"How long have you been in New York?" Peter asked.

"Oh, about a week now—but I've been here before," Meredith added quickly.

"How do you like it?"

"I find the intellectual climate here infinitely superior to the stuffy bourgeois suburbs of Connecticut. There is little there to engage the inquisitive young mind."

Peter's pleasant mouth lifted in a smile, and his eyes actually twinkled.

"I see. It sounds like you escaped just in time."

Meredith shrugged.

"I would have made do. Still, this is the place for me."

Peter smiled more widely.

"Well, we're jolly glad to have you here."

"Thank you," Meredith replied gravely. "Do you mind if I ask you a personal question?"

"Well, I guess not. What is it?"

"Do you have to take insulin injections?"

Peter looked startled.

"Meredith . . . " Claire began.

"No, it's all right," said Peter. "Why did you ask me that?"

"Well, you're a diabetic, aren't you?"

"How did you know that?"

"You're wearing a Medic Alert bracelet. I read what it said when you lifted your wineglass."

"Hmm. You're very observant, Meredith."

Meredith shrugged. "It's what I do," she said with an unsuccessful attempt at modesty.

"Why do you want to know about the insulin?"

"Just curious, I guess."

Claire felt she should intercede again.

"Meredith, it's none of your business—"

Peter put his hand on her arm.

"No, Claire, it's all right, really. How often do I get to talk to anyone so interested in my personal health? Yes, I do take insulin injections, since you ask. I've had this condition since childhood." He smiled ruefully. "It's a bloody nuisance."

"I'm sorry to hear that. Juvenile onset is much more serious, isn't it?"

Peter's smile faded. "Yes, it is."

Peter's eyes wandered around the room, and then he gripped Claire's arm.

"Bloody hell—Willard at one o'clock high and closing in. I need one more Scotch before I face him." Peter was partial to single-malt Scotch, and had probably brought his own bottle. He turned to Meredith. "It was nice meeting you. Stop by the office sometime and we'll give you the official tour."

"Thank you, I will."

Peter darted off through the crowd with surprising agility, given his stubby little body. Claire turned to Meredith.

"Why did you ask him about the insulin?"

"Just doing my job. The poison was most probably injected into the apples with a syringe, you know."

"You suspect Peter?"

"I suspect everyone and no one. The important thing is we have located someone with easy access to a syringe, though he wasn't necessarily the one who used it."

"But who . . . ? Do you mean someone could have—"

"Could have used it with or without his consent. Or

maybe it wasn't his syringe at all. I don't know yet . . . it's interesting, though."

"Well, presumably anyone could get hold of a syringe if they really wanted to."

Meredith's eyes narrowed and she bit the inside of her cheek. "Perhaps so . . . perhaps so."

Claire thought about Peter and what reason he could possibly have to want Blanche dead. If he was involved, she decided, there was a lot she didn't understand about human nature.

Just then she saw Sarah's cousin Marshall Bassett slinking his way through the crowd toward them. He was wearing a loose-fitting black Armani suit over a grey silk shirt, and the clothes hung well on his elegant slim frame. The way he moved showed that he looked good, knew it, and wanted you to know it. Claire smiled. With Marshall, clothes were more than just vanity; they were an expression of his joie de vivre. He took the same pride in looking good that Amelia took in cooking well, and Claire had to admire his style.

"Hello, ladies," he said, pulling up beside them. "So this is the famous Meredith."

"I'm hardly famous," Meredith said stonily.

"Well, you are in these parts, honey." Marshall laughed. "You're the hottest thing that's happening right now."

"This is Marshall Bassett," said Claire. "He's—"

"I'm the Dreaded Gay Relative of the Deceased," Marshall interrupted, winking at Meredith. "I only come out at night, of course, to prey on innocent straight people. I serve a useful function, however, as the black sheep in an otherwise exemplary family. But enough about me—let's talk about you. I hear you're going to find the murderer."

"That's right," said Meredith.

"How delicious." Then Marshall's face suddenly went slack and he dropped his sardonic tone. "I hope you do, you know. She was a good egg, Blanche was . . . a little crazy, but then, who isn't? She was a good kid underneath all that mascara and shoe polish she called makeup. Now there's only me and Sarah the Terrible left."

"Did you get along with Blanche, then?" said Meredith. Marshall smiled.

"What an interesting phrase. Let me see . . . I suppose I *went* along with her, which is what you did with Blanche. She was rather—headstrong, I think, is the term they use with horses and women like her. Come to think of it, she was rather like a highly strung young filly. Well, not so young, maybe, but then Blanche had an interesting formula for divining her age. I'm not sure, but I think it involved calculus and phases of the moon . . . what was I saying? Oh, yes— about Blanche and me. We were great buddies as children down in North Carolina, you know; Sarah was older and thought we were just too boring for words, so Blanche and I did everything together. She was a great storyteller, and liked to scare people even back then. She had me believing that there were man-eating bears out in the woods, and Indians still roaming around looking for white people to scalp.

"She and I spent one entire summer jumping out from behind trees, trying to outdo one another scaring each other to death. She got me good, she really did. She hid behind the shower curtain for half an hour, waiting for me to come in and use the bathroom, and then when I did, she stuck her hand out right in front of my face and snorted really loud. I did a standing broad jump backward and landed in the hall, and then we both fell down on the ground laughing. We couldn't stop laughing, it was so funny."

Marshall swallowed, and Claire saw that his eyes were moist. He took a sip of red wine. "Funny how when people die everyone tells stories about them, isn't it? Such a cliché, and yet . . . well, anyway, it's a pity more people didn't see that side of Blanche. Ever since college, what she presented to the world was her Southern Dragon Lady mask." Marshall shrugged. "Well, she lost the love of her life in school, or so she used to say . . . uh, speaking of dragon ladies, there's one approaching us off the port bow."

Claire followed his gaze and saw Sarah winding her way slowly toward them, her tall, lean body stately as a stork on its long thin legs. Marshall looked around for an escape, but it was too late; Sarah was upon them.

"Claire, how are you?" she said graciously, extending both her hands. Her grip was firm, and there was emotion in the squeeze she gave Claire. Sarah was just barely holding on, and the act of shaking hands seemed to help her maintain her strength.

"Hello, dear," she said to Meredith, who nodded in reply.

"Well, Sarabelle, it's a lovely party you've thrown; Blanche would have approved," Marshall said in a voice that Claire had trouble reading. It sounded sincere, but with Marshall the possibility of irony was always lurking behind every phrase.

"I'm so glad you think so," Sarah returned politely, and again Claire wasn't sure, but thought she sensed a frostiness under the polite Southern gentility.

"Will you excuse me?" Marshall said, addressing all three of them. "I have to go see a man about a dog. Nice meeting you, Meredith. I hope you succeed in your quest, and if you need any help, give me a call. I might know a thing or two that you could use."

As Marshall sauntered off Sarah looked after him.

"What on earth was he talking about?" she asked, the disdain in her voice evident now.

"He's going to help me find the murderer," said Meredith.

Sarah raised a thin eyebrow.

"Oh, really? How very charming of him," she said. "I'm sure he'll be a natural; he's good at poking his nose in where it doesn't belong."

"Why don't you like each other?" Meredith wanted to know.

Sarah looked at her and laughed.

"Good Lord, child, do you ever *stop*?"

"Only when I'm asleep."

"Meredith, I think you've done enough sleuthing for today," Claire said gently, with an apologetic glance at Sarah.

"Oh, come on—please?" Meredith begged, and the sudden shift from penetrating detective to whiny child made Claire laugh.

"Meredith, people have other things to do than answer your questions all the time."

"But—"

"I'll tell you what," said Claire, surprised to hear her father's Bargaining Parent tone in her voice. "Why don't we stay a little longer and then we'll go home and rent a video—anything you want, okay?"

Meredith sighed. "Okay," she said, as if she were making a great and generous concession just to humor Claire.

As they were leaving, Claire saw Sarah and Marshall huddled alone in a corner. Sarah was staring off into space, and Marshall was leaning toward her, talking.

"Don't worry, your little secret's safe with me," he said, and then he said something else Claire couldn't make out. She looked down at Meredith, and saw that she had been watching too.

"Come on," she said, feeling guilty for eavesdropping. "Let's go before the video store closes."

On the way home, Claire realized that she had not seen Anthony at the reception. She started to mention it to Meredith, but then checked herself. She couldn't imagine why Anthony would miss the funeral reception of the woman he had loved so intensely.

Chapter 8

The next day Meredith took the first train to Hartford. With the girl gone, Claire became restless. It was as though she had left some of her incessant energy and movement behind, to be absorbed by Claire through the air. She began taking long walks along Riverside Drive, and when she was in her apartment she found it hard to sit still. She added to Meredith's store of Pepperidge Farm cookies—Brussels, Mint Milanos, and Lemon Crunch—and ate them with tea in the evening after work.

She began taking more of an interest in the plots of her authors' mysteries. Though plot details had never been her strong point—she was always more interested in character, setting, atmosphere—now Claire analyzed them closely, suggesting clues and red herrings to her authors.

"What's gotten into you?" Willard said one day on the phone, after Claire suggested a couple of possible clues to use in his latest mystery, *Death Comes Unannounced*.

"What do you mean?" she responded, always on the defensive with Willard.

"Well, you've changed. What's all this interest in plot suddenly?"

"Oh, I don't know . . . broadening my horizons, I guess."

"It's because of Blanche's murder, isn't it?"

"What do you mean?"

"You're obsessing about solving Blanche's murder."

"No, I don't think so . . ."

Willard snorted, not exactly into the receiver, but loud enough so that Claire could hear him.

"All right, fine. I'm sorry I brought it up. When is the kid coming back?"

Willard always referred to Meredith as "the kid."

"A week from Friday."

"Good. Maybe you'll start acting like yourself then, and leave the sleuthing to her."

After they hung up, Claire decided Willard was just being possessive about his work. He never liked interference of any kind, and tended to regard any suggestion Claire made as interference. She shook her head and opened a new bag of Mint Milanos. Willard was such a pain. Many authors welcomed editorial advice—in fact, actively solicited her responses—but Willard was simultaneously arrogant and insecure, so that any suggestion she made was immediately perceived as a threat or a challenge. She had recently suggested to Peter that he consider assigning Willard to another editor—a man, perhaps—but Peter responded as though personally hurt by this idea. With Blanche gone, he pointed out, Willard was now their best-selling author.

"Think of what it would look like," he said. "Think of what they'll say—that you're losing your touch, that I've lost confidence in you, that you're on your way out."

Claire had to agree that it would look odd. She had been Willard's editor for five years now, and like him or not, he lent her prestige. Now that she had him, it seemed she was stuck with him. And so she endured the whiny phone calls and the complaining—his endless need for encouragement, for her assurance that his talent was indeed extraordinary, that he lifted the genre to a new level.

In fact, his books were little more than standard pageturners, but they were written with a spare and confident style. His books were brisk and commanding in a way that Willard himself could never manage to be in person. In fact, Claire consistently found it amazing how many of her writers transformed themselves in their work. Irritating, whiny Willard wrote with masterful terseness; flirtatious, distracted Blanche displayed a cool, collected intelligence in her books. It was as though the unexpressed or undeveloped aspects of their personalities found a home in their writing.

One of the things Claire had always liked about books was how words on a page always look the same as other words. A writer can communicate straight to the reader through these words, this black on white, without the intervention of physical appearance, voice, personality, or any of the other countless distractions involved in a face-to-face encounter. The words stood alone, the sole representation of the writer's mind and feelings, and thus the playing field was always level: the tools were the same, and the reader would not be put off by a homely face or unpleasing voice, a regional accent or an ungainly, unattractive social persona. The writer's voice resided solely in the arrangement of words on the page, and the reader could hear those words spoken in the voice of his or her choice, in the privacy of his or her own head. It was egalitarian and democratic: the only criterion for success was the writer's skill with words.

People are so complicated, Claire thought as she dug into the bag of Mint Milanos . . . *not like mirrors, but more like prisms, with their endless refractions of light*—Hesse had *talked about it in* Steppenwolf, *and Shakespeare had understood it, of course . . .*

"Each man in his time plays many parts."

Claire looked out onto 102nd Street and wondered what her parts would be . . . was she never to be a mother, never to hear the word "mother" spoken to her and only her? Meredith's presence in her life had filled a gap she had not even known existed. Much of her day now consisted of thoughts about things to do with Meredith, sights Meredith might like to see when she came back.

"Willst, feiner Knabe, du mit mir geh'n?
Meine Töchter sollen dich warten schön

*Meine Töchter führen den nächtlichen rein
Und wiegen und tanzen und singen dich ein."*

As the week progressed Claire fell into a funk. She began wandering around the apartment, moving things from one place to another. The phone rang several times over the weekend, and when she answered it the line went dead. This only contributed to her irritation, and she stopped overfeeding Ralph, who protested bitterly. For the first time even her beloved apartment felt confining, and she was restless and fidgety in it. She felt herself falling down a smooth slope of depression, with nothing to grasp onto. Everything seemed pointless and desultory, even eating and sleeping. She spent half the day Saturday in her ratty blue terrycloth bathrobe, dressing only to go out for milk—the only desire she seemed to have retained was her need for coffee.

She felt she was wasting time, letting it slip away, and yet the more she worried, the harder it was for her to do anything. She wished someone would call her, even just to talk—but then couldn't imagine whom she would want to talk to. All of her friends suddenly seemed foolish and predictable; she couldn't think of one she had anything important to tell. Her whole life in fact appeared ridiculous and pointless to her; here she was, a single, aging editor of run-of-the-mill mysteries, midwife to other people's mediocrity. She told herself not to dwell on these things, but the harder she tried, the more she hardened into an angry silence.

Claire was sinking into what her father used to call her "people are idiots" mode, in which she felt everyone around her was useless or irritating or both.

"Uh-oh," her father would say, "look out. Claire's on the warpath. She's decided we're all idiots and she's out to prove it." Sometimes his teasing would snap her out of her mood like a splash of cold water in the face, and sometimes it would just drive her deeper into her perverse determination to suffer—and make everyone suffer along with her if possible. Her mother would react with an icy silence of her own, and then the standoff would last until one of them grew tired, or until Claire's father prodded them both out of it.

She considered taking the train to Hudson and surprising Robert, but he had several jobs this weekend and wouldn't have much time for her. She couldn't see going all the way up there just to mope around his house. More than anything, she hated herself for falling into this black mood, hated the self-pity, but the more she tried to shame herself out of it, the more a part of her dug its heels in and refused to budge. Claire felt herself wallowing, slogging around in a mire of self-involvement. Objectively, of course, she knew she was one of the world's lucky ones, that her life was privileged and comfortable, but this weekend, faced with the confining walls of her apartment, her life seemed empty. She considered calling Robert and telling him how she felt, but something told her that he would just be impatient with her; he was very English that way.

Finally, at a loss for what to do, she turned on the television. Charlie Rose was interviewing an insistently robust, tanned man whose assertive jaw and swept-back blond hair gave him the look of a movie star. The caption on the screen read DR. BOB ARNOT, and Dr. Bob was energetically explaining to Charlie that to control your blood sugar was to control your destiny. Charlie, haggard and hunched over, nodded warily, his eyes trapped. Claire sighed and changed the channel.

Oprah was talking to three young black women and three white women. One of the white women, an expensively dressed blonde, was speaking to the black women.

"Don't you see that it's violence against women?" she said, her eyes pleading. Two of the black women looked stonily ahead, ignoring her question; the third, a large, very light-skinned African-American, shook her head violently.

"You just don' get it, do you? It's the same old story all over again: get the nigger!"

Claire winced at the sound of the word; it was so ugly, carrying behind it centuries of violence and racial hatred. The blonde in the expensive pantsuit looked deflated.

"But it's so clear he's *guilty*!" she said in a defeated voice.

One of the black women shook her head. "Maybe to you, white girl, but not to *us!*"

The audience hooted and roared. Claire turned off the television. The woman was right: as far as many black women were concerned, when push came to shove, racial empathy trumped sisterhood every time. Claire didn't understand it, and knew she couldn't understand it because she had never been where those black women had been.

Later that afternoon Claire called the video store and reserved three Buster Keaton films—but even *The General* failed to stir her from her apathy. It wasn't until Sunday evening that it occurred to her that she was missing Meredith. She wasn't even sure she liked Meredith—the girl could be very irritating—and yet the emptiness Claire felt was because of her absence. Sitting in the living room, she imagined Meredith opposite her on the couch, sipping tea, her thin legs pulled up underneath her, bony knees protruding like white knobs from under her skirt. Meredith in the kitchen, carefully arranging the latest cache of Pepperidge Farm cookies, alphabetically, Bordeaux to Zanzibar.

Sarah had suggested that Meredith might be autistic, and Claire scoffed at the idea, but, in thinking about her now, she thought maybe Sarah had a point. Maybe there were degrees of autism, variations on the condition that no one had yet discovered. Maybe Meredith was suffering—if that was the word—from a kind of autism . . .

When the phone rang Sunday night, Claire was more pleased than she expected to be when she heard Meredith's voice on the other end.

"Claire, it's me." Meredith sounded more childlike over the phone than in person.

"Hello, Meredith. How are you?"

"Oh, as well as can be expected, as they say, considering that I'm back in the Wasteland. Do you know, I think Eliot must have lived in Connecticut at some point."

"How are you getting along with your stepmother?"

Claire could feel the rolling of Meredith's eyes in her voice.

"One does not 'get along' with my stepmother, Claire;

one simply tolerates her, as one would a noxious odor—and attempts to remain sane."

"Well, are you doing that?"

"Oh, yes, I'm perfectly sane; *she's* the one who's bonkers. How my father could have gotten pulled into her undertow is something I'll never understand. His judgment must have been impaired by his excessive grief over my dear departed mother."

There was a pause, and then Meredith said, "Do you miss me?"

Claire took a deep breath.

"Yes," she said. "Yes, I do."

"I miss you, too," Meredith replied breezily, as though it cost her nothing. Claire wondered why she had held on to her own response so tightly, her emotions guarded currency to be spent frugally.

"So," said Meredith, "whatcha up to?"

Claire paused again. What, exactly, *was* she doing? Moping around, feeling ill-used by the world—in short, nothing; worse than nothing. Meredith, on the other hand, always seemed to be doing something.

"Oh, not much," Claire replied cautiously. "How about you?"

"Oh, research . . . cataloging clues, that sort of thing."

"Cataloging—"

"Clues. You know, who might be guilty and why."

"I see."

"Some people run on instinct, you know, but I have to organize my thoughts."

"Oh. Do you have any—"

"Any suspects? Oh, everyone's a suspect until proven innocent. Even you."

"Me?"

Meredith laughed. "Don't worry, I don't *seriously* think you did it. But you could have; like most everyone else, you had the means and the opportunity . . . whether or not you had the motive, I'm not sure. I don't think so. After all, Blanche was the goose that laid the golden egg, wasn't she?"

That was the second time Claire had heard Blanche referred to in this way since her death. *The third time it's comedy,* she thought. Just then she heard the beep of call waiting on her phone line.

"Meredith, I have another call."

"All right, I'll go. When do you want me to come back down?" There was a hint of a plea in her voice.

"Oh, I don't know . . . whenever you want."

"Good! I'll tell Dad he can bring me down Friday after school, okay?"

"All right."

"See you then!"

Claire pushed the button to click on the other call.

"Hello?" she said.

"Hello, Claire." It was Robert.

"Oh, hi!" Claire thought her voice sounded too bright, forced.

"I got a minute to myself, thought I'd call."

"How nice."

Claire heard music in the background.

"What are you listening to?" she said.

"Oh, that's Verdi's *Otello* . . . I was just in the mood for it." There was a slight pause, and then he said, "Do you miss me?"

How unlike Robert to ask that question, and how odd to hear it twice like this.

"Yes, I do."

"I miss you. Listen, why don't you come up next weekend?"

"Well, I . . ." Next weekend Meredith would be arriving.

"What's wrong? Don't you want to come?"

"Well, yes, it's just that—"

"What?"

"Well, Meredith's coming down on Friday."

"No problem; bring her along."

"Well, she's—"

"I know, I know—she's a handful. I don't mind; bring her. We'll find something to occupy her."

"Well, if you're sure . . ."

"Of course I'm sure. Don't give it a second thought, really."

After they hung up, Claire felt a little less depressed, but she was still restless. She hadn't mentioned her mood to Robert because she thought he would disapprove. She could imagine his response:

"Well, then go out and *do* something. Don't just mope about on your own."

Claire headed toward the kitchen to make some coffee. Ralph wove in between her legs, mewing pathetically.

"Did you miss me?" she said to him under her breath.

"Hey!" she yelped when he got under her feet, making her trip and almost fall. In response, he jumped up onto the kitchen counter, rubbing against the cupboard containing the cat food.

"You are so spoiled, do you know that?" Claire said.

Ralph sat and looked at her with wide, virtuous eyes.

"All *right*," she said, giving in, taking out a can of Tuna Treat.

Ralph jumped onto the floor, purring like a diesel, rubbing up against her ankles.

"It's not me you love," Claire muttered to him. "It's Tuna Treat. I'm just the vehicle for your digestive satisfaction." As she said it she was struck by the notion that it sounded like something Meredith would say.

After she fed him, Claire made herself a strong cup of decaf Kona blend, her favorite coffee, and went into the living room to drink it. She put on a recording of Rossini's *Messa Solenne* and lay down on the couch to listen. She sighed with pleasure at the first notes of the Kyrie, with its inventive and compelling bass line, and felt her stomach relax as the sopranos and altos made their entrance, eerily floating over the orchestra. *Kyrie eleison, Christe eleison . . .*

Chapter 9

Detective Wallace Jackson lay on the couch in his dark-ened study staring up at the play of headlights on the ceiling. He wore a wool sweater under his tatty grey trench coat; the heat in his building was malfunctioning again and the room had a distinct chill. He had gone to bed early, but unable to sleep, he wandered around the apartment for a while, until fatigue finally brought him to the couch in his study. Sometimes, when he couldn't sleep in his bed, he was able to fall asleep on the soft leather sofa in the study. He wasn't sleepy now—tired, yes, but not sleepy. His mind was working rapidly, about so many things that it was hard to keep track of them all.

Sleepless nights were not so frequent as they were a few years ago. Following the death of his wife, they had been the norm rather than the exception. He resisted taking the med-ication his doctor prescribed because his Scottish Presbyter-ian background held any and all such drugs in deep suspicion. Finally, though, as the circles under his eyes dark-ened and his hands began shaking with fatigue, he had ac-quiesced, sinking gratefully into nights of dreamless, drug-assisted sleep.

He got up from the couch and looked out the window,

where a light snow was settling on the fire escape. Anne had
loved snow—to her, extreme weather was an adventure, a
challenge. On more than one occasion she insisted on going
out in blizzard conditions just for the sheer exhilaration of it.
Jackson went into the kitchen and made himself a cup of
cocoa. He was just now beginning to pull out of the numb-
ness that had followed Anne's death. Food had regained its
taste, and the thick layer of sadness which hovered over his
life showed promise of lifting.

He went back to the study and put on a recording of the
Mozart *Requiem*. He sat down and leaned back to listen to
the opening bars of the first chorus. He closed his eyes—and
to his surprise, Claire Rawlings's face suddenly appeared in
his mind's eye. He didn't know why he thought of her just
then, but he allowed his mind to study her face—the high
cheekbones and thin aristocratic nose with its slight bump,
the full mouth and deep-set blue eyes. It was a good face,
plain in some lights and beautiful in others, but it was certainly a strong face.

Claire awoke to silence. She had slept through the entire
recording of the Rossini. She stretched and sat up. Her
shoulder bag lay open on the floor, and when she picked it
up to move it, a piece of paper fell to the floor: Detective
Jackson's business card. She picked the card up and looked
at the number written in ink on the back. Claire had an irrational desire to call him, to hear his soft, weary voice . . . she
imagined the heavy, sad eyes and rumpled grey hair. She
looked at the card again. She wondered if she called whether
a woman would answer. Remembering his tattered coat
with the missing button, she had an instinct that the answer
was no—but she had been wrong before.

Carefully, she put the card next to the phone and settled
in the red chair to drink her coffee, which was cold by now.
If she called him, she would have to have a reason or it
would. look odd. Something she had forgotten to mention
before, maybe . . . Claire tried to think if she might have
anything of real value to say to Detective Jackson. She
stared at the business card, at the phone number written in

his neat, precise hand. She pictured his hands, the long fingernails and firm palms. *I miss you,* she thought. *I miss you, and I don't even know you.*

She lifted the phone and dialed his number. It rang twice, and midway through the third ring he answered.

"Jackson here."

Hearing his voice over the phone, Claire realized for the first time that what she had interpreted as weariness was in fact pain.

"Oh, hello, it's Claire—Claire Rawlings," she said, suddenly out of breath.

"Yes, Ms. Rawlings."

Call me Claire, she wanted to say, *call me anything you want, as long as you call me.*

"I—I just thought I'd call and—" And then she realized she had nothing at all to say, that she just wanted to hear his voice. There was a pause, and then he spoke.

"Are you frightened?"

"Am I—?"

"Are you frightened?" The voice was patient, tired.

"Well, I don't know . . . I guess maybe; I hadn't thought about it . . ."

"Don't worry, it's perfectly natural to feel what you're feeling under the circumstances. Someone you knew well has just been murdered. It would be odd if you felt nothing."

Claire suddenly realized that Jackson was right—she *was* scared; terrified, in fact—and her depression was just masking the feeling of terror that lurked beneath the surface of her consciousness. *How did he know?* she thought. *How could he read my mind like that?*

"You know, sometimes people get help . . . I could give you some numbers to call."

"Well, that's very kind, but I don't think—"

She broke off, confused, afraid to reveal any more of herself to him.

"Well, let me know if you change your mind. You can reach me here or at the precinct."

"Thank you. Have you . . . have you made any progress in the investigation?"

"I'm sorry, but I can't really go into specifics. I'm sure you understand. It's department policy."

"Of course . . . sure. Sorry, I just . . ."

"I know; I'm sorry, too. We're doing everything we can, I promise you."

"Oh, I'm sure you are."

Another pause, during which Ralph came and wrapped his body around Claire's ankles, purring. "Well, listen, thanks," she said. "I appreciate talking to you. Let me know if there's anything I can do."

"I will—and in the meantime, if you think of anything that might be of use, call me."

"I will. Thanks . . . goodbye."

"Good night."

Claire hung up the phone and looked out the window at the early winter darkness settling over the West Side. Lights burned in the windows of the buildings across the street. She could hear the faint sound of a piano coming from one of the buildings, someone picking their way through a Mozart sonata.

> *Meine Töchter führen das Nächtlichen rein*
> *Und wiegen und tanzen und singen dich ein*

Claire stood looking out the window for a long time, then closed the curtains. Somewhere out there in the darkness was Blanche's murderer, and whoever it was, the killer might not stop with one victim.

Chapter **10**

At the end of the week, Meredith returned to New York to spend a three-day weekend with Claire. Once back in town, the girl was reluctant to leave "the scene of the crime," as she put it, but Claire wanted Robert to meet her.

"Is he handsome?" said Meredith as they wandered around the Museum of Natural History on Friday afternoon. She particularly liked the Gem Room, where she stood staring at the Star of India for some time. "It says here that it was stolen from the museum and then recovered," she said. "Someone should really write a mystery about that."

"I'm sure someone has," said Claire, watching a group of Japanese tourists listening to a tour guide explaining the reason some diamonds are colored. The tour guide was short with frizzy brown hair, and she carried a little orange flag like the one bicyclists sometimes use to increase their visibility to cars. The Japanese tourists were nodding, their faces frozen in a public mask of polite interest.

"You haven't answered my question," said Meredith. "Is he handsome?"

"Robert? Yes, I guess he is."

"Do you have a picture of him?"

Claire opened her wallet and took out the picture of

Robert standing in front of the Croton Reservoir. Meredith studied it for a moment and then gave it back.

"He's cuter than Detective Jackson," she said bluntly.

Claire realized that the Japanese tourists were now looking at her and Meredith. Embarrassed, she took Meredith's hand and pulled her in the direction of the exit.

"Hey, where are we going?" Meredith protested.

"Somewhere more private," Claire said grimly. "How about a cup of tea in the cafeteria?"

Meredith shrugged. "That's hardly more private."

Minutes later they sat sipping tea in the cafeteria in the basement of the museum. It was not exactly private, but the ambient noise of people talking and trays rattling echoed through the tiled floors and walls and created a kind of privacy. Meredith sat picking at a sweet roll, carefully removing the pecans before tearing off strips of dough and putting them delicately into her mouth.

"What's wrong, don't you like talking about Robert?" she said.

"I guess I'm just kind of private about these things."

"Do you have a crush on Detective Jackson?" Meredith plucked a pecan from her roll and deposited it carefully on the side of the paper plate.

"I think he's an attractive man."

"But Robert's cuter. Are you in love with Detective Jackson?"

Claire was caught off guard by the question. "Oh, what does that mean anyway, to be 'in love'?" she said feebly.

Meredith smiled a secret smile. "You are," she said. "You love Wallace Jackson," she said in the singsong voice of a child on a playground.

Claire couldn't think of a reply. Her stomach tightened and tingled. "Drink your tea," she said. She wasn't sure that she could allow herself to fall "in love" in the sense that Meredith meant. It seemed increasingly to Claire that growing older was a series of disillusionments, a letting go of expectations, a gradual freezing of options. She vaguely remembered a time when she had leaned eagerly into life, but now that seemed not only unrealistic but impossible. She no longer had the expectation of her needs being met by any one person. She felt ambivalent about most of the people in her life, and the truth was that she wasn't sure she could fall in love with anyone again. She looked at Meredith, busy dismembering her sweet roll, pale lips pursed, her kinky hair surrounding her face like an unruly orange halo. For just a moment she wished with all her heart she could be thirteen years old once again.

They decided to take the train up to Hudson on Saturday morning. Robert was photographing a wedding when they arrived, and so couldn't meet them at the station.

"If you take the later train I could come collect you," he had said over the phone Friday evening.

"Oh, it's not that much of a walk—it'll do us good," said Claire.

"All right, if you're sure. See you then."

Meredith had never taken the Lake Shore Line, and was very impressed with the scenery. It also seemed to have a tranquilizing effect on her; she sat staring out the window almost the whole trip.

As they walked up the hill from the train, Meredith huffed as noisily as possible to show her displeasure with the steepness of the hill. Meredith did not really like sustained physical exercise; she was kinetic without being athletic.

"There was a taxi place at the station," she said when they finally reached the part of Warren Street where the road leveled off.

"I know, but it's such a short walk," said Claire.

"Short but brutal. All I can say is you must really love him if you're willing to go through *that* each time you visit."

"Well, sometimes he picks me up."

Meredith was silent for a while as they walked along Warren Street. She looked at the calvacade of architecture with minimal interest, but studied any people they passed carefully. A dumpy woman with two small children returned her gaze, her pale eyes blank. The children were bundled in brightly colored snowsuits, but their eyes had the same dull glazed look as their mother's. When they had passed beyond hearing, Meredith shuddered.

"The living dead are alive and well in Hudson," she said.

When they got to Robert's house Claire knocked just to make sure he hadn't arrived early—Robert did not like to be taken by surprise—and then she turned the key in the lock and swung open the heavy green front door. The hall clock, an heirloom from England, struck four.

"Tea time!" cried Meredith, pulling out the packages of cookies she had stuffed in her bag as they were leaving. Claire had assured her that they sold Pepperidge Farm cookies in Hudson, but Meredith said she wasn't taking any chances and continued cramming her bag with packets of cookies.

Claire put on the kettle and then showed Meredith around the house. She seemed taken with it, and was suitably impressed with Robert's imaginative and quirky decorating style.

"Wow," she said, tugging on the heavy wooden sliding doors that separated the front and back parlors, "this place is really something. How did he find it?"

"It belonged to a painter friend of his who died. Robert bought it at the auction."

"Well, he got a good deal," said Meredith. "I don't know much about houses, but this one is really cool."

Just then the tea kettle split the air with its piercing whistle, and Meredith covered her ears.

"That kettle doesn't fool around," she said, wincing. "I'll get it." She moved toward the kitchen, hands still over her ears.

Claire wandered around the parlor, touching the furniture as she went. As she ran her hand lightly over a rosewood table, she was suddenly reminded of a scene she hadn't thought about in years: when she was eleven, just two years younger than Meredith, her family had left the big white house at the lake. There was a small grove of pine trees in the side lawn, and just before climbing into the car she had run tearfully to embrace each tree. She remembered grief filling her chest as she hugged each thin tree trunk, sticky with pine rosin, remembered her mother's sympathetic smile and her brother's snicker as she got into the car, wedged in between cardboard boxes full of china. Later Claire had written a rather bad and very sentimental poem about trees, which was published in her fifth-grade literary journal. She could still remember the feeling of missing each of those trees as if they were people—sentimental, perhaps, but real enough to her eleven-year-old mind.

Fifteen years later Claire learned the real meaning of grief when both of her parents died in a car crash. Afterward, she and her brother had drifted apart, stunned by the loss and not sure how to bridge the wall of pain that should have united but instead divided them.

Meredith emerged from the kitchen, carrying an enormous tea tray.

"Your tea, madame," she said, setting it on the rosewood table.

"Why, thank you," said Claire, taking a Bordeaux cookie from Meredith's dizzying assortment. She took a bite: butterscotch, her grandmother's specialty. She thought of her grandmother, baking, gardening; she was a woman of tremendous grace, which Claire had not inherited. She leaned back in an apricot upholstered wing chair and wondered what was triggering all of these nostalgic thoughts. She looked at Meredith, who was arranging her cookies on a blue flowered plate before devouring them. For Meredith, the past was all wrapped up in her mother's death, and Claire could feel the anger which simmered beneath the surface.

Just then Claire heard the front door open and Robert's voice came booming down the hall.

"Hello there—anyone home?"

"In here," Claire called.

Robert appeared in the doorway, a camera still slung around his neck.

"Aha—I see I'm just in time for tea. Hello," he said, seeing Meredith.

"Hello," she answered, her mouth full of cookies, fine crumbs spraying from her lips.

"You must be Meredith." Robert took off his camera and put it in the mahogany cabinet where he kept his equipment.

"And you must be Robert." Meredith swallowed and wiped the crumbs from her mouth.

Robert poured himself a cup of tea.

"Claire says you have quite a talent for detective work."

"Well, it would be false modesty if I denied it."

"Good for you!" said Robert in his hearty Schoolmaster voice, which always conjured up for Claire pictures of ruddy-cheeked English schoolboys running in for their cold showers after a game or two of rugby.

"Did Claire tell you what case we're working on now?" said Meredith.

"Oh, you mean that poor woman, her author friend? Yes, I know about it, but aren't the police working on that one?"

"Well, yes, but . . . well, you know how blind the police can be."

"Can they? I always thought they were rather clever over here. You know, like on television."

"Oh, it's nothing like on television," said Meredith.

"So you're going to show them how, are you?" said Robert, and Claire wondered if Meredith noticed the faint condescension in his voice.

"Well, *someone* has to help them," Meredith replied.

"Well, there you are," Robert said cheerfully. He turned to Claire. "What do you want to do tonight?"

"Oh, I hadn't thought about it, really."

"Well, I'm going to go up and shower and you have a look through the local rag and let me know what you decide," he said, and went upstairs. That was Robert: exits and entrances, not staying long anywhere, never wearing out his welcome, even in his own house.

"He didn't finish his tea," Meredith noted when he had gone.

In the end they decided to go to a small cinema in town playing second-run movies. The building, built around the turn of the century, was once a vaudeville theatre. The owner was slowly restoring it; in the meantime he had installed a little electric organ in the front of the theatre, and on weekends a local woman gave organ recitals before the film.

"Oh, we must go to the organ recital," Robert said. "It's too much, really. You have to see it."

They were the first to arrive, and Robert said he wanted to go across the street to get some coffee (the theatre didn't yet have a full concession service). Meredith insisted on accompanying him, so Claire sat by herself in the darkened theatre. She sat silently, her knees pulled up to her chest, imagining what it would be like to be enormously gifted, driven, and ambitious. She wasn't sure that it would be altogether pleasant, but it would be exciting, and she couldn't help feeling regret for a life she would never have. Only a few people could be stars, and the rest would orbit around them like planets in a solar system, grateful for the glow of their reflected light. Meredith was one of these stars, and Claire just hoped that she would not burn out before her time.

Looking around the empty theatre, Claire felt her body relax. She grew up in the country, but had quickly become accustomed to city life. It was only in stepping away from it that she realized how complicated the smallest things could be in New York. Life was so much easier in Hudson. Simple errands, such as a trip to the post office, were no longer ordeals. Instead of a half-mile walk followed by waiting in line for forty minutes, you just got in the car, drove to the post office, delivered your package, and went home. After living in New York City, Claire no longer took anything for granted. She enjoyed doing errands in Hudson, marveling at the ease of everything up here, the privacy of driving everywhere, the pleasure of simply loading groceries into a car instead of carting them home several blocks. In Hudson, she relished the opportunity to run small errands: she loved to wander around the cavernous, uncrowded aisles of the A&P, the shelves packed with consumer goods. There was even enough room in the aisles for two shopping carts to pass side by side, while in the city she often stood interminably behind a slow moving cart waiting to pass. Claire liked New York—the city had resonance for her—but the crowded quality of life there tapped into her claustrophobia. She sometimes felt as though she were constantly pushing through throngs of people in order to get anywhere, and then she would experience her old fear of entrapment.

Robert and Meredith returned just in time for the organist's entrance. She was an elderly woman and wore a blue sequined blouse over a red cotton skirt, silver lamé belt, all topped off with a rhinestone necklace. Her playing was uneven, with some numbers being better than others. Her third selection, "This Land Is Your Land," was not one of her better numbers. She kept having to slow down to accomplish the various ornamentations and runs in this particular arrangement. The effect was one of a phonograph record playing on a turntable whose motor was turning slowly and unevenly, and Claire found herself leaning forward every time the woman slowed down, as if by doing so she could push her back onto the tempo.

In New York the woman would not even have been a rehearsal pianist for an Off-Off-Broadway company, but here in Hudson she had a job, and Claire was glad for her. She even enjoyed the performance for its flaws and inconsistencies, because the very imperfection of the woman's playing testified to the difficulty of her task: unpolished, raw, she still loved the music enough to sit in front of strangers and make mistakes. Of course, she may have thought she was better than she was, but Claire forgave her that, and even admired her hubris, because Claire had little of it herself. She admired qualities in others that she herself lacked: Amelia's saintliness, Sarah's stoicism, Meredith's breathless ambition, Marshall's wicked wit. Claire sometimes thought that she herself was so perfectly ordinary, so lacking in qualities that would set her apart, that she wondered what someone like Robert saw in her. She wouldn't have thought she was his type, really, and yet . . . *Well, there was no accounting for taste.*

The movie playing that night was *Forrest Gump*. As they were walking out Meredith said, "Well, I guess it's good to be stupid if you're going to be a real American hero."

Robert laughed so loudly that all the other patrons looked

at him. Claire felt her face heat up, glad for the darkness so that no one could see her blush.

That night in bed, she said, "Well, what do you think of her?"

"She's a force of nature," Robert said, and then he bit her ear. "Speaking of nature . . ."

Claire rolled over and met his lips. For a moment she imagined that it was Wallace Jackson she was kissing, then felt so guilty she kissed Robert with more ardor.

"Mmm . . ." he said, "what's gotten into you?"

Claire came downstairs the next morning to find Meredith sitting on the living room floor with Robert's *Complete Works of William Shakespeare* on her lap.

"What are you reading?" said Claire.

"Othello."

Claire leaned down and looked over Meredith's shoulder. The page was turned to the moment in the play where Othello resolves to murder Desdemona.

> *Like to the Pontic sea,*
> *Whose icy current and compulsive course*
> *Ne'er feels retiring ebb, but keeps due on*
> *To the Propontic and the Hellespont,*
> *Even so my bloody thoughts, with violent pace,*
> *Shall ne'er look back, ne'er ebb to humble love,*
> *Till that a capable and wide revenge swallow them up.*

"In college I had an English professor who said Shakespeare must have been drunk when he wrote those lines," Claire remarked.

"Yeah?"

"Yeah."

"Hmm," said Meredith.

"The odd thing was that he said it with admiration, as though it were the most natural thing in the world."

Just then Robert walked into the room.

"And why not get drunk?" he said. "What does it mean, to get drunk? To forget for a few moments the everyday anxieties and fears we all carry around with us, the fears that lurk around us when we go to bed and are there again when we wake up. Why not get drunk indeed? To live with the awareness that God's in his heaven and all's right with the world. The gift of the grape is right up there with faith and hope and charity. So it diminishes judgment—well, look where our judgment has brought us so far. I say to hell with our judgment, because it is fatally flawed anyway. I say that we should be allowed our forgetfulness for a while, a waking forgetfulness in which the world around us loses its terror, and we allow ourselves to imagine that there is a possibility of redemption after all. If Shakespeare wasn't drunk when he wrote those lines, he should have been."

Meredith stared at Claire, who felt like she should applaud or something.

"Well, well," she said. "What's that from?"

Robert shrugged modestly. "Oh, a play I wrote when I was a foolish, callow youth. I played the hero, who delivered that speech in the second act. Kind of makes you appreciate Shakespeare, doesn't it?" he said to Meredith, smiling.

"Well, at least you *wrote* it," Meredith said with uncharacteristic diplomacy. She lay on the floor, her thin legs waving back and forth in the air, ankles crossing and uncrossing. Something about the motion reminded Claire of the flicking of a cat's tail.

Claire laughed. "Well, my professor was fired shortly afterward for alcoholism. He made an impression on me, though, and I always wondered what became of him."

"Well," said Robert, "are we ready to go out for our little sojourn?"

"Sure!" said Meredith, jumping up from the floor.

The three of them spent the day on a tour of Olana, the home of Hudson school painter Frederick Church. Robert loved the place, and as they wandered around the spacious rooms, with their Turkish-fantasy-palace decor, Meredith talked about Othello.

"How come he believes Iago?"

"Well, people are gullible . . . and his thing is that he's jealous."

"You mean it's his 'tragic flaw'?"

"Yeah."

Just then Robert came up behind them and put his hands around Claire's waist.

"Whose tragic flaw?"

"Othello," Meredith said. "We're talking about his jealousy."

"Ah, yes . . .

"'It is the green-eyed monster which doth mock
the meat it feeds on; that cuckold lives in bliss
Who, certain of his fate, loves not his wronger;
But, O! what damned minutes tells he o'er
Who dotes, yet doubts; suspects, yet soundly loves!'"

"Very impressive," said Claire.

Robert shrugged. "The result of an English public-school education—more rote learning than wisdom, I'm afraid."

"What's a cuckold?" said Meredith.

Robert cocked his head to the side. "Hmm . . . I don't think she's old enough for that, do you?" he said to Claire.

"In Elizabethan times it was a man whose wife had been unfaithful," said Claire. Just at that moment one of the museum curators passed. He was a thin, ascetic-looking man with a long bloodless face, and he raised a disapproving eyebrow at their conversation. Robert chuckled when the man was out of earshot.

"Maybe *he's* not old enough for it, either."

Claire laughed.

"Hmm," said Meredith. "The Elizabethans were really into that, I guess, huh?"

"Into cuckoldry? Hmm . . . that's an interesting notion," said Robert, giving Claire a squeeze.

"No, I mean they thought that was a really big deal," said Meredith.

"Some people still do think it's a big deal," said Robert.

"But not as much, not anymore."

"It depends on who you talk to."

As they approached the front door of the mansion, Claire looked at her watch.

"It's lunchtime. I'm starving."

"All right," said Robert. "Lunch is on me. Come on," he said to Meredith. "I'll race you to the car."

Meredith stopped walking. "I'm not really very physically inclined," she said.

"Too bad." He started off in the direction of the parking lot.

"Oh, go ahead," said Claire, "be a kid for once. It won't kill you, you know."

"All right," said Meredith, as if doing her a big favor, "if you insist." She started after Robert unenthusiastically, running in an ungainly trot.

"Come on," Robert called over his shoulder, "don't let an old man beat you."

Meredith ran a little faster, loping awkwardly on her long thin legs. Claire stood and watched as the wind picked up her fluffy orange hair and tossed it behind her like a banner.

That night Claire had trouble sleeping. She awoke from a dream and lay for a while looking at the ceiling. Robert slept serenely beside her, breathing in the slow, easy rhythms of peaceful slumber. She couldn't remember what she had been dreaming about, except that the lines from "The Erl King" once again roamed through her head.

> *Mein Vater, mein Vater, und hörest du nicht*
> *was Erlenkönig mir leise verspricht?*

She rolled over and readjusted her pillow, and as she did she inadvertently saw the clock on the bedside table: it was two o'clock. Claire was no stranger to insomnia: put to bed too early by her well-meaning mother, she spent many nights thrashing around in bed trying to sleep as a child. Sometimes as she lay awake, rolling back and forth between the sheets, it seemed to her the very sounds of the crickets in the night summoned her to action, to life. She longed to squeeze life as if it were an orange, extracting each last drop of juice. Sleep, that misty interrupter of consciousness, was her enemy, a last resort. Her mind fought its insistent tug as though it were the pull of its relative, death. As a child she bounded out of bed early each morning, eager for experience, but as an adult she found that transition also difficult to bridge. Once she had fallen into the cavern of sleep, the climb back into consciousness was laborious as the departure had been. She dreaded waking up the next morning, and the inevitable fatigue that would hit her in the middle of the day.

The truth was that Claire had recently begun to feel a resentment toward Meredith, and she was feeling guilty about it. She realized that her resentment was born in part from her growing attachment to the girl. She knew, too, that resentments are often deepest toward the people we care about the most, but somehow that did not allay her guilt. Although being in therapy had helped her come to terms with her mother's sometimes pious altruism, it was creeping into her subconscious again like a weed whose roots had been left in the ground. She once asked her mother if it was boring being stuck in the big house on the lake with no neighbors and two children, and a husband who spent long hours as an associate professor working on a doctoral thesis.

"Oh, no," was her breezy reply, "I was never bored. I found you fascinating." Not having children of her own at the time, Claire could only nod and suppose her mother was telling the truth, or some form of it. *It must be different when they're your own,* she remembered thinking at the time. Now, with Meredith, she realized the complexity of human relationships extended very much to those between children and adults—and realized also that her mother must have resented her and her brother, at least sometimes. Claire was certain she must have thought of the life she could have had without them. Now her mother was gone, and Claire would never know what she really thought.

Claire realized that her mother had done her best to spare her any guilt, any feeling of being unwanted, but she was sorry that her mother could never speak of these things to her, unable to voice the inevitable regrets that come with any choice. *Open a door and another is closed behind you.* We each choose our own truths, the codes by which we live, Claire thought, avoiding certain truths as we embrace others. Claire's mother's truths were good and noble and generous, and for the most part truly felt, but they were her truths. Claire would have to find her own—and so would Meredith. Meredith's obsession with detective work was her way of finding palpable, knowable truth: *this person is guilty,* and that's the end of it. Such truth, such hard facts, were all well and good, and give a sense of knowledge and control that she evidently desperately needed; but it was the more elusive truth Claire was concerned with—the endless forms of human interaction—which Claire needed to decode. Perhaps this was why she had become an editor; vicariously, through her writers, she might come to know what she needed to know. Like Meredith, her job was the endless search for the criminal: at the end of a mystery, the comforting label of Guilty was pinned upon the murderer like a scarlet letter, letting the rest of humanity sink gratefully into a righteous sense of innocence. *Well, I'm not perfect, but at least I'm no murderer;* that was the mantra that every reader could recite at the end of a good mystery novel.

Claire got up from the bed, being careful not to wake Robert, and crept down the hall toward Meredith's room. The door was ajar, and Meredith lay sprawled out on the bed, asleep. Mouth open, her springy red hair spread out all over the pillow, she was an unlovely sight, but as Claire watched her she felt the bond between them tightening, until it wound itself around her heart and she began to forget her life before Meredith entered it. There was so much about the girl that was irritating: her intellectual smugness, her presumptuousness, her air of superiority, but Claire could always see the frightened, abandoned child underneath all of it, and it pulled at her maternal instincts like a magnetic field.

She longed to speak of these things to Robert, to tell him of her uncertainties, but her relationship with him was built on a mutual undeclared pact: that both of them not speak of certain things, not release certain demons. At first she had been grateful to Robert for offering her this relief from the vagaries of her subconscious; she even felt guilty that she needed to speak of dark feelings she thought she had conquered after years of therapy, but after a while she wished that she could talk to Robert. She began to want to redraw the ground rules, to escape the need to "put on a happy face"; her face wasn't always happy, and she wanted Robert to know that. But when she was around him, she felt somehow that it was childish of her to want more.

Claire sat on the edge of the bed. A flash of lightning suddenly illuminated the trees outside, and Meredith stirred in her sleep.

> *Er hat den Knaben wohl in dem Arm,*
> *Er fasst ihn sicher, er hält ihn warm.*

Outside, thunder tore through the sky like the growling of a rabid dog, and lightning ripped across the heavens in jagged streaks, slashing the night in half. Watching from the window, Claire felt the exhilaration that extremes of weather always produced in her. She loved the raw fury of nature. Meredith was like a thunderstorm: furious, rampant, mercurial, and Claire watched her with the same kind of awe, a little afraid, but liberated by her willful power. Meredith rolled over and opened her eyes.

"I'm scared," she said.

"What are you frightened of?" said Claire.

Meredith shivered.

"I'm . . . I'm afraid of the thunder and lightning." She leaned her body against Claire, and Claire put her arms around the girl's thin shoulders.

"It's all right; there's nothing to be afraid of. Nothing's going to hurt you," she said, stroking her hair until she felt Meredith's body slowly begin to relax.

> *Siehst, Vater, du den Erlkönig nicht?*
> *Den Erlenkönig mit Kron' und Schweif?*

They sat like that for a long time, watching the storm together, until Meredith fell asleep again. Claire pulled the blankets up over her and tiptoed out of the room. A few last thin streaks of lightning lit up the old willow tree, pallid in the white light.

> *Mein Sohn, mein Sohn, ich seh' es genau,*
> *Es scheinen die alten Weiden so grau.*

Chapter **11**

After their return from Hudson, Meredith went back to Connecticut to attend school, and again Claire was restless all week long. On Friday she went into Meredith's room to straighten it up a bit for her arrival. To say that Meredith was untidy was like saying that Ralph liked to eat: the girl was a virtuoso of untidiness, a maestro of mess. The door to her room had been closed for several days and the room was musty, so Claire stepped over piles of discarded clothes and opened the window. A sudden breeze lifted a pile of papers from the bed and spread them around the room. As Claire knelt down to the pick them up, the top page caught her eye. Feeling guilty but too intrigued to stop herself, she sat on the bed to read it. It was a poem written in Meredith's sprawling hand:

> ### GOD
> *You leave us stranded at the shore of our sorrow*
> *You leave us standing at the gate of our grief*
> *You give us pain and ask us to find meaning*
> *You send disaster and expect us to find relief*
> *You toll our death knell and look for thanks*
> *You desert us in our suffering and watch from above*

Removed, silent, impassive; you tell us nothing
And then ask for our love

Claire put down the poem and looked out onto the street.
The subtext was all too clear to her: Meredith resented her
mother's death, feeling abandoned by her and by God. The
poem was an expression of the girl's tightly controlled rage,
a rage that found limited expression in her overly developed
intellect, which she wielded as a shield against feeling. Yes,
that was it: Meredith used her intelligence as a defense
against the world of feelings, which explained her disdain
for her father's affection; she was afraid to accept it because
that, too, might be taken from her someday.

Claire had never realized what a sad child Meredith was.
Meredith herself had seen to that, with her sharp, breezy
manner and rejection of feelings as sentimentality. Claire
felt strongly that the girl had never grieved properly for her
mother's death, that there were many unresolved feelings
swarming inside of her all the time. She wondered how she
could talk to Meredith about these things, or whether it was
wise even to try.

And so when Meredith returned the following weekend,
Claire was on the verge of saying something so many times
that she finally gave up the idea and decided that Meredith
could bring up the subject if she wanted to talk about it.

If she could, Meredith would live on tea and Pepperidge
Farm cookies. She and Claire returned from a trip to
D'Agostino's with a six-pack assortment of her favorites:
Bordeaux, Orange Milanos, Nantucket, Brussels, Chesa-
peake, and Lemon Crunch. Claire saw them every morning
when she took out her coffee; Meredith had lined them up
neatly in the cupboard, a tidy row of sentinels.

Meredith also loved pizza, and she declared that New
York pizza was second to none.

"In Connecticut they skimp on the cheese; everyone's
afraid of clogging their arteries."

When Claire took her to V&Ts, the venerable establish-
ment up by Columbia University that had been open since
1945, Meredith ate an entire small pie by herself.

"Now *this* is what I call *pizza!*" she said, a beacon of grease shining on her chin.

For her first night back, though, Claire wanted to make dinner, so she made her mother's vegetable beef soup recipe, using some leftover beef from the night before. While Meredith sat in the living room reading a true-crime book Claire had bought for her while she was away, Claire worked in the kitchen, rinsing vegetables, cutting lemons, sponging off counters as she went, taking pleasure in the brisk efficiency of her movements. She remembered her mother, her quick long hands chopping carrots for soup, or canning pickles. Her mother was a miracle of motion in the kitchen: smooth, steady, and relentless. She thought of her father, standing in the doorway, arms folded, watching her mother work.

Before her brother was born, Claire felt surrounded by her parents' love, wrapped securely in the knowledge that she didn't have to share it with anyone else. She basked in the contentment of being the only focus of her parents' affection, and remembered resenting the change and her loss of status as only child. Meredith was an only child and likely to remain one, as she once pointed out in the acid tone she always used when speaking of her stepmother:

"At least I don't have to worry about siblings; Jean Cummings Lawrence may be many things, but she is not a breeder. God forbid she should gain five pounds on that drug-infested body of hers, let alone thirty-five."

And so Claire and Meredith continued in their little fauxfamily unit, caught in the fantasy of playing house together. While Claire was chopping vegetables the phone rang and Meredith answered it.

"They hung up on me," she said, replacing the receiver.

"Yeah, that's been happening a lot lately," said Claire.

"Maybe you should tell Detective Jackson about it."

"Oh, I don't know . . . I don't think I should bother him with it. It's probably nothing."

"Yeah, but it might be important. I think you should tell him."

"Okay, maybe I will."

While Claire was making the soup, Meredith set the table, putting out some candles she brought from Connecticut.

"They don't sell anything useful in Connecticut," she said when she gave them to Claire, "only things like candles and scented soap."

After dinner they watched television together. Meredith especially liked *Mystery!* on Channel 13, and tonight was part one of a Detective Allyn mystery.

"I just think he's so dreamy," she said of Patrick Malahide, the show's star. Claire looked down at her, lying on her back on the floor—Meredith loved to lie on the floor—toes twitching, knees swaying, fingers fidgeting on the rug. She was all motion, all the time, this girl.

After Detective Allyn the evening news came on. On the news, a bunch of people were waving Confederate flags and singing "Dixie." The women were middle-aged with thick, hard faces. The men were bearded and fat with beer bellies; some of them wore grey Civil War uniforms. Confederate flags were everywhere: on their cowboy hats, on their sleeves, T-shirts, and belt buckles. Claire half expected one of them to pull down his jeans to reveal a flag tattooed on fleshy white buttocks.

The people sang in tuneless, unlovely voices:

> *I wish I was in the land of cotton*
> *Old times there are not forgotten*

The men wore dreamy half smiles on their bloated white faces, as though remembering their first prom. The women had hard, set jaws and dead eyes, staring straight ahead at an angle away from the camera. The announcer's voice broke in:

". . . the town has asked that the group not display the Confederate flag, but a spokesperson for the group says they are ready to take the matter to court if a ban is enforced." The television reporter was a young Asian woman, and she stood fifty yards or so away from the crooning racists. "The group is also threatening to hold the convention elsewhere next year," she said. Her carefully painted face was rigid with politeness, a mask of professionalism.

"What group?" said Meredith blandly. "Racists-R-Us? Bigots United? Assholes Anonymous?"

"Meredith!" said Claire reflexively.

"What? That's what they are, you know—assholes."

Claire sighed and changed the channel. She didn't want to look at these people's faces anymore, didn't want to hear their singing. They probably thought of themselves as game individualists, survivors in a public-opinion war on free thought, rebels against political correctness. She imagined the women sniffling over *Gone with the Wind,* the men having an extra beer or two while watching *The Deerhunter,* getting good and angry at those damn gooks, misty-eyed at the singing of "America the Beautiful" in the final scene.

"Nothing unites like a common enemy," said Meredith cheerfully from the floor.

Claire sat up on the bed and looked down at her. Meredith was flicking a shoelace back and forth over Ralph's back. The cat watched the lace, his tail jerking fitfully, ears back. Ralph did not like exercise of any kind, but even he was helpless in the face of the universal Feline String Instinct.

He pounced, clawing and biting the shoelace.

"What did you just say?" said Claire.

"Oh, I said that nothing unites like a common enemy."

"What did you mean by that?"

Meredith shrugged.

"I was just thinking about those good ol' boys, and how they might not wave their stupid flags around if there weren't so many people telling them not to. They get their jollies from annoying the rest of us."

"Oh, so we're the common enemy?"

"Right. It helps them define themselves, having something to rail against."

Meredith was right; it was in part a matter of self-definition. I am not that, therefore I am this. But why did *that* have to be bad, to be wrong? Why can't it just be different? Let it go at that; why should the process of self-definition for some people involve dismissing, despising, or destroying everything which was Not Me? And why always dichotomies? Surely the world was wide enough to encompass all of the variations of its citizenry; why hadn't man's brain evolved beyond the need for such dangerous simplifications?

"Hey, did you see in the paper that there were some FBI agents at the Good Ol' Boy Roundup?" said Meredith gleefully.

"No." Claire's head was beginning to hurt.

"Yeah. They were reprimanded by the FBI, but I'm not surprised."

"Meredith, it's past your bedtime."

Meredith jumped up on the bed, releasing Ralph from the thralldom of the shoelace.

"Aw, come on," she began. Sometimes Meredith actually sounded like the thirteen-year-old child she was, and when she did, Claire found it startling; she had grown so used to regarding Meredith as a genre unto herself.

"No arguments," Claire said. "If I let you stay up you'll just be tired tomorrow."

"Aw, man," said Meredith. "I wanted to watch the rest of the news."

"No, you didn't," said Claire. "All that's left is sports and weather, and you don't care about either. You just don't want to go to bed."

"Well, who ever *wants* to go to bed?" said Meredith crossly.

Claire had to admit she had a point, though right now she was exhausted.

Chapter 12

Amelia Moore called on Saturday morning and invited
Claire over for brunch. Claire asked if she could bring
Meredith.

"She's just here for the weekend," said Claire. "Then she
has to go back to school."

"Of course you can bring her; she's a lovely child."

Claire could not imagine anyone except Amelia ever referring to Meredith as "lovely."

Claire and Meredith walked up Riverside Drive to 116th
Street, where Amelia lived. A few dried, faded leaves skirled
around their ankles as they walked, heads bent into the cold,
biting wind which blew in from the north. October had
given way to November, and the days were growing shorter
as the nights got colder.

The doorbell rang hollowly through Amelia's long front
hall. At first there was no answer, then Claire heard Amelia's
quick, delicate footsteps coming down the hall. There was
the click of many locks, and then the door opened.

"I'm sorry—I was down the hall drying some mushrooms," Amelia said as she let them in. It was so like Amelia
to apologize for not being immediately at other people's
beck and call. She led them into the south living room;

Amelia's apartment was so big that it had a north and south living room. The south was the smaller of the two, and Claire liked it better. The walls were painted a soothing terra-cotta, and a baby grand piano stood in one corner, draped in a green flowered shawl. The room, warm and homey, was quintessentially Amelia.

While Amelia fussed about, taking hats and coats, Meredith wandered casually around the room, inspecting everything. She picked up a book lying open on the coffee table and read the title aloud.

"The Audubon Society Field Guide to North American Mushrooms." Meredith opened the book and studied it. "Wow," she said, "here's a mushroom called the Destroying Angel—and here's one called the Death Cap. How Gothic."

Amelia stopped on her way to the coat closet.

"Oh, yes—they're both members of the amanita family."

"Some family. Are they really deadly?"

"Oh, yes, very. They're poisonous in extremely small doses."

"Wow." Meredith indicated a small bowl of dried mushrooms on the coffee table. "Are these poisonous?"

"Good heavens, no!" Amelia laughed. "Those are some morels a friend of mine sent me. No, I would never pick an amanita, let alone bring it home."

"Because you never know who might eat it?" said Meredith.

"Well, yes . . ."

"Have you ever seen them; these—ama—"

"Amanitas? Oh, yes, I see them in the woods—but I leave them there."

"But aren't there some safe mushrooms that *look* like poison ones?"

"Oh, yes; that's why people eat them and die. I don't believe in taking that kind of chance, though. I guess I'm too much of a coward."

"Oh, you're not a coward," said Claire, "you're just cautious."

"Well, cautious or cowardly, I for one don't want to die that way. It's . . ." Amelia's face sagged and her shoulders dropped. "Poor Blanche," she said softly. "Poor, poor Blanche. No one should have to die like that."

There was a sad silence, and even Meredith seemed chastened. Claire was aware of the sound of traffic outside on Riverside Drive.

"It was a nice funeral, wasn't it?" Amelia said forlornly. "Blanche would have liked it, don't you think?"

"Oh, yes," Claire said quickly, as if the funeral were another of Amelia's parties. "She would have approved. It was really very nice." Amelia was so in need of comfort, much more so than Sarah.

Amelia sighed. "It's funny, but I couldn't help thinking that the one person missing, the one who would really like it . . . well, it's ironic, isn't it?"

"I never thought of it that way," said Claire. "I guess it is sort of ironic."

"Well, I . . . I just hope she didn't suffer too much, that's all," said Amelia.

"It's all over now, at any rate," said Claire, with a glance at Meredith, who had seated herself on the couch and was studying the mushroom guidebook.

"It's funny," said Meredith, putting the book down, "but it's a cliché of crime investigation that poisoning is a traditionally 'feminine' method of killing someone. It's because of the lack of overt violence, plus the whole 'ingestion' thing, you know. It's a kind of perversion of the 'nurturing mother.' "

"Did you know that Blanche left me all her papers?" Amelia said suddenly. "She gave her clothes to Sarah, but she left me all her letters and scrapbooks and things."

"Does that include her research notes?" said Claire.

"Oh, you mean from her books? Yes, I suppose it does."

Claire didn't mention Peter's request that she finish Blanche's Klan book; there was time enough to talk about that, when Amelia was feeling less vulnerable.

"Don't worry," said Meredith, looking up from the mushroom book. "We'll find her killer."

Amelia smiled wanly.

"I certainly hope somebody does, dear," she said.

Just then Amelia's doorbell ran.

"I wonder who that is," said Amelia. "I wasn't expecting anyone."

"I'll get it!" cried Meredith, jumping up from the sofa and heading toward the front hall. When Meredith had disappeared down the hall Amelia turned to Claire.

"You're very brave to take her," she said, with an expression of wonder.

Claire laughed.

"Oh, she's not so bad once you get used to her."

Meredith appeared in the doorway.

"It's Marshall. Shall I let him in?"

"Yes, of course."

When Meredith had gone, Amelia turned to Claire.

"I wonder what Marshall could want."

Meredith reappeared in the doorway, followed by Marshall Bassett. He was dressed in tight black jeans and a shiny black shirt, which emphasized his thinness.

"Hello, Amelia; hello, Claire. What a pleasant surprise, finding you here."

"Hello, Marshall." Claire knew Marshall's flattery was just that, but she enjoyed it anyway.

"What can I do for you, Marshall?" Amelia said with unaccustomed directness. Claire had the impression she was a little peeved at being disturbed without warning.

"Forgive the lack of ceremony in my dropping in like this," said Marshall, settling his long body down on the most comfortable armchair in the room, "but I was in the neighborhood."

He took out a pack of cigarettes and extracted a thin, dark cigarette from it. "Oh, do you mind if I smoke?" he added nonchalantly when he saw Amelia staring at the cigarette.

"Uh . . . I guess not," she answered. "I'll just open a window."

Claire was annoyed; annoyed at Marshall because it was clear that Amelia *did* mind, and annoyed at Amelia for being such a pushover. Sometimes she wished Amelia would just take a stand and say no to somebody—anybody—instead of letting everyone walk all over her.

"I'm sorry," Meredith said suddenly. "I'm an asthmatic, and I'm violently allergic to cigarette smoke."

Marshall looked at her as if he didn't believe her, but Meredith stared right back at him. He sighed and put out his cigarette.

"Ah, well . . . one can't even kill oneself in peace these days. Such is modern life."

There was a pause, and then Marshall said, "Look, I'm sorry to break up your party. I just wanted to borrow the key to Blanche's apartment."

Amelia looked startled.

"The key?"

"Yes—you have it, don't you?"

"Well, yes, Blanche did give me a copy."

"So could I borrow it, please?" His tone was impatient.

"Well, I don't know . . ."

"What do you mean? I'm her cousin, for God's sake!"

"Sarah has a key; why didn't you ask her?"

Marshall snorted.

"Don't tell me you are the only person in New York who doesn't know that Sarah and I don't get along."

"Look, Marshall," Amelia said with uncustomary firmness, "I'm not even sure the police will let you into Blanche's apartment. After all, it *is* a crime scene."

"My God." Marshall leaned back on the sofa. "If the police aren't finished gathering clues by now, they're slower than I thought."

Claire was surprised to see herself reacting with indignation at Marshall's insult.

"They're doing a perfectly good job," she said quickly.

Meredith turned to Marshall.

"You might not want to insult the police in front of Claire," she said with a sly smile.

"Why?" said Amelia innocently. "Does Claire have some friends on the force?"

"Not *exactly*," said Meredith with the same Mona Lisa smile.

"Hmm . . ." said Marshall, sitting forward. "You intrigue me. What on earth are you talking about?"

"Let's just say that there's a certain *frisson* in her relationship with the police these days," Meredith replied.

"*Frisson*, eh?" said Marshall. "Good word. You don't hear it much these days, now that there is a national movement against literacy." He turned to Claire. "Well, Claire? Dish, dish—what is your young ward here referring to?"

"Oh for God's sake, Meredith," Claire said weakly. "It's all in her head." She couldn't help feeling that she was utterly unconvincing.

"What's in her head?" said Amelia, always a beat behind everyone else.

"The *romance,* for God's sake," Marshall said impatiently. He turned to Claire. "So, no hanky-panky at the precinct, no swooning in the patrol cars, no bodice ripping at the station house?"

"Absolutely none."

Amelia patted Claire's hand. "Don't worry," she said in a soothing voice, "you don't have to tell us anything you don't want to. And now if you'll excuse me, I'm going to get us something to drink." She rose. "Claire, would you like a Bloody Mary?"

"That sounds wonderful," said Marshall.

Amelia ignored him. "Meredith, what about you? Soda or juice? I have orange and cranberry."

"Oh, juice, I think—either one is fine."

"I like my Bloody Mary on the spicy side," Marshall called after Amelia as she trundled toward the kitchen.

Meredith turned to Marshall. "So, why do you need to get into Blanche's apartment?"

"She has—had—a letter of mine and I'd like to get it back."

"It must be an important letter." Meredith's tone was bland, nonconfrontational.

"Not really, it's just that I'd like to get it before Sarah goes through the apartment."

"Why?"

"Because she might throw it out."

"Why would she do that?"

"Because she's Sarah." Marshall paused and looked

longingly at the unlit cigarette he still held in his right hand. "Surely you noticed there was a certain amount of—tension—between us."

"Oh, I noticed it all right." Meredith nodded. "I just haven't figured out why yet."

"Well, then there's something to keep you occupied on these long winter nights," Marshall replied wearily, again eyeing the cigarette. He stood up abruptly. "Look, I must have a cigarette, so I'm going outside to smoke this." He looked at his watch. "Come to think of it, maybe I should just go now. I've interrupted your little party long enough."

Just then Amelia entered the room with a tray of drinks.

"What about the Bloody Mary?" she said, sounding disappointed.

"Oh, so you made me one after all," Marshall observed, looking at the tray. "All right—thank you."

He took the drink and sat down again, but looked so nervous that Claire almost suggested that he go ahead and smoke the cigarette.

"How's that handsome boyfriend of yours?" he said to Claire.

"Oh, fine. He's very busy now, with the holiday season and everything."

"Does he ever come to town and visit you?"

"Mostly I go up there. He says the city makes him nervous."

"That's the whole point," Marshall said. "It's kind of like drinking too much coffee; it's exciting and unpleasant at the same time."

Claire looked at Meredith, who sat on the sofa, legs dangling, sipping her juice. Amelia had put an orange slice and a maraschino cherry in the glass.

Marshall rose from his armchair.

"Well, I really must be going. It's been delightful seeing all of you. We must do this more often." He turned to Amelia. "What about the key?"

Amelia put down her glass. "How about if I go over there with you?"

Marshall shrugged. "If you want to do it that way, it's all right with me."

"How's tomorrow?"

"Fine. I'll be in the city in the evening and I'll come over here around seven, all right?"

Amelia agreed and Marshall made his exit.

"It's a good thing he smokes, or he might have stayed for brunch." Amelia sighed as she sat down again.

"Oh, he wouldn't really have done that, would he?" said Claire.

Amelia stirred her drink. "The longer I know Marshall, the more I have no idea what he's capable of. That whole family," she said, shaking her head. "Well, you just never know *what* they're going to do."

Meredith plucked her cherry out of her glass and popped it into her mouth. She chewed it slowly and then sucked on the stem thoughtfully. "I wonder what's in that letter."

The next day Meredith and Claire were sitting at the counter at Rumplemeyer's sharing a pot of hot chocolate. Rumplemeyer's cocoa was Meredith's absolute favorite treat, and she would beg Claire to go there, promising anything in return. Claire had never seen anyone with a sweet tooth like Meredith's. Unless the weather was really bad, they would walk the length of Central Park, following the horse trail on the West Side, and then over to Central Park South, where Rumplemeyer's pink-and-purple awning beckoned to them like the beacon of a lighthouse. By the time they got there, the cold and the exercise had created an even more intense craving for Rumplemeyer's renowned pot of hot cocoa, handmade from huge lumps of semisweet chocolate.

"Why does Marshall torment Sarah like that?" Meredith said, stirring her chocolate.

"I don't know why the two of them are so hard on each other," Claire answered thoughtfully, watching the whipped cream in her cup slide slowly into the deep swirl of chocolate below, white and brown merging into a dark caramel color.

"It's almost as though he were a spoiled younger brother or something."

"I know," said Claire. "It's odd, isn't it?"

"I have the feeling that there's something between them, something only they know about," said Meredith.

"What do you mean?"

"I'm not sure exactly; it's only a feeling. I don't know; it's like Marshall *has* something on her . . . that he's holding something over her."

"You mean a secret?"

"Yeah, like a secret or something." Meredith paused for a moment. "Was Sarah ever married?"

"No, not that I know of—why?"

"Oh, I don't know . . ." Meredith spooned some whipped cream directly into her mouth, leaving a small white mustache on her upper lip. "I'd sure like to see that letter Marshall wrote to Blanche," she said, licking chocolate from her fingers.

At the other end of the counter two little old ladies in extravagant hats—archetypal Rumplemeyer's customers—were eavesdropping on Claire and Meredith. They stirred their chocolate and pretended to talk in low voices between themselves, but Claire could see that they were listening to every word of her conversation. She thought it unlikely that either of them knew Sarah or Marshall, but decided it might be better to change the subject.

"Uh, Meredith, do you want to buy some catnip for Ralph on the way home?" she suggested.

"What?" answered Meredith, and then, seeing the ladies, winked at Claire. "Sure, why not? Even a cat needs to get high once in a while."

Claire didn't even look at the ladies to see their response. She paid the check and hustled Meredith out the door without looking back.

Chapter **13**

That week, in the middle of November, the temperature suddenly shot up to seventy degrees and stayed there for several days. People wandered around in shirt sleeves, dazed looks on their faces, as if the world were about to come to an end but they were determined to enjoy what time they had left.

Claire didn't go into the office on Monday. She read manuscripts at home all morning, and then went down to Chinatown to do some shopping. Meredith was back in Connecticut for the last week of school before the holiday break, and Claire wanted to buy her a Christmas present before she returned. Afterward she walked up through Little Italy and SoHo to the East Village. As she walked past Italian cafés and SoHo art galleries, she thought about Blanche, and wondered if Blanche had ever walked this same route up Mulberry Street, on one of her "think walks"—while working on her books, Blanche would take long strolls to think.

By the time she reached the East Village, Claire was tired and hungry. She paused on the corner of Fifth Street and First Avenue. Peering down the street, she could just see the stone building that housed the Ninth Precinct. She wondered what Detective Jackson was doing right now, but she re-

sisted an impulse to drop by and find out. Instead, she
walked north on First Avenue, toward the nexus of Indian
restaurants on Sixth Street. As she walked, enticing smells
filled her head—a mixture of exotic spices, cardamom,
curry, anise, nutmeg—all blended into a beckoning breeze
that made her light-headed with hunger.

She stopped in front of a restaurant on First Avenue
called the Royal House of India. GARDEN OPEN!" the hand-
painted sign said, and next to it was a review from *The Village Voice*. She went down the steps and through a beaded
curtain into the restaurant. A handsome dark-skinned man in
a turban met her at the door, and asked her if she would like
to sit in the garden. She said she would, and he led her
through the restaurant, past a tank of water containing a
huge silver fish swimming languidly back and forth. Claire
noticed half a dozen small goldfish swimming nervously in
a cluster at the bottom of the tank. She didn't need to be told
what the goldfish were for.

She was conducted out into the back garden, festively
decorated with brightly colored banners, potted plants, and
paper lanterns hung on poles. In the corner of the garden,
alone at a corner table, sat Detective Jackson. Claire saw
him before he saw her, and walked toward him.

"Hello," she said at the same moment he looked up and
saw her.

"Hello," he said, standing up so quickly that he knocked
over his chair.

"Oops—sorry," said Claire reflexively.

The waiter, hovering nearby, reached for the chair at the
same moment as Claire and Detective Jackson, and the three
of them laughed. The waiter replaced the chair with an embarrassed smile, then left them alone.

"Please join me," said Jackson, indicating one of the
empty chairs at the table.

"Thank you," said Claire, and sat down.

The waiter reappeared to take her order. He was a thin
dark man with a wiry little mustache and thick black hair.
Claire ordered the chicken tandoori lunch special and the
waiter disappeared again, leaving them alone. There were

no other customers in the garden. There was an awkward pause. Claire could hear the faint hum of traffic from First Avenue, mixing with the soothing clatter of kitchen noises coming from inside the restaurant. She took a deep breath.

"Do you—do you come here often?" she said. "I mean, since your office is around the corner?" she added lamely.

Detective Jackson laughed.

"As a matter of fact, I do. I've tried just about all of the places on Sixth Street, but this is my favorite."

There was another pause, and then he said, "What brings you down to this neighborhood?"

"Oh, just shopping. And I thought I'd wander through Blanche's neighborhood. She was writing this book, and I'm going to sort of finish it for her. I mean, it's mostly done, and I'm really an editor, not a writer, but . . ." She trailed off, wondering why she felt she had to explain. Peter had practically begged her to finish the book, and now she was falling all over herself apologizing for it.

Jackson nodded as though it were quite natural.

"The Klan book, you mean?"

"Yes, how did you know?"

"Well, it's part of my investigation into her murder."

"Oh? You think there might be a connection?"

"Not necessarily, though it's possible. We're trying to learn everything we can about the victim, in the hopes that it may lead us to her killer."

"Oh, I see."

"I haven't read any of the book myself. So you have a copy of the manuscript?"

"Yes, would you like a copy? It would be easy to copy the computer diskette."

"Yes, thank you." He paused and studied his hands. "Actually, I was going to ask you if you come across anything you think might be helpful that you let me know. Would you mind doing that?"

"Well—no, not at all. But how would I know what would be helpful?"

"You might not. But if you do see something, I would appreciate knowing about it."

"Sure. I'll be glad to help if I can."

The thin waiter returned with their food. Claire was glad for the distraction, though she suddenly didn't feel much like eating.

"Is it a difficult job, being a book editor?" Jackson said as he helped himself to lentils and boiled cabbage.

"Oh, not as hard as being a police detective, I'm sure," Claire said. Jackson didn't answer, so she continued. "What made you—I mean, why did you become a policeman?"

"Well, I didn't set out to become a homicide detective . . . it was kind of a default plan, I guess you might say."

"Oh, really?"

"Yes, I was teaching high school English by day and by night taking a stab at writing the Great American Novel."

"What happened?"

Jackson stroked the lip of his water glass, and again Claire noticed how beautiful his hands were.

"I had a chance to experience a homicide close up," he said softly.

"What happened?"

"My wife, shot once through the head as she sat in her car." Jackson looked off in the direction of the door. "It turned out to be some punk out on a spree, but after that I couldn't go back to teaching. It seemed pointless, when all I wanted to do was catch people who killed other people and put them in prison." He took a sip of water and then looked toward the exit again. "It's funny, though; unlike most cops, I don't believe in capital punishment."

"Why not?"

He shrugged. "A bunch of reasons. For one thing, I don't really believe that it's a deterrent to crime, and for another thing, it's racially biased. And I don't believe the state should have the power to kill anybody."

There was a silence between them, not an uncomfortable one this time, but Claire suddenly had an irrational fear that he knew what she was thinking. What she was thinking was that she would like to get him alone, and massage away all the pain and misery of his past, to make him forget losing a woman he loved—and, if possible, forget the woman herself.

Claire's skin ached just being near him, and she couldn't eat much of her food.

"There's only two reliable ways to lose weight," Blanche had once said, "grief and love. Given a choice, I'll take love anytime."

Claire agreed with this, though what she felt right now was so acute, so sharp, that it felt as much like grief as it did love.

"I'm sorry," she said. "That's terrible about your wife."

"I've tried hard to put it behind me, because I think personal matters cloud your judgment, as they say. There's a danger that every time I'm after a criminal . . . well, you know, that I'll be looking to avenge Anne's death."

Anne. So her name was Anne. Claire imagined her: tall and willowy, with light brown hair and doe eyes, a wise and noble, and yes, sainted creature, gentle as a summer's day . . . and then she looked back at Jackson, sitting across from her, looking so forlorn. Was it just pity, this feeling she had for him, an expression of her long dormant maternal instincts, jolted into life now with the presence of Meredith in her life? She turned to the waiter, who was hovering nearby, wiping off tables.

"May I have some more water, please?"

Jackson looked at her plate.

"You're not eating very much. Don't you like it?"

"Oh, yes, I do! I just, uh—I guess I wasn't as hungry as I thought," she replied, feeling foolish.

"Well, I guess I'd better get back," said Jackson, looking at his watch.

"Oh, yes, of course." Claire jumped up from her chair. "I didn't mean to keep you."

"Oh, you didn't keep me." Jackson smiled at her. "I kept myself. Don't worry; they don't make me punch a clock at the precinct."

Out on the street, he said, "By the way, where's—"

"Meredith? She's in school in Connecticut."

"Oh, so she doesn't live with you?"

"Not really, no. I'm just . . . looking after her for a while."

"Oh." Jackson looked up and down the street, as if reluctant to leave. "She's really something, isn't she?"

"Yes, she is."

"Well, tell her if she comes across anything useful to give me a call."

"Oh, that's very nice, really," said Claire, but Jackson looked at her seriously.

"No, I mean it," he said. "Between you and me, we're stuck on this case, we really are. The killer just hasn't left any of the tracks you might expect in a case like this. It's as though he—or she—has vanished into thin air."

There was another pause, and then Claire said, "Well, Meredith would be only too thrilled if she could help somehow. She's a real armchair detective, you know."

Jackson smiled. "Well, we all have to start somewhere."

"Oh, by the way, Meredith thought I should tell you this, though I don't know if it's important or not," said Claire.

"What is it?"

"Well, sometimes my phone will ring and then when I answer they hang up."

"They don't say anything?"

"No, nothing; they just hang up. Do you think it's relevant?"

Wallace Jackson ran a hand through his thick grey hair.

"I don't know," he said. "It may be nothing, or it may be the key we're looking for."

Chapter 14

A t work on Friday Claire's phone rang just as she was about to go to Peter's office for a meeting. She picked up the receiver but regretted it instantly. It was Willard Hughes.

"Hello, Claire," he said, and she knew immediately he wanted something from her.

"Hello, Willard," she said, and waited.

"What are you doing this afternoon?" he said sweetly. "I thought we might have lunch."

Claire sighed. Her first impulse was to put him off for a week or so, as she usually was booked for lunch far in advance, but it so happened that an agent had called to cancel a lunch date with her just this morning. She decided she might as well get it over with.

"As it happens, I'm free. Shall we meet at Keens at twelve-thirty?"

Willard was so surprised to hear her suggest Keens that he just stuttered an affirmative and Claire was able to get him off the phone quickly. She looked at her watch; it was ten, which meant she had two and a half hours of freedom before she faced Willard. She headed for Peter's office.

"Chin up," said Peter when she explained the reason for

her grim expression. "At least you have an excuse to leave early."

Claire did have another author coming into the office at three o'clock, and so lunch with Willard would have to be fairly short.

"Give my regards to Willard the Dread," Peter said cheerfully as Claire grabbed her coat and headed for the elevator a couple of hours later.

Claire glanced at herself in her pocket mirror as she stood waiting for the elevator. She considered putting on some lipstick, but as the elevator arrived she decided not to bother. It was only Willard, after all. She was running a little late but felt like walking, so she set a brisk pace and walked the twenty blocks down to West Thirty-sixth Street.

Keens Chophouse had become one of Claire's favorite restaurants from the first time she ate there, courtesy of Peter, who had taken her there to celebrate her hiring at Ardor House. She loved the rows of thin-stemmed meerschaum and clay pipes on the ceiling left by past and present customers, the mahogany paneling, the nineteenth-century London club atmosphere, carefully wrought but nonetheless convincing, and was still a little thrilled by it every time she went there. When she saw Willard sitting by himself at a table along the wall, a little of the thrill evaporated, but Claire took a deep breath and vowed that even Willard would not ruin this lunch for her. When she approached the table he raised his eyebrows in a gesture that was clearly a reproach for her lateness—all seven minutes of it—but Claire ignored this and greeted him cheerfully.

"What are you drinking?" she said, indicating the glass in front of him.

Willard looked up at her and blinked. It was common knowledge that he was in The Program, as he liked to call it, and did not drink. (Claire personally thought his writing had been better when he *did* drink, an opinion she shared with Peter once over a glass of Merlot.)

"Uh, ginger ale," Willard replied, and Claire noted with satisfaction that his left shoulder was beginning to twitch.

"I'll have a pint of Bass," she said to the waiter in the

long white apron who approached their table. Sometimes she felt guilty about drinking around Willard, but she was damned if she was going to face him sober today.

Claire looked around the low-ceilinged dining room, which was beginning to fill up with the usual lunchtime trade, mostly businessmen and women mixed in with the occasional party of tourists out on a spree at Macy's. The tourists were conspicuous in their bright mall clothes and shiny, open faces, while the business customers wore expensive suits and spoke in subdued tones, glancing around to see who might be listening.

Claire listened to the waiter recite the list of daily specials even though she knew exactly what she was going to have: the mutton.

"I never even *think* about ordering anything else here," Peter had said at that first lunch. "Trust me; I know what I'm talking about."

And so Claire followed his lead that day and many days since, always amazed at the huge, juicy slab of rare meat which transcended any lamb she ever had in her life. It was almost impossible to imagine that meat could be as good as Keens's mutton, which was aged on the premises. Every time she ate it, she felt herself slipping further away from any notion she ever had of becoming a vegetarian.

When they had ordered, Willard put his elbows on the table and leaned forward.

"The reason I wanted to talk to you was that I have the idea for my next book."

"Oh, good." Claire hoped she sounded interested.

"I want to write about Blanche's murder."

"What?"

"Oh, I'll fictionalize it, of course, but I just think it would make such a great hook for a story: mystery writer killed, and all that."

Claire looked down at her beer and scratched her left palm, which was beginning to itch.

"It's been done before, you know."

"Oh, I know, I know; it's just that being based on fact and everything—well, you know—it'll help sell books."

Claire had never seen anyone so obsessed with his own success as Willard. He was forever coming up with ideas for selling his books, marketing schemes, promotional concepts. Willard could nudge you to death until you gave in from pure exhaustion.

"If he were half as interested in doing his job as he is telling us how to do ours, he'd be a halfway decent writer," Peter muttered once in a moment of uncharacteristic grumbling. (Some people in the office referred to him as Peter the Positive.)

Claire took a big swallow of Bass ale. It was cold and sharp on her tongue, but already she could feel the warmth of it going down, relaxing her body.

"I think a more important question would be why do you want to write this particular story?" she said.

Willard's left shoulder twitched impatiently. He ran his hand over a thin oily strand of hair which threatened to slide from its carefully arranged perch atop his bald head.

"It's as good as any other story," he said irritably. "It's what you *do* with a story that counts."

Claire had to admit he had her there. She tried to think of a reply, but was saved from the effort by the arrival of their food. She looked at the plate of sizzling mutton in front of her, warm in its own juices, with just a hint of garlic. *Not even Willard can spoil this pleasure,* she told herself with grim determination. The mutton cost twenty-seven dollars on the lunch menu, and as Claire savored the first bite she thought it was worth every cent—an easy conclusion, since Ardor House was footing the bill.

Blanche had been much too delicate ever to initiate a free meal, but Willard always made sure he got his share of expense-account lunches. If Claire didn't call him for a while, he would invent a pretext and suggest they meet (the unstated rule, of course, being that Ardor House would pay).

The one thing Claire did like about her relationship with Willard was that it was totally financially based, and both of them knew it. Neither one pretended that it was anything else, and that allowed for a certain honesty between them. Willard was irritating, but he didn't look to Claire to solve his personal problems. She knew very little about his private life, in fact. He lived on the Upper East Side, and Claire knew his address, his phone and fax numbers, but not much else. She had no desire to know more. Having lunch with Willard was as close as she ever wanted to get to him. She wouldn't have been surprised to learn that he worked for the CIA (unlikely, since he hadn't gone to Yale and was heterosexual, as far as she knew), or that he was a member of a satanic cult, or was raising ferrets in his basement. Anything was possible with Willard, but somehow you just didn't want to know.

Meredith was different, of course.

"You know that weird author of yours—Willard Hughes? What's his story?"

Claire would then explain that she really knew very little about Willard and that she liked it that way. Meredith would complain about her lack of curiosity, and that would pretty much be it. Then a few hours later Meredith would mutter something about Willard being an ideal murder suspect, and they would start all over again.

Now the ideal murder suspect sat across from Claire devouring his mutton with religious fervor. Willard ordered the mutton not because he liked it particularly but because it was the most expensive thing on the menu.

"You know," he said, chewing and speaking at the same time, so that Claire had to look away, "that inspector fellow has been 'round to see me."

"Oh, you mean Detective Jackson?" Claire said, feeling the blood rush to her face as she said his name.

"Yeah, him," said Willard, spearing a crisp homemade potato chip.

"What did he want to know?"

"Oh, he asked me a lot of questions about 'my relationship to the deceased.' You know, the usual thing." Willard smiled, revealing a piece of spinach that clung to his teeth. "He told me he's read some of my books."

"Oh?" Claire decided not to mention the piece of spinach. As usual, Willard was beginning to get on her nerves.

"Yeah—he said he even got some ideas from one of them."

"Oh, which one?"

"I think it was *Death Pays a House Call*." Willard always had some form of the word "death" in his titles; he claimed that it sold books. Willard impaled a piece of cucumber on his fork. "He told me he likes mysteries."

"Well, he should; he's a detective."

"Yeah, but he doesn't *seem* like a detective, you know? He seems more like . . ."

"Like what?" Claire enjoyed talking about Jackson, even if it was only with Willard.

"Oh, I don't know . . . like a history teacher or something. He just doesn't seem like most of the cops I've known."

Willard liked to hang around police stations doing research for his books. He was a familiar figure at the Nineteenth Precinct, where they called him Twitchy.

Right now his shoulder was relatively calm as he sat concentrating on ingesting large amounts of mutton chop. Claire managed to get through the meal without letting Willard prey on her nerves too much, and she promised to tell Peter of their conversation about the proposed book.

"Send me an outline," she said as they parted, and Willard seemed satisfied with that. His eyes had the glazed expression of a man with a very full stomach.

Claire had had a little too much to drink and a lot too much to eat, so she decided to walk back to the office. She passed a bookstore on Sixth Avenue with a mystery display featuring the very book Willard had mentioned, *Death Pays a House Call*. She stood looking at the display and wondered exactly what Wallace Jackson had seen in that book which caught his eye.

That night on the phone, Claire asked Meredith if she had read the book.

"Oh, sure, I read that one."

"Willard said that Jackson told him he got some ideas from it."

"Really?" Meredith sounded immediately intrigued. "Do you have a copy?"

"Somewhere, I think."

"Or you *could* just ask the good detective himself," Meredith suggested slyly.

"Yes, I could, but I'm probably not going to."

"Suit yourself. Sounds like a perfect pretext for a phone call to me."

"Oh, come on, Meredith. Why would I want to call Detective Jackson?"

"Beats me," said Meredith, "but do you have to have a reason?"

Claire insisted on playing dumb. "I have no reason. I'm not a part of his investigation."

"Oh, that's where you're wrong," said Meredith. "We're both a part of it, whether we want to be or not. May I remind you that it ain't over till the fat lady sings?"

Meredith's comment made Claire think of Amelia—not exactly fat, and not exactly a singer, but the closest person she knew who fit the bill.

Chapter 15

When Amelia arrived at Blanche's apartment on East Fourth Street that Saturday afternoon, Marshall was waiting in the lobby. With him was a young, round-faced policeman who introduced himself as Officer Gubbins. As next of kin, Sarah had contacted the police about unsealing the apartment, and they sent Officer Gubbins to do it. The three of them rode the elevator up together in silence, and after Officer Gubbins had broken the bright yellow seal, he withdrew, leaving Amelia and Marshall to enter the apartment alone.

Amelia went in first, pushing the door open as far as it would go. A stack of newspapers in the entry hall prevented the door from opening all the way, so Amelia was just able to fit through the opening. Turning sideways, she slipped through, followed by Marshall, into the foyer of Blanche's apartment.

Blanche DuBois had been a pack rat. Stacks of newspapers and magazines leaned at precipitous angles from every wall of the front hall; heaps of clothes lay piled upon chairs in the living room; books and tapes and papers littered every surface of the bedroom. Take-out menus were everywhere—on top of the television, stuffed in between the radiators and the walls, on top of the refrigerator. Marshall walked with delicate, carefully chosen steps, as though he were afraid he might step in something. The phone rang, a startling sound in the forlorn, deserted apartment. Amelia picked it up.

"Hello, this is Amelia Moore speaking," she said, and then there was a pause. She held the receiver away from her ear for a second and then replaced it.

"Who was it?" said Marshall.

"I don't know; they hung up as soon as I answered."

"I'm going to start by looking in the bedroom," he said, and disappeared into the back of the apartment.

Amelia stood in the middle of the living room and looked around. Even the disorder of Blanche's apartment had a distinctly genteel quality, a kind of well-bred delicacy: there was virtually no dust, and the stacks of papers were neatly ordered. There were several years' worth of *The New Yorker*, and other piles consisted of back issues of *Vanity Fair*, *Premiere*, and *Town and Country*. Knickknacks were everywhere: china angels, crystal decanters, Chinese fans and figurines. Amelia tried to imagine Blanche—elaborately coiffed, impeccably turned-out Blanche—emerging from this ocean of objects. Standing there, looking at the leftovers of a life suddenly and brutally ended, Amelia felt sad, so sad that she needed to sit down. Carefully moving a stack of *Gourmet* magazines, she sat on an upholstered burgundy satin chair. Next to her was Blanche's writing desk, and Amelia ran her hand over its mahogany lid. As she did so her hand brushed against something hard protruding from the side of the desk. She craned her head around and looked at it: it was small and round, and appeared to be a knob, though she couldn't imagine its function. It looked like a lever of some kind. Idly, she pushed on it. Nothing happened. Then she tried pulling on it, and the instant she did a small drawer shot open from the side of the desk. Startled, Amelia jumped back, and then she looked in the drawer.

The lone object in the drawer was a slim, silk-bound volume, and before Amelia even picked it up she knew it was Blanche's diary.

Marshall had rummaged through more stacks of papers

than he cared to think about when he finally came across a stack of letters, bound by a red ribbon. He sat on the bed and began looking through the letters, amused by Blanche's adherence to certain clichés: tying her letters with a red ribbon, for example. He soon found what he had come for. He recognized his own handwriting, and, reading through the letter quickly to make sure it was the right one, he stuffed it into his jacket pocket and went back down the hall to find Amelia. He thought he heard the sound of her voice, and when he reached the living room he saw her, sitting next to Blanche's writing desk, a perplexed look on her face.

Manny Alvarez was on duty in the lobby when Marshall and Amelia left, and he noticed them because they were such an odd couple: the short, round woman with the tall, angular man walking just slightly in front of her. The woman, he noticed, looked preoccupied, even troubled. They did not speak, but the man nodded to him as they went by. If asked, he would have said they reminded him of a couple who had just had a fight.

Consuela Rodriguez had been a teller at Apple Bank on Fourteenth Street and Fourth Avenue for ten years, and did not think it particularly unusual when the small plump woman with the delicate features asked for a safe-deposit box. The neighborhood, while not particularly dangerous, had its share of burglaries, and some of the local residents, many of whom were immigrants, preferred to keep their valuables locked up in bank vaults instead of in their apartments. Consuela did her best not to stare at what the woman put in the box, but she did think it was strange that the only item she placed in the box was a single torn sheet of handwritten paper. *It took all kinds in this city*, she thought; but she had seen stranger things, much stranger, in her ten years at the bank. The woman was well dressed and soft-spoken, not obviously *loca,* and Consuela assumed she had her reasons. Consuela's grandmother in Ecuador used to say, "People all have their reasons, you can be sure of that—even thieves and murderers; they all have their reasons." And so

when the woman returned the box to her, Consuela shrugged
and handed her the receipt and box number.

Amelia Moore stepped out into the bright November sun-
shine and hailed a cab. She knew it was dangerous to deliver
her message to Claire by hand, but she mistrusted answering
machines. A Luddite by nature, she disliked most technol-
ogy; and besides, when she called from Blanche's apartment, Claire's machine had delivered such a long beep that
she was afraid the tape was full. She had left a somewhat
confused message on the machine, but then decided to take
the chance of coming over to deliver the note by hand.

Vasily Kronja did not like his job as doorman at 346 West
102nd Street. He knew he was destined for greater things,
and was impatient to get on with his life. He ignored his
mother's suggestion that he was at least better off than the
poor souls back in his native country, the former Yugoslavia;
he did not even remember Yugoslavia, and could not concern himself with the lives of people halfway across the
world. What Vasily knew was that his job as doorman was
boring and demeaning, opening doors for people no better
than himself, people who did not have the blood of counts
running through their veins as he did.

Vasily's claim to noble blood was based on a story his
uncle Nicolai had once told him, a story that had something
to do with being the illegitimate descendant of a Slavic
count. The fact that his uncle was very drunk at the time did
not matter; Vasily at once recognized the ring of truth in the
story. And so, unsubstantiated as the rumor was, Vasily had
pinned it to the center of his identity, and wore it like a crest.
He knew it was true, because he *felt* different from other
people; he could feel the stirrings of his noble destiny within
him. He did not know what that destiny was to be, only that
it was great and that someday he would be admired by all
the people who now barely glanced at him as he opened the
door for them, day after dismal day.

Vasily was at his post when Amelia entered the building,
and he opened the door for her politely. He recognized her—
she was a nice lady. She always smiled at him sweetly, and

once she had given him a box of Christmas cookies. Vasily smiled at her and even tipped his hat, but she seemed distracted, and hurried by with barely a nod, her face set and worried. Vasily would remember this later as being unusual. Shortly after Amelia entered the building, Vasily began to feel very sleepy. He had been up late talking to his girlfriend about all the great things he would accomplish someday, and now he was afraid he might fall asleep on his feet. He glanced around the lobby. It was a quiet day, with nothing much happening, so he stepped out to the deli across the street for a cup of coffee. Vasily's timing was unfortunate, because that was when the murderer, in disguise, entered the building, slipping a credit card over the door lock.

Chapter 16

Meredith was performing in a school play Saturday night and so wouldn't visit Claire until the following week. Claire spent Saturday afternoon at the Met, wandering from room to room. She felt vaguely restless, unrooted, as though there were something she should be thinking about, but she couldn't remember what it might be. She hung around the Impressionists, staring at Monet's haystacks until the museum guard began to look at her suspiciously. When the museum closing announcement came, she filed out behind a group of Dutch tourists, their straw-blond hair white in the dying evening sun. She walked across Central Park, taking the horse trail along the reservoir, hoping to see a rider. Today she was in luck: a woman on a little bay mare cantered by, the horse's hooves kicking up clods of dirt behind her. Watching the horse recede, Claire felt happier, a sudden rush of affection for the city filling her heart. How many cities could boast of such beautiful riding venues as New York, with its leafy trails winding through Central Park?

As Amelia rode the elevator up to Claire's apartment she hoped Claire was home, but was not surprised when her ring received no answer except Ralph's hoarse, lonesome meow.

She waited a moment, her heart thumping, and then fished around in her bag for her notepad. *At least I remembered the notepad,* she thought. Amelia was absentminded, as everyone knew; most of her friends had received late-night phone calls from her when she locked herself out of her apartment. Amelia had distributed keys to a half dozen of them just for such emergencies. Now she wished she had a key to Claire's apartment so she could wait for her here—she didn't feel safe on the street—but Claire was a private person who didn't give her keys to anyone. Amelia dug in her bag for the notepad, leaning against the wall to steady herself, and wrote a note to Claire.

> *Dear Claire, I have some very urgent information—I must see you—I don't feel safe at home, so when you get this* please *come immediately to the Life Café at Avenue B and Tenth Street.*

She looked at her watch: it was four-thirty. She hoped Claire would return soon. She slipped the note under the door and walked rapidly to the elevator. The car was on its way up to the twelfth floor, where it paused for a long time. Amelia leaned wearily against the wall and closed her eyes.

In the stairwell, the murderer waited for the sound of the arriving elevator and then, after the door had closed and Amelia was on her way back down to the lobby, stole out and went up to Claire's apartment. In her haste, Amelia had not slid the note very far under the door, and Ralph, bored with being alone, amused himself by batting the slip of paper around, so that now a corner of it protruded from under the door. The murderer slid the note out, quickly read it, then shoved it into a coat pocket.

Amelia, short and round, moved slowly, and the murderer easily caught up with her as she left the building. Unfortunately for her, Vasily had wandered down to the basement to chat with the night porter and so was still not at his post when she walked through the foyer. Perhaps it would have made no difference; perhaps Vasily would not have seen the murderer lurking behind a marble column in the lobby as Amelia left the building, unaware that she was being followed. But now there was no witness as the murderer trailed Amelia out into the street, keeping a safe distance and blending in with the crowd of people on Broadway. She had no way of knowing the murderer was among the group of people who followed her down the stairs to the IRT subway. Perhaps if Amelia had taken a cab instead of the subway, she would have been safe—but it was rush hour and she figured the subway would be at least as fast as a cab, and being in a crowd of people just then was comforting.

There was no safety in numbers for Amelia, though, and as the Broadway local came screeching into the station and the crowd pressed forward expectantly, no one saw the hand that pushed her toward the gaping chasm of track. In fact, only a few people saw her clutch the air and fall into the blackness in front of the oncoming train, a scream caught in her throat. These same people turned away immediately, instinctively closing their eyes in horror at the sight in front of them. No one saw the slip of paper she clutched in her hand which fluttered loose and was caught up in the wind created by the oncoming train. By the time anyone knew what had happened, the murderer was up the stairs and back out into the street, walking rapidly away in the gathering twilight.

When Claire arrived home the machine was blinking six times. There was a message from Robert, and then four messages from Meredith—long, rambling monologues about how boring Connecticut was and how anxious she was to return to New York. Then, after the beep, and a long pause came Amelia's voice, sounding frightened and shaky. "Claire, it's Amelia. I—I hope you get this message. I'm scared, Claire—I need to talk to you. I'm afraid to stay here, so I want to meet you—come to the Life Café in the East Village as soon as you get this—I'll be waiting there for you." There was a pause, and then she continued, "I . . . please hurry." Then there was a click and the tape machine rewound. Claire sat on the bed and looked out the window. Ralph came in and wound himself around her feet, and Claire stroked him absently. Amelia really sounded distraught on the phone; even though Amelia was excitable, the tone of her voice shot a tingle of fear through Claire's stomach. Claire put her coat back on and left. As she rang for the elevator Ralph's peevish protest could be heard behind her.

When Claire got out of her cab at the corner of Avenue B and Tenth Street, night was falling. The Life Café faced Tompkins Square Park, and had all the offbeat atmosphere an East Village restaurant should have. Small tables were scattered around the colorful inlaid tile floor; the tops of the tables were covered with lacquered newspaper clippings from the fifties and sixties; and the thin, sallow staff members had hair dyed in colors you might see in a box of Crayolas. The sun had sunk behind the buildings and the waiters appeared with candles for each table. Outside in the park basketball games continued into dusk, the hard *punct* sound of the balls hitting the concrete court mingling with the hoarse yells of the players.

"Yo, Edward, here, man!"

"Oh, foul me, why don't you—"

"Hey, hey—I'm clear!"

"Nice shot, man."

A man walked by with a tatty black collie. A woman jogged by pushing a stroller. A Labrador retriever, leashed to the stroller, trotted along next to her. *Killing three birds with one stone,* Claire thought: *walk the baby, exercise the dog, stay fit.* Robert would approve of that kind of efficiency.

The café stereo was playing a Bach concerto, one of the Brandenburgs. A girl with hair dyed the color of a new penny walked by the window. Claire sipped her coffee, which was strong and bitter. To her disgust the man behind her was smoking. At the table in front of her a young woman with blond hair as smooth as glass picked at a health food salad. Was it her imagination, or was everyone in this neighborhood impossibly young?

As dusk fell outside, inside the café it was dark and cozy. The candles on the tables, reflected in the window, became dozens of candles extending out into the gathering night. Claire thought about Robert, and wondered if they would make it as a couple. He was so tightly wound, so kinetic and compulsively active. He only seemed happy when he was at work, doing "something constructive." Claire, on the other hand, had fantasies of complete and total rest; she longed to give in to the pull of inertia. Sometimes she wanted nothing more in life than to have a place where she could sit, read, and watch the sun go down. It was down now, with only a few thin pink clouds hanging above the trees.

Claire needed so much time to think, to reflect; she had often thought of Robert's constant activity as a dodge, a distraction to keep him from thinking too much about things. She had never dared to suggest this to him, however—their relationship was not a mutually analytical one. After several relationships with men with whom she had taken turns playing therapist—it was a particularly New York thing to do—Robert's private nature was something of a relief. Eventually, she thought, too many mutual revelations of the soul can become a bit cloying. No fear of that with Robert, with his English heritage. He didn't make her feel responsible for his feelings all the time, which she appreciated. And yet . . . you could get only so close to Robert, and then a wall went up . . .

People came and went in the café, and Claire thought about how many lives existed in the city which she had no part of. The city was like not one hive, but like hundreds of thousands of hives or colonies all intermingled. Claire looked at her watch. She had been there for half an hour already. She wondered if she had gotten the place right. She pulled the crumpled receipt from her bag on which she had written the name: the Life Café. She had definitely come to the right restaurant.

A girl in black tights and leather jacket, her hair the color of a purple crayon, came into the café. She spoke to the waitress in an excited voice.

"There's been an accident on the subway."

"What happened?"

"A lady was killed. She fell on the tracks. I heard the police think she might have been pushed."

Claire felt a cool dread creeping over her like a narcotic, paralyzing her. It was as if the report of the subway death triggered a terror that she had been holding on to without even knowing it. Suddenly she felt extremely claustrophobic: the restaurant was too crowded, the tables too small, the cigarette smoke stifling; she must get out. Claire turned toward the waitress to ask for her check. She had to make a phone call, had to talk to—who? She scratched around frantically in her purse for her wallet, found it and paid the bill, not even glancing at the change the waitress placed in front of her. She staggered up from her seat and pushed her way out into the street, almost tripping a jogger, whose glare was lost on her. She forced her mind to concentrate as her eyes searched the corner for a phone booth. Seeing one across from Tompkins Square Park, she ran across the street, ignoring the light, and lifted the receiver with trembling hands. She had to concentrate to remember the precinct number: the ninth. She dialed the number the operator gave her, her heart leaping at every ring.

Finally, after seven rings, a thick voice said, "Ninth Precinct."

"Detective Jackson, please."

"Who's calling?"

"Claire Rawlings."

"He's not here right now."

"When will he be back?"

"I dunno."

Claire felt panicky. Then she remembered the precinct station house was a few blocks away from where she stood. She could go there and wait for him to return.

"Did you wanna leave a message?"

"Uh, no, that's okay." She hung up. It suddenly occurred to her to call Amelia's apartment, just in case . . . but after the tenth ring her dread deepened, a cold, rising tide of fear in her stomach.

She walked through the park, past the homeless people living out of shopping carts, past the dogs romping together on the hill, past old men playing checkers on the stone tables. She turned and walked on Fifth Street, until she stood in front of the heavy grey stones of the station house. She pushed open the thick door and stood inside, panting. The room was no more bustling than it had been on her last visit: blue-clad policemen stood around smoking cigarettes and drinking coffee. The phone rang steadily. The blond woman's desk sat in its corner by the door, but there was no sign of her. Claire felt a draft behind her, and turned to see the door open just as Detective Jackson entered. She had an impulse to rush to him but stood where she was, mouth open, until he saw her. He stopped in front of her, his face grim.

"There's been a death on the subway, and I have to go investigate."

"I heard," Claire said. "Do they know the victim's name yet?"

"Amelia Moore."

Claire stood still, staring at him.

"What?" Claire heard her own voice, small and distant.

"Amelia Moore—she was an acquaintance of Blanche DuBois's. You knew her, too?" he added, seeing her face.

"She was my friend."

Claire felt a sudden, strong need to hug someone. Detective Jackson stood before her, a rumpled trench coat slung over his sloping shoulders. She flung herself into his arms, knocking him off balance. He staggered, recovered, and hesitated a moment. Then his arms folded around her like a comforting cloak.

Chapter 17

Amelia had a mother on Long Island and a brother in North Carolina, but since her life had centered in New York, her funeral was held in Riverside Chapel, on Riverside Drive and 122nd Street. This time Meredith was allowed to attend, and she was very well behaved, even subdued. She had liked Amelia, and was as shocked as everyone else to hear of her death.

"It's my fault," she said bitterly when Claire told her the sad news. "If only I had worked faster, this wouldn't have happened." Meredith was convinced that the same person who killed Blanche had pushed Amelia onto the subway tracks—an opinion shared by Wallace Jackson. He, too, attended the funeral—looking for suspects, Meredith said—in the same shabby grey trench coat he always wore.

"I am considering this a homicide," he said in response to Meredith's inquiry as she and Claire slid into the pew next to him. Claire hadn't wanted to sit by the detective, but as soon as Meredith saw him, she begged to sit with him, and Claire acquiesced. She thought she saw Marshall Bassett smile at them when they sat down next to Jackson.

Nobody felt much like smiling during the service, though; there was audible weeping as the minister gave the eulogy. Claire saw a lot of unfamiliar young faces in the crowd, and supposed they were Amelia's voice students. Anthony Sciorra sat alone near the back, his face rigid. He had already lost the woman he loved, and now he had lost the woman who loved him. Amelia's death made the front page of the Metro Section of the *Times*, and a few reporters loitered about the church, though the taking of photographs was strictly prohibited during the service.

WOMAN'S DEATH RULED "SUSPICIOUS," the *Times* headline read, and then the article went on to quote the captain of the Twenty-fourth Precinct, who said noncommittally that Amelia's death was "under investigation." As a detective in the Ninth Precinct, Wallace Jackson was not officially involved in any way—and his superiors on the force evidently did not share his opinion that the two deaths were necessarily linked, because they did not assign him to the investigation.

"Of all the stupid, pigheaded things!" Meredith ranted when she heard this. "Of *course* they're related; you don't have to be a rocket scientist to see that!"

As they were leaving the church Claire saw Sergeant Barker. He and Jackson were having a conversation, heads bent together, voices low. Claire thought the sergeant looked a little thicker than the last time she saw him. When he saw her and Meredith, he bounded over toward them.

"Hello," he said, doing his best to look solemn but not succeeding; it was simply inherently impossible for Sergeant Barker to look sad.

"Have you gained weight?" Meredith asked sourly in response to his greeting.

Sergeant Barker looked pleased by this question.

"Ah, you noticed! Yes, I have to gain twenty pounds for a role I have to play next month." He produced a flyer from the depths of his coat. "You should come see it; we're doing *H.M.S. Pinafore* at the South Street Seaport. Neat, huh?"

Meredith didn't respond. Claire took the flyer and looked at it; there was a drawing of several sailors saluting a plump woman who she supposed was Little Buttercup.

"Well, I've got to go," said Sergeant Barker, and he scurried off through the crowd.

Claire went to the reception just long enough to pay her respects to Amelia's mother, a small, sad woman with Amelia's delicate features and curly hair, except that hers was grey. At the sight of Amelia's mother Claire couldn't help thinking that this would have been Amelia herself someday if she had lived a normal life span.

After a few words with Amelia's mother and brother, both of whom were distraught with grief—both shared Amelia's emotional intensity as well as some of her mannerisms—Claire took Meredith and went home.

As they walked along Riverside Drive Meredith said, "What's going to happen to Amelia's mail now?"

Claire watched a squirrel running along the stone wall bordering Riverside Park. The squirrel had been keeping up with them for some time now, stopping every once in a while to sniff the air, evidently hoping for handouts.

"I don't know," she replied. "I suppose it will go to her mother."

"I have a better idea," Meredith suggested. "It should be forwarded to the police. There may be a clue in the mail."

Claire stepped carefully over a rough section of the path. Meredith had already made an arrangement with Sarah to look at Blanche's mail as soon as it was forwarded to her; Claire was surprised, actually, that Sarah had been so amenable to the idea.

"Well . . ." she said.

"I think we should call Mrs. Moore and ask her."

Sometimes Meredith's presumptuousness amazed Claire. She imagined the poor, bereaved woman having to make such a decision so soon after her daughter's death.

"All right, we'll ask Detective Jackson what he thinks. But wait a few days, all right?"

Meredith scuffed her shoe on some gravel along the side of the path.

"All right."

In the aftermath of Amelia's death, everyone was frightened and depressed. Sarah was particularly upset. She called and asked Claire and Meredith to come over the next day.

"What did she ever do to anyone—that good, kind woman?" she said, blowing her nose into a pink lace handkerchief she had inherited from Blanche. Sitting across from her in Sarah's living room, Claire looked out onto Bethune Street, where a light rain was falling. She felt a sense of unreality. It did seem impossible that anyone could consider Amelia a threat—sweet, trusting Amelia who just wanted to hunt her mushrooms and give parties. Claire turned back to Sarah.

"I don't know," she said lamely. "I can't figure it out."

"She knew something," Meredith said from the couch. She sat hunched in the corner of Sarah's stiff-backed antique sofa, her hands clasped over her thin knees. Claire knew the girl felt personally responsible for Amelia's death, because she sat staring at the wall, refusing Sarah's offer of cookies.

"She knew something," Meredith repeated, "and I'm going to find out what it was. That will lead me to her killer."

Sarah rubbed her eyes wearily.

"That's very good of you, but what makes you think you can accomplish something the police haven't been able to do?"

Meredith looked at Sarah, her eyes almost yellow in the lamplight.

"Because if I set out to do something, it will get done," she said with such conviction that Claire was impressed. Sarah just smiled sadly.

"Well, I for one wouldn't know where to start."

"Oh, that's the easy part," said Meredith. "Amelia knew something that no one else knew, something she tried to communicate to Claire. The murderer must have known this, and that's why they killed her."

"Yes, but what did she know, and why was she trying to tell Claire and not the police?"

"That's just *it,* don't you see?" cried Meredith. "That's exactly the right question: why *did* she want to tell Claire and not the police?"

"I can't imagine," Sarah replied dully. Claire thought she was more moved by Amelia's death than by her sister's; certainly it was no secret Sarah had liked Amelia better. But Claire couldn't think of anyone who didn't like Amelia. She was different from Blanche, who could irritate people just by the way she walked into a room.

Claire remembered Peter's suggestion that she ask Sarah about finishing Blanche's book. Since Amelia's death, everything seemed fragile and transitory, and the book had taken on an importance for her that she could not quite explain.

"Sarah," she said, "my editor wanted to know if you would have any objections to my finishing Blanche's last book."

"Oh, that Klan thing she was working on? You want to finish writing it?"

"Yes; she completed a first draft before she died. It mostly just needs editing."

Sarah got up and walked over to the French window and looked out into the street.

"I can't imagine why she made me her literary executor." She laughed, a dry, mirthless chuckle. "Blanche's last revenge, getting me involved with her writing after she's gone—and I haven't even been able to bring myself to go through her apartment."

"What did she leave Marshall in her will?" said Meredith.

"Oh, books, furniture—she and Marshall both went in for antiques, you know."

"Anything else?"

"Oh, and a certain percentage of the Klan book, if it's published."

"Did you know Claire and I were in Amelia's will?" Meredith said.

"You?" Sarah looked puzzled. "But Amelia barely knew you," she said to Meredith.

"Oh, she just left me her books on mushrooms, because she thought I was interested in them," Meredith replied.

"Are you?"

"Not really—except the poisonous ones. She left Claire some nice china, I guess because they used to have tea together."

Sarah sat down on one of the straight-backed chairs. "But that would mean that Amelia's will was done—or at least added to—quite recently."

"That's right."

"Do you think—"

"That she knew she was going to die?" Meredith wrapped her thin arms around her body. "I've thought about it, and I'm not sure what to think. She was frightened about something. Marshall told me he noticed something strange about her the day they went to—the day she was killed."

Sarah shook her head. "Good Lord," she said, and turned to Claire. "Go ahead, finish the book. Maybe you'll discover the key to her murder."

Claire had been going over the manuscript, and as she did she wondered what had caused Blanche to turn from her lucrative mysteries and do the enormous amount of research necessary for a book like this. She had never asked her, but she wondered what in Blanche's own life made her want to tackle such a project, what personal event or events had led her to an interest—an obsession, maybe—deep enough to devote so much time to the subject of racism. She mentioned this to Sarah.

"Well, we haven't spoken about it much since school, but . . ."

"What?" said Meredith, unable to contain herself.

"Oh, there was a boy at school, a lovely man, really—a scholar and an athlete, and I think Blanche actually loved him."

"What happened?"

"He disappeared."

"How?"

"Well, I remember she had just thrown over this one fellow, James White, a handsome art major, a Southerner—from Virginia, I think. He was very angry at her, thought that she had led him on, and he turned out to be a very vengeful, ugly person, and—though we didn't know it at the time—a racist. Anyway, the young man Blanche fell for—his name was Cliff—happened to be black, and when James found out about it, he confronted them in public and said some really horrible things. Blanche and Cliff were classmates at UNC, and one day they were strolling together in Chapel Hill when James approached them and . . . well, I wasn't there, but Blanche said he physically threatened them. A few days after that Cliff disappeared."

"Was a body ever found?" asked Meredith. Sarah paused and looked away, and Claire noticed that her hands gripped her wine glass tensely.

"Not exactly."

"What do you mean 'not exactly'?"

Sarah put down her glass and stared at the carpet.

"It's been years since I've allowed myself to think about it, so please excuse me. It was so—horrible . . ."

"What?" Meredith leaned forward expectantly. Sarah looked at the child as if she were not quite human, then addressed herself to Claire.

"Shortly after Cliff's disappearance Blanche received a package in the mail." She paused again and shuddered. "It was a heart."

"A heart?" Meredith's voice was tight with excitement.

"A human heart."

"Was it his?"

"There was no way to tell for sure without the rest of the body, but Blanche was sure it was Cliff's."

"And the police?"

"There was an inquest, of course, but without a body—"

"That was in the days before DNA testing," Meredith said thoughtfully. "Were there any other clues as to who might have . . . ?"

Sarah leaned back against the couch and rubbed her forehead.

"I've tried so hard not to think about this . . . wait a minute; yes, there was something else. About a week before Cliff disappeared Blanche received an envelope with nothing in it except five little seeds."

"The Five Orange Pips!" Meredith cried, leaping from

her chair, sending Sarah's cat fleeing to the safety of the kitchen.

"What?" said Sarah.

"It's a Sherlock Holmes story: 'The Five Orange Pips.' A 'pip' is a seed. In the story the seeds are sent to the murder victims to warn them of their impending demise. Holmes figures this out and finds the murderer."

"Who is it?"

"A former member of the Ku Klux Klan! See, the Klan used to—"

"Yes, yes, I grew up in the South, you know," Sarah said a little impatiently. "We knew that one of the methods the Klan used to intimidate their victims was sending them seeds in the mail. Blanche showed the seeds to the police when she received them, but they laughed at her. They said a few seeds in the mail didn't constitute a legal threat."

Meredith waved her hands dismissively.

"Where real finesse is required, the police are next to useless." She looked at Claire and then quickly added, "Except for some of them, of course."

Sarah rose and went to the window, pulling back the white lace curtain to look out onto the street, where a light rain was falling more steadily now. Under other circumstances, Claire would have found the whoosh of car tires upon the rain-soaked street comforting.

"I don't know if I should say this . . ." Sarah began.

"Oh, go ahead," Meredith said, but Claire glared at her.

"Well, I always suspected that Jean knew something about it . . . something she never told anyone."

"Jean as in Jean my evil stepmother?" said Meredith.

Sarah let the curtain drop, ignoring her.

"It isn't anything concrete, just that she seemed very nervous after that, and then when she transferred to UNC Greensboro, none of us ever heard from her again."

"So the plagiarism incident was after this?" said Meredith.

"Yes; it was a few months later."

"Maybe she did it on purpose, because she was looking for an excuse to leave," Claire remarked.

Sarah shrugged. "Well, I don't know about that. It's possible, I suppose . . ."

Meredith leaned back in her chair. "As a colleague of mine once said, 'Once you have eliminated the impossible, whatever remains, however improbable, must be the truth.' "

Chapter 18

Yet you know, Meredith's the ultimate *egoist*," Claire said to Peter Schwartz over lunch at Keens. "She knows she's smarter than most people, and doesn't feel guilty about it or think she should hide it."

"She'll have to find a hell of man to take her on someday," he said, adding quickly, "that is, if she ever—I mean, not that she necessarily *will* want to . . . but if she does . . ." He sighed. "I keep trying to play by the rules, but I'll probably end up getting sued someday. It'll be something stupid, like telling a woman she looks good in red. She'll think I'm sexually harassing her and she'll sue me. You'll testify in court for me, won't you?"

He looked at her over his Scotch glass, his brown eyes sad as a beagle's. The left corner of his mouth twitched upward, though, and Claire smiled back at him.

"Of course I will," she said. "I'll even say you're gay, if you want."

Peter wrinkled his nose. "You don't have to go overboard," he said indignantly, and Claire laughed again. She couldn't resist teasing Peter; he was so huffy, like a little bantam rooster, when his sexuality was in question.

"Do you know, we used to play a game when I was in

graduate school," Peter said. "If someone was heterosexual, they had to say who they would sleep with if they *had* to have a homosexual affair, and then the reverse for someone if they were homosexual. They had to say who of the opposite sex they would choose."

"Interesting," said Claire. "Who did you pick?"

"Well, my first choice was Alan Ladd, but if he wasn't available I would have taken Basil Rathbone or Humphrey Bogart."

Claire laughed. "I'm not sure I see a pattern there," she said.

Peter shrugged and took a bite of mesclun salad. He was always dieting.

"Does there always have to be a pattern?"

"I don't know," said Claire. "Meredith seems to think so."

"Meredith wants life to imitate fiction," Peter sighed, "but it doesn't. It's much messier than she realizes."

"I could be wrong, but I think Meredith may see patterns where other people just see chaos."

"Jolly good for her," said Peter. "Maybe she should have been a quantum physicist."

"It's not too late," said Claire, taking a sip of red wine. "It's funny you should say that, because ever since Amelia died I've been thinking about the passage of time . . ."

"Uh-oh, maybe I should order another drink."

Claire made a face at him. "It's just that when I'm around Meredith, I notice her ability to immerse herself entirely in the moment, and I sometimes think I've lost that ability. She uses her time simply and naturally, as though it were a gift, whereas I hoard it, obsess about it, and worry about its passing."

Peter nodded. "That seems natural enough. I do the same thing."

"But is it a function of growing older, do you think?"

Peter shrugged. "I don't know. Maybe."

"You know, this may sound strange," Claire said slowly, "but today I suddenly realized that I expected Amelia to . . .

always *be there*. I mean, I guess she seemed beyond death in some way. Does that make any sense?"

Peter nodded. "I think we all have people like that in our lives. When we're young it's our parents, but then later I think movie stars and athletes often perform that function. We can even accept our own aging as long as we can point to someone who doesn't—a delegate, if you will, for our own secret hopes of immortality."

Claire sighed. "You're so wise, Peter."

Peter smiled and took a sip of Scotch. "Ooo, you take advantage of my poor male ego. Flattery will get you everywhere. Be careful, or I may ask you to marry me."

Claire laughed, but something like a sob caught in her throat. Amelia had been the true core of their little group, and now that she was gone Claire knew that the center had not held. Lately she had been obsessing about the people who were no longer in her life, either because of death or geography or just apathy, and she was beginning to feel that over the years she had shed people like a snake sheds its skin. People were like comets, whirling in and out of solar systems, spinning through space, orbiting around each other like lost planets. Claire ran her finger over the lip of her wineglass, making a faint ringing sound. A couple of overfed business men in expensive suits looked up from their rack of lamb, but she didn't care.

"Do you know what Willard wants to do?"

Peter sighed. "Please, not while I'm eating."

"He told me he wants to write a book based on Blanche's murder."

Peter put down his fork. "Good Lord, that man's capacity for tackiness really does continue to amaze."

"Peter," she said slowly, "you don't think Willard . . ."

"What? Do I think Willard killed Blanche?" He smiled and shook his head. "Wouldn't that just be too perfect?"

"What do you mean?"

"I can just see the headlines: 'Best-selling author kills competition.' We're not in Texas, you know."

"Texas?"

"I was thinking of the mother of the cheerleader who put a contract out on her daughter's competitor."

"Oh, right. Still, do you think . . . ?"

Peter balanced a piece of arugula on his fork, studying it as if it were a laboratory specimen. A sudden eruption of laughter burst in from the bar in the next room; it was Friday afternoon and the office crowd was beginning to gather for their weekly ritual.

"Willard is . . . well, let's just say he's not my favorite person in the world. But it's hard to imagine him . . . I mean, it's hard to imagine anyone I know doing something like that."

Claire nodded. "I know what you mean. I've gone through the list of everyone I can think of, and . . . it just seems inconceivable."

Peter signaled the waiter for another Scotch. (His diets always included a certain allowance of single malts.) "Yes, well, that's what the police are for. By the way, I understand your swain Robert has some competition from a certain detective."

Claire looked at him. "I don't know what you're talking about."

"Never mind, never mind . . . rumors will circulate. Forget I said anything."

But Claire couldn't forget. She spent the rest of the afternoon wondering who had spread the rumor—and why.

Sarah and Claire made an appointment to go to Blanche's apartment together the next day to gather Blanche's notes on her book. Meredith asked if she could come along, and Claire agreed on the condition that she not get in their way. She was afraid that Meredith would send one of the stacks of magazines crashing to the ground with one careless fling of an arm.

They picked their way cautiously through the piles of things and went into Blanche's living room. Blanche used a computer for her final drafts, but there were sheets of scribbled research notes everywhere on her writing desk. Claire sighed when she saw them, and Sarah laughed her dry little laugh.

"Well, you have your work cut out for you, as the saying goes. Good luck."

Claire sat down at Blanche's writing desk and looked at the scattered sheets of paper with dismay. Meredith roamed the room like a bird dog, poking into everything. Claire glanced at Sarah to see if she was annoyed yet, but she was just sitting on the edge of the sofa, staring into space. Claire turned back to the desk, and noticed a mirror with an ornate brass frame hanging on the wall over the desk. Tucked into the corner of the mirror was an elegant tortoiseshell comb. She picked up the comb and ran her finger over its smooth edges. *Mirror, mirror on the wall, who's the fairest of them all?* Blanche had certainly been fair, but it had not saved her . . .

"That comb was a gift from Anthony," Sarah said.

"It's beautiful."

"Yes, isn't it? It's from Italy. He brought it back after one of his trips there."

"Does he go back very often?"

Sarah shrugged. "I don't know. He has family there, in Palermo, I think."

Meredith appeared at Claire's shoulder.

"Find anything? I haven't found a damn thing," she said, leaning on the desk.

Claire was about to reprimand her for swearing when she noticed the little drawer pop out of the side of the desk. Meredith saw it at the same moment, and pounced on it.

"Look! What's this?" she said, extracting a small book from the drawer. "It's Blanche's diary!" she said loudly, holding it up for Sarah to see.

"You don't have to shout; I'm right next to you," said Claire, thinking more of Sarah, who hated loud noises.

But Sarah was staring at the diary.

"Good Lord," she said, "I didn't know she kept a diary. Can I see it?"

Meredith handed it over reluctantly, then proceeded to read over Sarah's shoulder.

"What? What does it say?" she said, wriggling with excitement.

"Look," said Sarah, holding it up for Claire to see, "the last page has been torn out."

"Oh my God," Meredith murmured. "Oh my God."

For once Claire didn't think Meredith was being overly dramatic.

The Ninth Precinct was just a few blocks from Blanche's apartment. The blond woman was at her desk, eating a bagel with cream cheese, when the three of them arrived.

"Can I help you?" she said, her cheeks puffing out like a chipmunk's.

Meredith started to speak but Claire put a firm hand on her shoulder.

"We'd like to see Detective Jackson, please," she said as calmly as she could.

"Do you have an appointment?"

"No, but—" Meredith began, squirming away from Claire's hold on her.

"No," said Claire with a look at Meredith. "He knows us, though. Tell him—tell him Claire and Meredith are here."

"And Sarah," Meredith added, determined to be involved.

"Wait just a second," the blond woman replied. She heaved herself out of her chair and lumbered over to Jackson's cubicle. In a moment she returned and motioned them over.

"Go ahead and go in." She resumed her vigil with satisfaction, delicately spreading the cream cheese around the bagel with her index finger.

Claire saw Sarah roll her eyes, but fortunately the blond woman was oblivious to such nuances of behavior. The three of them walked over to Jackson's cubicle, arriving just as Sergeant Barker shot out of it at a trot.

"Oh, hello," he said. "Sorry, I gotta dash. I'm late to an audition."

"What does that man *do*?" said Sarah, looking after him.

"I don't think even he knows," said a voice behind them, and they looked up to see Detective Jackson standing there, the familiar trench coat slung over his arm, the same weary slope to his shoulders.

"Would you mind very much joining me for lunch?" he said apologetically. "I haven't eaten all day. Is the Veselka all right with you?"

The Veselka was all right with everyone, and ten minutes later they were all seated in the back room amid potted plants and blackboards listing the day's homemade soups. Even in a neighborhood full of Russian and Ukrainian restaurants, the Veselka was a landmark: open twenty-four hours a day, it boasted the best borscht in the East Village. Anytime of day you could find poets, businessmen, and anarchists side by side, hunched over the rickety crowded tables, sipping soup and reading the *Times*—or the *Anarchist News*.

It did not take long for Detective Jackson to peruse the diary and agree that it was a most important find.

"A secret compartment?" he said, leaning back in his chair and rubbing his forehead. "Would I insult your sister if I said 'how clichéd'?" he said to Sarah.

Sarah let some air escape her lungs—not a laugh, not a snort, but something in between.

"She's past insulting, Detective, and besides, it *is* clichéd! I think Blanche reveled in that sort of thing. It was all part of her playacting."

"Well," said Jackson with a glance at the waiter delivering his soup, "the most obvious question, of course, is who tore out that last page. Was it Blanche, or was it—"

"The murderer!" Meredith exclaimed.

The waiter stared at her. Tall and thin, sallow-skinned, with a bristly crew cut and little wire-rim glasses over a narrow nose, he resembled a young Bertolt Brecht. Sometimes Claire thought everyone in the East Village looked like they were in costume. She supposed this young man was an anarchist—or, at the very least, a socialist.

"It might have been someone else," said Jackson. He turned to Claire. "Didn't you tell me that Amelia and Marshall went to the apartment right before she was—"

"Yes, yes, that's right," Claire interrupted, not wanting to hear the awful word.

"So it could have been one of them!" cried Meredith, nearly upsetting the plate the waiter was trying to set in front of her.

"Yes, it could have," said Jackson. "I just regret that our boys didn't find the drawer when we searched the apartment. Frankly, we found it tough going. No offense," he said to Sarah, "but it was hard work, sorting through everything there."

"Did you really go through *every*thing?" Sarah sounded horrified at the idea.

"Well, maybe not everything, but we did our best," he answered. "Evidently it wasn't good enough."

"Oh, don't feel bad," said Meredith. "Even I would have missed it if I hadn't happened to lean on it by accident."

"So good of you to admit that it was an accident," Claire observed dryly, but her sarcasm was lost on Meredith.

"Oh yes," Meredith went on cheerfully, "this is a difficult case, really quite difficult."

"So what do we do now?" asked Sarah.

"Nothing," said Jackson. "Don't tell anyone about this. The fewer people who know about the diary the better."

"Because one of them could be the murderer, right?" said Meredith, tackling the hamburger on her plate energetically.

"That's part of it. We also don't want the press to get ahold of any details," he said to Claire, "because that can really hamper our investigation."

"Right—got it; no press," said Meredith.

Sarah looked at her.

"What do you do when you're asleep?" she said. "Or *do* you sleep?"

For some reason the remark struck all of them as funny, and they all burst out laughing, even Meredith. The combination of anxiety and fatigue made it difficult to stop, and they were still laughing when the bemused waiter came to clear their plates.

Chapter 19

Meredith was lying on the living room rug reading *Madame Bovary* while Claire sat on the red leather chair reading manuscripts. A soft autumn rain fell outside. It was one week before Thanksgiving, and Claire had left the office early to work at home.

Meredith suddenly snorted and rolled over on her back. "Ugh!"

"What?"

"This description of her death! It's disgusting."

"Oh, when she poisons herself . . . yes, I remember it was pretty gruesome."

"What a yucky way to die."

"Yes, it is." Claire put her manuscript down for a moment. "I hope Blanche didn't suffer too much."

"Yech," said Meredith. She closed the book up and wriggled on her stomach in the direction of Ralph, who had been sitting just out of the danger zone. He saw her coming and fled, and Meredith rolled over onto her back again. Absently, Claire began scratching her left palm.

"You know, that spot on your hand is linked to a chakra," said Meredith.

"What?"

"That spot you're always scratching—it's linked to a chakra. There's an imbalance of energy somewhere in your body."

Claire decided to humor her.

"Oh, really—where?"

Meredith shook her head.

"I think it's linked to your heart meridian."

"You mean heart as in cardiovascular health, or heart as in romance?"

Meredith shrugged. "Take your pick. The Chinese don't dichotomize the mind/body relationship the way we do; they believe more in the connected nature of all things."

"I see."

"It's become a commonplace in Western medicine now that there's a connection between emotional health and physical health, but the Chinese were there way ahead of us."

"Yes, well, this is very interesting, Meredith, but I really have to finish reading this manuscript today."

"All right, all right." Meredith rolled over onto her stomach and resumed her reading. After a few minutes she said, "I wonder what concentration of cyanide would have been used in the crime? Who would know the answer to that?" Then she raised herself up on her elbows and looked at Claire.

"I know—Anthony! I'll call Anthony. Where did you say he worked—Hoffman LaRoche?"

Claire sighed and put down her manuscript. "I don't think that's a good idea, bothering him at work," she said, but Meredith was already dialing.

"Hello? May I speak with Anthony Sciorra?" she said, lowering her voice and doing her best imitation of an adult. There was a pause and then she said, "Anthony Sciorra, please." There was a longer pause and then Claire heard her say, "Oh . . . do you know where he can be reached?" Then another pause and Meredith hung up. A moment later she appeared around the corner, her face dejected.

"They said he doesn't work there anymore."

"What?" said Claire, surprised. "Since when?"

"They didn't say. They couldn't even tell me where he went."

"That's strange," Claire mused. "Anthony's been at Roche for a long time. I wonder why he left."

"So do I," said Meredith, "so do I."

Peter Schwartz walked into Claire's office the next morning and tossed a packet of photos onto her desk.

"Well, what do you think?" he said, plopping himself down on the couch.

Claire looked through the photos. They were all of Peter, taken in his office.

"They're good; what are they for?"

"Oh, it's for a magazine article. They said I could provide my own photos if I wanted."

"Who took them?"

"Don't you recognize the style?"

Claire looked at the photos again. They were really very good; in them, Peter looked ten pounds lighter.

"Was it Robert?" she said.

"*Naturellement*—who else?"

"When did he take these?"

"Oh, a few months ago—just before you started dating, actually. Right after the book party where you two met."

Peter took the photographs and put them in his jacket pocket.

"Listen, I have some tickets for the theatre tonight. Would you like to come?"

"Well, that sounds nice, but Meredith—"

"Oh, bring her along."

"Well, thank you . . ."

"Here's the address," he said, scribbling it on a scrap of paper. "Don't worry," he said as he left Claire's office, "it's suitable for children."

Suitable for children. Claire thought of Meredith and smiled at the inappropriateness of the phrase.

Claire had heard stories about the kind of shows Peter liked to see. To say that he had a taste for the avant-garde was an understatement—but Meredith thought it would be good for her to see something weird.

"Oh, come on; it'll expand your horizons," she said over tea and a bag of Nantucket cookies.

And so they showed up that night at the appointed place, a loft in TriBeCa where they had to use the service elevator to get to the theatre, which was on the second floor. The production was a Swedish theatre company's rendition of the story of Kasper Hauser, and the first twenty minutes consisted of a man slowly working his way out of a large black garbage bag. He did not talk, though he made sounds from time to time that suggested a bull moose during rutting season. He was then joined onstage by two other men, and the three of them made sounds that evoked a bear with a particularly virulent attack of gas.

At intermission Claire considered pleading that she had a headache—which would not have been far from the truth—but Peter looked so pleased that she didn't have the heart.

"Isn't it smashing?" he said, offering her a glass of red wine from the wobbly makeshift bar that was set up in the lobby. "It really calls into question everything—the whole dynamic of entertainment, the nature of the audience's relationship to the actors. It makes us so aware of our *expectations*."

"It's really boring," said Meredith.

"Oh, but boredom is good for the soul," said Peter. "Just don't fight it."

"The only thing I'm fighting is sleep," Meredith replied sourly.

Claire smiled, glad that she had brought Meredith after all, because the girl could say everything Claire was too polite to say.

During the second act the boredom became a physical sensation, acutely painful, like a toothache. There was a mime scene performed by bad mimes, and then a young man with red dreadlocks chased some other people around for a while. During this, a large woman sat in the corner beating a drum. Peter was enraptured, and as they left he suggested dinner.

"We can't end an evening like this so abruptly. I won't fall asleep for hours now, I'm so stimulated," he sighed happily.

"He's weird," Meredith whispered to Claire as they wound through the streets of TriBeCa on their way to Chinatown, where Peter said he knew a terrific noodle house on Mott Street.

The noodle house was tucked away in the crook of Mott Street as it turns to intersect the Bowery. Peter insisted on ordering for all of them, and when the food came, Claire had to admit his taste in cuisine was better than his taste in theatre.

"You know," Peter said in between mouthfuls of shrimp lo mein, "I once saw a production of a Peter Handke piece which consisted of an actor who stood absolutely still without speaking for thirty minutes."

Meredith looked up from her hot-and-sour soup. "You mean, you *paid money* to watch someone stand there without saying anything?"

"Oh, yes . . . I got to musing about the nature of theatre, and what it all means." He took a bite of noodles and thought for a moment. "A lot of people left."

"But not you."

"No, I stayed the longest."

Meredith rolled her eyes.

"So you got your money's worth."

"I'll say I did; it was very stimulating."

"John Cage did a similar thing, you know—sat there until the audience walked out," said Claire.

"Oh, this was *before* John Cage," said Peter, as though the comparison were an insult. "The second act was even more interesting; it was all about a man and his doppelgänger."

"His what?" said Meredith.

"His doppelgänger. It's a German word which literally means 'double-goer,' but it's often used in literature to mean someone's evil genius or demonic side—"

"Oh, you mean like Dr. Jekyll and Mr. Hyde?"

"Exactly."

"Hmm . . . that's interesting." Meredith turned to Claire. "Maybe I'm your doppelgänger," she said playfully.

"They say that everyone has one," said Peter, digging into a plate of crabs in garlic sauce.

"Who's yours?" said Meredith.

Peter paused, holding a crab in midair with his chopsticks. "I don't know. How about Willard?" he said with a wicked grin, and they all laughed.

"I like that idea," said Meredith. "Doppelgänger . . . I wonder if Detective Jackson has one?" she whispered to Claire.

"Well, don't get too excited about it," said Peter. "In literature, the appearance of the doppelgänger often heralds death."

"Cool!" said Meredith.

Claire shivered.

Wer reitet so spät durch Nacht und Wind?

They ate in silence for a while, and every once in a while Peter said something to the waiter in Chinese. He had learned to speak it during the Vietnam War, and was very proud of himself. Claire had to admit that Peter was a good host, and he even managed to charm the waiter, who joked with him in Chinese.

"So how are you enjoying New York?" he said to Meredith, lifting a piece of asparagus to his mouth.

"Oh, it's a big improvement over Hartford-on-Auschwitz," Meredith said.

Claire felt herself tighten, and she glared at Meredith. Peter looked startled, but then he laughed. "Is that what you call it?"

"Yeah, I guess . . ." Meredith shrugged. "I mean, I don't mean to be insensitive or anything, it's just that it fits."

"Is Hartford that bad?"

"Well, it's just really constraining and conservative, you know, and there's very little culture for an inquisitive mind."

"Like yours."

"Like mine, or anyone who is serious about the life of the mind."

"But what about the life of the body?" said Peter, pouring himself and Claire some more Tsing Tsao beer.

Meredith shrugged.

"I have no objection to it on principle, but the unexamined life and all that, you know."

"Yes, I know," Peter said, "but don't you think the examination thing can be overdone? I mean, aren't you a little tired of all of the whining that's going on in our society now, with people blaming their traumatic childhoods for every little neurosis or personality quirk? God, it seems like there's a support group for everything these days. I wouldn't be surprised if they form a support group for support-group addicts."

Meredith snorted disdainfully.

"I don't think that's the kind of examination Meredith's talking about," said Claire.

Just then there was a loud crashing sound in the kitchen. Conversation in the restaurant stopped abruptly, and there were a few nervous giggles; a couple of people applauded.

"People are so strange, aren't they?" said Meredith, shaking her head. "Everyone loves a disaster, even if it's only a tray dropping in the kitchen."

"We all have a dark side," said Peter, his mouth full of lo mein. "Oh, listen, speaking of strange, I wanted to tell you something."

"Oh? What's that?"

"Do you remember asking me about my insulin injections?"

"Yes."

"Well, I seem to have misplaced my spare syringe."

Meredith's eyes brightened, and her whole body shot up to attention.

"What do you mean, you misplaced it?"

"Well, normally I keep one at home and one in the office just in case, and the other day I looked and it wasn't there."

"Did you look everywhere you might have left it?"

"Well, yes; at least, I think I did. I don't know what to

make of it. Do you think I should tell the police, or would that be silly?"

"You should absolutely tell the police," Meredith said, "and no, I don't think it's silly at all."

"But who would—I mean, who could possibly have—"

"That's what I intend to find out," said Meredith, with a look in her eyes that Claire had already come to recognize. She then launched into a lecture, about leaving no stone unturned and how the smallest thing may be of significance. Peter listened politely, and when Meredith paused for breath he turned to Claire.

"It sounds as though you have another future mystery author on your hands."

"Oh, I'm not a *writer,* " Meredith said, as though the word were an insult. "I'm a *detective*. There's a difference, you know."

"Yes, I'd heard that," Peter said, and ordered himself another beer. Claire thought about Meredith's stepmother and her drug habit, and wondered if being around Meredith had exacerbated it.

When they had finished eating Peter suggested a cappuccino in Little Italy, but Claire was exhausted.

"It's way past Meredith's bedtime," she said. "Maybe another time."

"Aw, come on," Meredith begged. "I'm not tired at all."

"Well, you may not feel tired, but it's very late," said Claire.

"It's Friday night," Meredith whined.

"You'd better do what she says," said Peter. "You don't want to press your luck with Claire; believe me, I know."

Claire had no idea what Peter was talking about, but she smiled at him gratefully.

Meredith grumbled a little, but she climbed quietly into the cab when they got to Canal Street.

"Cheerio," said Peter, closing the door of the cab.

Meredith settled into the back of the cab as it rattled up Centre Street. "I like him," she said, looking out the window. "He's weird, but I like him. He seems like a good guy."

"Yeah," said Claire, "he's all right."

"Of course, that doesn't mean he's not on my list of suspects."

"Really?"

"Oh, sure. Do you believe the story about the misplaced syringe?"

Claire thought about it. "I guess I do, yeah. Do you?"

Meredith shrugged. "I neither believe nor disbelieve. I keep my mind open to all possibilities so that when the truth emerges I'm prepared to recognize it. I'll tell you one thing, though: If Peter isn't the killer, it's almost certainly someone who knows him well enough to know he has access to a syringe."

Claire was silent. She found it difficult to picture Peter Schwartz as a cold-blooded killer. But then, someone had killed Blanche DuBois and Amelia Moore—and if it wasn't Peter, who was it?

Chapter 20

"You know what I'm not looking forward to?" said Meredith the next morning as they sat on the terrace of the boat café in Central Park watching a couple of mallards paddling around on the lake. The fall continued to be unusually mild, and Claire sat with her jacket unbuttoned. A patch of sunlight filtered down through the dried vines that wound around the wooden trellis.

"What are you not looking forward to?" said Claire.

"Being an adult and dealing with all that stupid stuff adults have to do, like remembering to buy toilet paper." Meredith looked up at her, squinting, from where she sat on a little bench in the shade. Meredith hated sunlight—her pale eyes were sensitive to any kind of strong light, and she worried obsessively about skin cancer. "Silent killer," she would say, studying her white arms, completely devoid of freckles, "especially for fair-skinned people like us."

Claire took a sip of coffee, hot and bitter and comforting. They were alone on the terrace except for an elderly man in an old-fashioned suit and a fedora; he was reading the *Times* and eating a bagel.

"You know what I mean?" Meredith continued, picking apart her Danish into tiny pieces, which she ate one by one.

Meredith was always pulling her food apart before consuming it. She seemed to have a need to rearrange everything before she put it in her mouth—for instance, she liked to pull all the cheese off her pizza to eat it, then eat the crust separately. Sometimes she would dismantle an entire sandwich and eat all of the components separately—first the tuna salad, then the bread, then the lettuce, and finally the tomato.

Claire tried not to look too hard at the implications of this behavior. Something about the girl made Claire not want too pry too deeply into what was troubling her. Though she knew Meredith missed her mother, she wasn't sure that she wanted to delve too deeply into the girl's loss. The truth was Claire was jealous of Katherine; feelings she had been able to repress at school now bubbled to the surface. At Duke, Claire had successfully convinced herself that she and Katherine were not really in competition. But now that Meredith was part of the equation she was sure the girl was comparing the two of them, and feared that whatever the scale of measurement, Claire would always come out second best.

As if reading her thoughts, Meredith said, "You know, my mom always said she hated that kind of thing, too—you know, having to remember what to get at the store and stuff."

Meredith threw a piece of Danish in the direction of the ducks. It landed out in the water beyond them, and they rushed toward it, tilting forward, heads bent, paddling madly. The male reached it first, and the female circled him, disappointed. He ate greedily, his beautiful green head bobbing up and down in the water as he pecked at the bread.

"My mom was"— Meredith paused, and Claire braced herself, but to her surprise the girl said—"funny that way."

"What do you mean—funny what way?"

Meredith shrugged.

"Oh, I don't know . . . she hated what she called the 'dull throb of everyday existence.' "

Claire didn't know what to say, so she pulled off a piece of her own Danish and threw it to the ducks. It landed a few yards away, closer to the shore this time, and the ducks turned around abruptly and paddled frantically toward it. Meredith laughed.

"They're so silly," she said. "Scrambling after a little piece of bread."

"Do *you* hate it?" said Meredith.

"Hate what?"

"The dull throb of everyday existence?"

Claire thought about it. "Sometimes," she said. "When I remember to think about it . . . I guess it doesn't bother me most of the time."

"Why not?" said Meredith.

"Why not?" said Claire. "Well, I guess because it's all we have."

"Right," said Meredith. "It's all we have . . . I guess you have to learn to love it, huh?"

"Yeah," said Claire, "I guess you do."

"I wish I could have told my mom that," Meredith said wistfully. "She always wanted . . ."

"What?"

"I don't know. I'm not really sure what she wanted, just that—"

"What?" said Claire, holding her breath.

"Oh, why did she have to die before she found it?" Meredith said in a voice that was somewhere between a wail and a sob. She buried her head in Claire's lap. The elderly gentleman with the newspaper looked over at them, a startled expression on his face.

Claire's hand, uncertain at first, stroked the girl's hair. It was rough and kinky, with the texture of hemp.

"Shh," she said, "it's going to be all right. Everything's going to be all right."

Claire looked out over the lake. A gust of wind ruffled the surface, the fluted ripples of water shivering in the breeze.

> *Sei ruhig, bleibe ruhig, mein Kind;*
> *in dürren Blättern säuselt der Wind.*

Claire looked down at the ducks. This time the female had reached the bread first, and the male had to watch as she ate it. He circled her anxiously, flicking his tail feathers impatiently. "Good for you," Claire whispered softly to the female, "good for you."

When they got home there was a message from Marshall Bassett on Claire's machine.

"I'm in a frivolous mood. Come join me for lunch at 21. Be there by one if you get this."

Claire looked at the clock; it was twelve-fifteen.

"Do you want to go?" she asked Meredith.

"*Do* I?" said Meredith, "Of *course* I do! They know about 21 even in Connecticut!"

They changed quickly—the best thing Meredith had to wear was a brown corduroy jumper—grabbed a cab, and were there by 12:55. Marshall was already seated at the bar.

"Well, well, you made it," he said, draining the last of his martini. "I wasn't even sure if you were in town when I called."

They were seated at a corner table, and the staff treated Marshall in a way that indicated he was a regular.

"Wow, this is *cool*," said Meredith, looking around.

"Yes, just try not to gape too hideously much, or I'll lose the respect of the staff," Marshall remarked dryly.

Meredith laughed. "I'll try not to act like a tourist from Connecticut." Claire was glad to see her enjoying herself.

"Order whatever you want," Marshall said breezily. "I'm going to write this off as a business lunch. I came into town to keep an appointment with a dealer but he forgot about the meeting, so I'm entitled to enjoy myself."

"I didn't know dentists had business lunches," said Meredith.

"I'm an oral surgeon, not a dentist," Marshall said a little huffily. "The difference is three more years medical school and about fifty thousand dollars in student loans." He lit a cigarette and inhaled deeply. "Anyway, today I missed seeing a Union canteen and ammunition box circa 1861, and so I shall drown my sorrows in béchamel sauce."

Claire ordered the turbot, Marshall ordered oysters, and Meredith had a steak sandwich.

"You know, I thought of asking Cousin Sarah to join us, but there's nothing like a meal with Sarah to spoil your appetite," Marshall said as he speared an oyster from his plate.

"What *is* it with you and Sarah?" said Meredith.

Marshall laughed and removed the olive from his martini. His laugh was a thin needle of air, flat and dry as a gust of winter wind.

"This new bartender they have doesn't understand that olives belong in salads, not martinis," he muttered, looking around the restaurant. "Have you ever heard Sarah mention anything about a—boyfriend?" he said, addressing his remark to Claire.

"Um . . . no, I guess not," she said.

"Right. Neither have I. In fact, neither has anyone." He paused to let the import of his comment sink in. Marshall had a sense of dramatic timing all his own.

"What are you saying?" said Meredith.

"Good Lord, surely it doesn't take a rocket scientist to figure it out!"

"Oh," said Claire. "Oh."

"Right," Marshall replied smugly.

"*Oh,*" said Meredith. "So *that's* it! That's the Big Secret!" She shrugged. "Big deal. I wonder why she's so sensitive about it."

"My dear," Marshall replied dryly, "you have to realize that not all the world holds the same open views as yourself about homosexuality, especially when it comes to a woman of Sarah's august social and professional standing. Can you imagine Arlene Lucien's reaction if they were to learn that their precious head of marketing thinks more about dykes than dyes, that she's a genuine *lesbo*? I imagine once they sensed the metaphorical pink triangle on her lapel, the very real pink slip would follow soon after." He lit a cigarette, blowing the smoke straight up into the air.

Claire was still stunned. "I can't believe I never—I mean, I never really thought about it. I always saw Sarah as so—"

"So remote, beyond the lure of base sensuality?" Marshall offered, smiling. "Oh, you'd be surprised. Of course, that was what she *wanted* people to think, but her official image as Southern Ice Princess hides a dark and deeply erotic nature." His tone was sarcastic and flippant, and he settled back in his chair, cigarette held gracefully aloft, legs crossed, a sardonic smile on his face, like a character out of a Noël Coward play. Claire always believed that Marshall's cynicism was partly a function of his life as a homosexual, and that his analysis of Sarah's mask came easily because his own was so firmly in place. *Well, I suppose we all wear a mask of some kind,* she thought.

"So Sarah likes girls?" said Meredith, trying to impress Marshall with her bluntness, Claire supposed.

Marshall laughed.

"Well, hardly," he said. "I mean, she's not a pedophile or anything like that . . . though I do sometimes wonder at her taste in women."

"Well, that could explain her undercover behavior," Meredith said thoughtfully.

"What?" asked Marshall.

"Meredith thinks there's something furtive about Sarah. She told me so after she first met her," said Claire.

"Oh," said Marshall. "Yes, I suppose being 'in the closet' is a little like being undercover . . ."

"How come you know about it but no one else does?" said Meredith.

"Well, darling, it takes one to know one, doesn't it? Actually"—he snuffed out his cigarette on his salad plate— "to be perfectly honest, I didn't really know for sure until about a year ago. I mean, I had my suspicions, of course, but then I ducked into Henrietta Hudson for a lark one night and saw her. It's an upscale lesbian hangout in the Village," he added in response to Meredith's blank look. "She tried to explain it away," he continued, "but—well, it was quite clear, and the young thugette she was courting wouldn't go away just because her dear cousin Marshall had arrived."

Marshall shuddered. "I always thought Sarah would go for the pearls-and-round-collar types, but I was dead wrong: she likes the East Village punks—you know, the ones who have mistaken their bodies for pin cushions. This particular one had a skull-and-crossbones leitmotif going on—very Wagnerian, blond braids and all." He shrugged. "Well, you know what they say about accounting for taste and all that. Still, it was a bit of a shock to imagine Sarah and that refugee from *Treasure Island*."

"What type do *you* go for?" said Meredith.

Marshall displayed his sunniest smile.

"Pretty ones," he said. "Plump and pretty. None of this iron-man thing—I like them soft and sweet. But enough about me," he said, seeing the alarm in Claire's eyes.

"So is that why Sarah's mad at you?" Meredith asked.

"Well, I wouldn't say she's *mad* at me," Marshall answered cheerfully. "Just frightened of me. She's terrified I'll spill the beans, and that puts her in a bad mood around me." He sighed. "I suppose I *have* spilled the beans—but you won't tell anyone, will you?"

"No," said Meredith, "why should I?"

"I don't know. No reason, but now if it gets out, it'll be my fault. I shouldn't have said anything, but I suppose I was getting tired of the responsibility . . . it's a lot to carry around, you know."

"I can't believe no one else at Arlene Lucien is gay," Claire remarked.

"Well, if they are, they ain't talkin', honey," Marshall told her. "Either that or no one's listening, and it amounts to the same thing. Of course, Sarah is certain that if she even hinted at it, she would be the center of a firestorm of controversy, and she's probably right. Corporate image and everything, you know . . . How's the investigation going, by the way?" he said to Meredith.

"Well, we haven't had that much luck so far."

"I'm sorry." Marshall sounded sincere for once. "It's really been hard on Sarah, you know. Her sister *and* her best friend . . ." He stared out the window, shaking his head. Claire suddenly realized that Marshall's cynical persona had prevented her from really looking at him, but now as she studied him she saw what a good-looking man he was, his leonine face handsome and dignified in repose, the heavy eyelids lending him an air of gravity.

"Well, I'll see you later," he said after he signed the check.

"Thanks for lunch," said Meredith.

"My pleasure. Do me a favor, though—don't take this detective thing too seriously, okay? Two people have already died."

"I know." Meredith nodded.

Marshall looked at her with a curious expression on his face.

"Don't be the third," he said, and then, nodding to Claire, turned and left the restaurant.

"Hmm," said Meredith, looking after him, "I wonder why he felt he had to warn me."

Claire was wondering the same thing.

Chapter 21

Later that afternoon Claire was sitting on her bed reading over the manuscript of Blanche's Klan book while Meredith sat on the bedroom rug brushing Ralph. Meredith held him firmly pinned to the floor with one hand, hairbrush in the other; the cat miserably tolerated her grasp, waiting for the moment to escape. Claire looked down at them, and Ralph's eyes pleaded with her for release.

"Are you sure that cats need to be brushed?" Claire said.

"Oh, yes. It's good for them; it stimulates their hair follicles." Meredith applied more energy to the task as if to prove her point.

"Well, do his hair follicles really need stimulating?" Claire asked. "I mean, he sheds plenty as it is."

"Well, this will help with the shedding, because the excess hairs will end up on the brush instead of your rug." Meredith held up the brush, which was full of white cat hairs. At that moment Ralph saw his opening and took it, squirming out from under her grasp and bounding toward the kitchen.

"Damn!" Meredith got up to follow.

"Oh, let him go. He's had enough for tonight . . . and don't swear."

"Do you really think bad language warps a young mind?"
Meredith asked. "I mean, what difference could it possibly
make, given all the trash that's available on TV all the time?"

"I don't know," Claire responded wearily, "but I'm sure
your parents don't want you to swear, and so I—"

"My 'parents,' as you call them, don't care much *what* I
do, so long as it doesn't interfere with their plans," Meredith replied icily.

"Oh, come on, Meredith, your father loves you; you
know he does."

Just then the phone rang, and Claire picked it up. As if on
cue, Ted Lawrence's cultivated voice said, "Hello, Ms.
Rawlings, it's Ted Lawrence. I just thought I'd call."

"Hello," said Claire, and almost added *we were just talking about you,* but decided against it.

"How are you getting along?" he said, an edge of apprehension in his voice. He sounded as though he had been
drinking. There was a softness around the edge of his consonants.

"Oh, fine," she said. "Do you want to talk to Meredith?"

"Yes, thank you, if she's there."

Where else would she be? Claire thought, and handed the
phone to Meredith.

"It's your father."

Meredith sighed and took the phone.

"Hi . . . oh, I'm fine; how are you?" Meredith pulled the
phone across the bed and lay on her back on the floor. "Oh,
nothing much," she said, "just trying to solve a murder.
Well, actually, there have been two now, though not everyone knows it. I mean, some of the police don't know how to
put two and two together . . ."

There was a pause, and Meredith looked up at Claire.

"The Wicked Witch is saying something to him. She always does that. She waits till he gets on the phone, and then
she yells at him from the other room." Meredith put her feet
up in the air and swung them back and forth. "That's okay,
I'm still here," she said into the receiver. "What was she saying to you?" There was another pause. "She's talking again,"
Meredith told Claire.

Claire felt that the phone conversation was none of her business, so she left the bedroom and went into the living room. She was uncomfortable with Meredith's attempt to pull her into a conspiracy against Jean Lawrence. She didn't like the woman, who, it was clear, wasn't the world's best stepmother, but she didn't want to join a cabal against her. She intended to remain as neutral as possible, at least in front of Meredith. She had left her manuscript in the bedroom, and rather than go back in and get it, she turned on the little television in the living room.

Claire felt a little decadent owning two televisions. She'd had the little television for years, and then when it broke she found the big one on sale and bought it, intending to throw out the little one, but she hated throwing things out, so she went ahead and had it fixed anyway.

When she turned on the set the screen flickered into life. She changed the channel to NBC, where *Dateline* had yet another set of spin doctors talking about the ongoing O. J. Simpson drama. The lawyers were going on and on about how racially divided the country was. The Goldmans had just made another statement regarding their upcoming civil suit, and the news media were already licking their chops over the coverage of yet another Simpson trial.

Meredith walked into the room, the instrument of Ralph's torture still in her hand.

"Ugh," she said, throwing herself dramatically on the couch.

"What's wrong?"

"Oh, she's just so—so *icky,* you know?"

"What did she do?"

"Oh, she didn't *do* anything; she never *does* anything—except take drugs—it's just her attitude."

"About what?"

"Oh, *every*thing. She's got this idea now that I shouldn't be investigating the murders, and she's got my father all worried about it."

"Worried about what?"

"Oh, she's telling him that something will happen to me. *I* don't know . . ." Meredith rolled over on her back, her legs in the air, clutching a pillow to her chest. Just then Ralph entered the room tentatively; seeing Meredith, he backed out again.

"They want me to come back up for *Thanksgiving*. My cousins will all be there."

"Well, maybe you should go."

Meredith flopped over onto her stomach.

"I *hate* my cousins."

"Look, Meredith," Claire said, "you can't just turn your back on your family."

"I don't see why not. They're all stupid and boring."

Claire walked over to the couch and sat down next to the girl.

"Sometimes you have to try to get along with people even if you think they're stupid and boring."

"All *right*," said Meredith. "I'll go, if you insist."

"I don't insist; it's just that I'm sure they would like to have you there."

"All *right*, I get the picture. I'll go, okay? Are you satisfied now?"

Claire tried to think of something else to say, but Meredith buried her face in the pillow. Claire decided to leave her alone for a while, and went back into the bedroom. She knew that Meredith's anger wasn't really directed toward her.

Claire picked up Blanche's manuscript. She had been avoiding diving into the project of rewriting it, held back by a strange reluctance, but she was doing her best to fight it. She opened the manuscript to the chapter she had been reading. It was entitled "The Greensboro Massacre" and was about the killing of five people by Klansmen during a march in Greensboro in 1979. Claire had already left North Carolina when it happened, but she remembered reading about it. The incident had been a nasty example of police complicity: an armed convoy of Klansmen had fired, almost casually, into a group of civil rights marchers who were holding an anti-Klan rally in a residential neighborhood, fatally wounding five marchers, as the police looked on. Later, it became clear that one of the gunmen had somehow been able to elude arrest, in spite of the presence of many witnesses. As Claire read Blanche's account her admiration for the woman grew; behind the silly pink-and-powdered Southern-belle facade had lurked a social conscience after all.

On one of the pages, Claire noticed a number scribbled in the margin in pencil. It was faint and faded, but it looked like a phone number. She recognized the 919 area code: North Carolina. She reached for the bedside phone and then hesitated. There was no name next to the number; how would she know whom to ask for?

She picked up the manuscript and looked at the number again. Then she lifted the receiver and dialed. It rang twice, then a machine answered. A man's voice with a Southern accent said, "Hi. You have reached Jeff's photographic studio. I'm in the darkroom right now with a hot little number, so leave *your* number and I'll call you when I can." Claire listened until she heard the beep, but then hung up abruptly. She didn't even know who this person was, or why his phone number would be written in Blanche's book.

"Whatcha doing?" asked Meredith, appearing in the doorway. She was apparently over her snit.

"Oh, just working on the manuscript," Claire replied.

"Who were you calling?"

"I'm not really sure."

"What do you mean?"

"Well, look." She showed the number to Meredith.

Meredith took the manuscript and looked at the number.

"Did anyone answer?"

"I got a machine. It's a photography studio of some kind."

"Did you leave a message?"

"No. I don't even know why Blanche has this number."

"Hmm . . . I wonder." Meredith sat on the edge of the bed. She looked at the number again, then picked up the phone and handed it to Claire. "Call and leave your number, only say you're Blanche DuBois."

"Why?"

"I just have a feeling about this."

Claire didn't know where Meredith was headed but she picked up the phone and dialed the number. To her surprise, a man answered this time.

"Jeff's Photos." The voice was the same as the one on the machine—high and reedy, with a cultivated Southern accent.

"Uh, hello," Claire said.

"What can I do for you?" the man asked, all business.

"Well, I—I want to check on some photos," Claire answered, feeling her way. Meredith stood beside her, watching tensely, coaching her with gestures.

"Okay, what's your last name?" said the man.

"Uh, DuBois—Blanche DuBois."

Meredith nodded energetically.

"Just a minute," he said, and Claire heard the sound of paper rustling.

"What's he doing?" Meredith whispered.

"He's looking it up."

The man returned to the phone.

"Yes, Ms. DuBois. I didn't send them because I never received your check. It says here that you were supposed to send a check"— the man consulted his records—"over a month ago, but it never arrived. Do you still want the pictures?"

"Uh, yes—yes, I do," said Claire.

"All right, I've still got them."

"How much is it?"

"Well, that'll be eight dollars for the large blowup and then a couple dollars for any smaller prints."

"Do you take credit cards?" said Claire.

"No, ma'am, I don't. A personal check will be fine, though. Just make it out to me, Jeff Dumont, and I'll send the photos right off to you."

"I'm kind of in a hurry to get them."

"Well, you can use overnight mail, and if you want to reimburse me for it, I'll do the same from my end," Jeff Dumont offered.

In the end they agreed to use Federal Express. Claire wanted to ask the man about the subjects of the photographs, but was afraid of arousing his suspicion, so she said nothing.

After she hung up, Meredith said, "We've got to tell Detective Jackson about this right away."

"Right now?"

"Yeah."

"But—we don't know that they have anything to do with Blanche's murder."

"True," Meredith replied, sitting on the bed, "but I have a feeling about this. I think we should call Detective Jackson."

"All right," Claire agreed, her stomach in knots.

When the detective answered the phone he sounded sleepy.

"Jackson here."

Claire looked at the clock on the VCR; it was only ten-thirty.

"Am I calling too late?" she said.

"Uh, no—that's all right; I guess I just drifted off . . . Is this Claire Rawlings?" he said.

Claire was pleased that he recognized her voice.

"Yes," she said. "I just came across something that I thought might be of some interest."

When she had told him the whole story, he said, "Well, I think you did the right thing."

"Do you think it might be anything important?"

"It's impossible to tell until we see the photos. It could be something; you never know. Call me when you get them."

"All right."

"Thanks for calling."

"You're welcome," she said. There was a pause, and then she said, "Goodbye."

"Good night."

"Well?" Meredith demanded after she had hung up. "What did he think?"

"He said to call him when the photos arrive."

"Right." Meredith turned and swooped down on Ralph, who had just entered the bedroom. She was too slow, though; he escaped through her legs to the sanctuary of the clothes closet, hiding himself behind the winter coats and cross-country skis.

"Damn," Meredith muttered, "I almost had him that time."

Chapter **22**

"By the way," Meredith announced over breakfast Monday morning, "I did a little research on Anthony's abrupt departure from Hoffman LaRoche."

Claire took a bite of buttered onion bagel.

"Oh? What did you find out?"

"I'm pretty sure that he was let go because they suspected him of stealing drugs."

"*What?* How did you find that out?"

"I have my methods. Actually, I'm afraid if I tell you you'll disapprove."

"Maybe I will, but I still want to know."

Meredith shrugged.

"Well, you remember on Friday when I told you I was going to spend the day at the museum?"

"Yes."

"I didn't. I took a bus to Nutley, New Jersey."

"Meredith!"

"I *knew* you'd disapprove—"

"But you should have told me!"

"Would you have let me go?"

"Probably not."

"All right, I've proved my point!" Meredith fiddled with

her shoelace, sulking. "Well," she said finally, "do you want to know or not?"

Claire felt that she should take a superior attitude and pretend not to be interested, but she was too curious.

"All right, tell me. How did you find out?"

"Well, everyone has a barber, right?"

"Yeah, I guess so."

"Nutley's not a very big town, and there's a little barbershop close by Hoffman LaRoche, so it was a good bet Anthony went there, and a lot of his colleagues as well."

"So how did you—"

"I'm coming to that. Actually, to be honest, the idea of the barbershop only occurred to me when I got off the bus. I just came to poke around a little, and then I saw it—and I had an impulse to go in. One of the guys getting his hair cut worked at Roche, and—well, you know what gossip is like. I said I was waiting to meet my father there, and that he worked at Roche—"

"Didn't the man ask who your father was?"

"Oh, sure, but I said he had just started. In fact, I said he had been hired to replace someone who had just been fired. I didn't even mention Anthony's name, and the man just said, 'Oh, yeah—you mean Anthony Sciorra.' I hardly had to ask him anything; he volunteered most of the information, about how Anthony had been suspected of stealing drugs and everything. You know how much people love scandal. Then I thanked him, pretended to call my father, said the plan had changed and that he wanted me to come meet him at Roche. I left the shop, got back on the bus, and came home."

Claire shook her head. "Poor Anthony," she said.

"Well, maybe poor Anthony, and maybe not," said Meredith.

"Did you find out exactly what kind of drugs?"

Meredith shook her head. "No, only that when he was confronted with it, Anthony didn't deny the charges. Apparently Roche had decided not to prosecute him, probably because it would be bad publicity."

"Do you think we should tell Detective Jackson all this?"

Meredith smiled and took a bite of a bagel.

"I already have," she said.

The next morning as she was getting ready for work, the phone rang, and Claire answered it.

"Hello?"

"Hello, darling." It was Robert.

"Oh, hi. How are you?"

"Fine, thanks. Listen, how would you like to come up for Thanksgiving weekend? I know it's short notice, but—"

"Oh, that sounds nice, actually. Meredith is going back to Connecticut for Thanksgiving anyway, so I'd be all alone. Yeah, that sounds great. Mind if I bring some work?"

"Do I ever? Bring anything you like."

"Oh, listen, do you mind if I have a package sent to your house while I'm there?"

"No, why should I mind?"

"Oh, no reason; just thought I'd ask. I'm having some research photos sent from North Carolina by Express Mail."

"Sounds exciting. What are they?"

"I don't know yet; it's something Blanche was working on when she—"

Robert cut her off tactfully, sparing her the awful word.

"Listen, don't you worry about it. Have them ship whatever you like. I've got to run. I'll see you Thursday."

Claire looked at her watch.

"Oh, God, I've got to go. I'm late for work."

"Have a nice day," Meredith called after her from the kitchen as the door closed behind her.

When Claire returned from work that night the apartment was empty. She threw her stack of mail on the couch and went into the kitchen. There was a note from Meredith on the counter. *Gone out for supplies—back soon—M.* Claire smiled; "supplies" probably meant Pepperidge Farm cookies. She made herself a cup of tea, then settled on the couch to read her mail. There were a couple of catalogs and a postcard of Key West from one of her authors. Pink flamingos stood in a shallow pond, and inset over them was a florid blue script that read *Exotic Key West.* Claire read the postcard and then picked up the last piece of mail, a plain white envelope with her name and address printed on it in block lettering. There was no return address. The aroma of oranges floated up from the envelope.

When Meredith returned to the apartment she found Claire sitting on the couch.

"Hi," Meredith called, putting down the bag of groceries she was carrying.

Without answering, Claire held out her hand, which had five small white seeds in it.

"Oh, my God," said Meredith. "Did these arrive in the mail?"

Claire showed her the envelope, her name written on it in black ink, with its fragrance of oranges.

"We've got to call Detective Jackson immediately," Meredith said.

Claire nodded, fighting panic, reminding herself to breathe.

Jackson had left the precinct for the day, so they called him at home. When they told him about the seeds, he said he would come right over.

Half an hour later Wallace Jackson sat on the couch in Claire's living room studying the five small white seeds he held in his hand.

"No note or anything with it?"

"No—nothing," Claire replied. A couple of glasses of red wine had calmed her panic, and she looked at the situation as if from a distance: curious, interested, but with a sense that this couldn't be happening to her.

"So what do you think?" said Meredith. "Are these from the murderer?"

"Well . . ." Jackson began, his voice serious, "it is possible that someone is playing a practical joke on you."

"Who would do that?" Claire interrupted him. "None of my friends thinks this is funny, and I can't imagine who would be sick enough . . ." Her voice trailed off.

"Someone doesn't want her to finish Blanche's book," Meredith said, "and this is their way of telling her. Don't forget that Blanche received the same threat."

"Who knows you're working on the book?" said Jackson.

Claire shrugged. "I don't know. It's no secret. And just about anybody could find out about it if they tried hard enough."

"I'll have to ask Peter Schwartz who he's told," Jackson thought aloud. "It was his idea, wasn't it?"

"Yes, it was."

"Hmm . . ."

"You don't suspect him, do you?" said Meredith.

"Oh, I can't really rule anyone out," Jackson answered, "but, no, I don't particularly suspect him." He put the seeds back in the envelope and stood up and stretched. As he did, Claire noticed the long muscles of his back under his creased white shirt. He was always slightly rumpled, which went along with his absentminded air, as though he had more important things to think about than clothes. It was easy to see in him the high school teacher he had once been. "Unfortunately," he said, "these seeds, without a written note of some kind, don't really constitute a legal threat."

"But you must realize—" Claire began.

"Oh, I realize it, all right." Jackson cut her off, an edge of anger in his voice. "The problem is, no judge would recognize it as a legal threat. That means our hands are officially tied in terms of protecting you. However . . . there are means, and then there are means."

"Oh, by the way, I wanted to ask you," Meredith interjected, "what was it about Willard Hughes's mysteries that gave you ideas?"

"Oh, it's an old idea, really," Jackson said, "but I wanted to put a little fear of God into him."

"Why?"

Jackson cocked his head to one side, considering the question. "I'm not sure . . . I guess it's because I don't like him."

"Claire doesn't either," said Meredith.

"Meredith!" Claire tried to sound irritated.

"Well, you *don't.*"

"But you still haven't told me what idea you got from his book," said Meredith.

"It's simple, really. It's the notion that the murderer always returns to the scene of the crime."

"But why would they do that?"

Jackson leaned back on the couch.

"Oh, different reasons. To check on their handiwork, to gloat, to taunt the police . . . or maybe all of the above."

"Do you think that it's true, here, that the killer will return to the scene of the crime?"

Jackson looked out the window into the night outside.

"I intend to find out," he said.

Chapter 23

"Would you rather be boiled in oil or buried alive?"
Meredith looked up at Claire, awaiting an answer. She sat cross-legged on the couch in her office. Claire was seated at her desk, trying to read a manuscript.

"Well?" Meredith said impatiently when Claire did not respond.

"Uh . . . oil, I guess."

"Why?"

Claire thought for a moment.

"Because it would be faster?" she said hopefully.

Meredith looked disappointed.

"Maybe, but much more painful, don't you think?"

Claire looked at Meredith, her face so serious and expectant. She had been on a kick lately, and Claire wondered how long it would last. The topic was always death: ways to die, unusual means of death—the more bizarre the better. All morning Meredith had been offering Claire a choice between violent forms of death. No matter which form Claire chose, Meredith always seemed vaguely disappointed, as if Claire had failed her in some way.

A few minutes later Meredith said, "Would you rather starve to death or freeze to death?"

Claire put down the manuscript.

"Look, Meredith, I really need to get some work done. We agreed that you would come into the office today only if you could amuse yourself." She waited, but there was no response. Meredith was looking down at the floor, one leg swinging back and forth from the couch. "Isn't that right?" Claire said, hearing her mother's tone of voice in her own. *Isn't that right, Claire? We agreed, isn't that right?* The roles were reversed, but now Claire had to stick to her part, just as Meredith was bound to play hers.

"But I *am* amusing myself," Meredith said in her whiny voice. When she wanted to, Meredith could sound like any thirteen-year-old.

"You and I both know that 'amusing yourself' does not mean interrupting me every five minutes to ask me how I would prefer to die."

"I'm sorry," Meredith said in a small voice, and then she burst out laughing. "Would you rather be nagged to death," she said through her giggles, "or—"

Claire had to laugh, too. Meredith sat on the couch, her body shaking; Claire leaned back in her chair, and they both laughed.

"Would you rather die laughing . . ." said Claire, "Or—"

Just then Claire heard a commotion out in the hall, and she got up and opened her door. Detective Jackson and Sergeant Barker stood in the hall, and with them was Peter Schwartz.

"What are you talking about?" Peter was saying loudly.

"If you cannot afford an attorney, one will be provided for you. Do you understand?" Detective Jackson was saying.

"What the bloody hell is going on here?" Peter yelled as a small crowd of Ardor House employees gathered to watch.

"Please don't make me use the cuffs," Jackson said softly, with a glance at Sergeant Barker, who cheerfully held up a pair of handcuffs.

"Use your bloody head!" Peter shouted. *"Why would I kill my best-selling author?"*

Jackson nodded to Barker, who slipped the handcuffs on Peter with a practiced gesture.

"Please, Mr. Schwartz," said Jackson, his eyes tormented, "we'll explain at the station."

If he saw Claire and Meredith standing there, Jackson offered no acknowledgment of it, but as they went by, Sergeant Barker looked at Claire and said, "Sorry, really—this wasn't our idea. Just following orders—the higher-ups, you know." He rolled his eyes in a gesture meant to indicate sympathy but that looked like something out of a comic opera.

Jackson and Barker managed to escort Peter out of the office. He put up no physical resistance, but continued to complain loudly all the way to the elevator. When they were gone there was a stunned silence in the office. Several people looked at Claire and Meredith. Claire's secretary, Kathy Cochoran, went over to them.

"What's going on?" she said quietly. "Why did they arrest Peter?"

"I really don't know," said Claire firmly, "but I intend to find out."

"Wow," said Meredith. "Now you sound like me."

Forty minutes later Claire and Meredith were seated in the Ninth Precinct station house awaiting Detective Jackson's return. The blond woman didn't even ask who they wanted to see. She looked up from her falafel on pita bread and said, "He's out right now."

"We'll wait," said Claire. The blond woman shrugged, flicked a spec of parsley from her lip, and pointed to the dingy yellow plastic chairs lining the wall.

Meredith fidgeted for a while in her chair, then got up and walked around the station, looking up at the plaques on the wall. Claire glanced around the station. The desk sergeant was a youngish, ruddy-faced man with closely cropped brown hair. Cops came and went, alone and in groups, and a few of them glanced at Claire and Meredith. Claire had the impression it was a quiet day; several of the policemen stood and gossiped with the desk sergeant, some of them laughing and looking surreptitiously at Claire as they did. She didn't think they were necessarily talking about her, but she was an outsider to their club, and to be watched with some suspicion.

When they had waited twenty minutes, Detective Jackson came in, followed by Sergeant Barker. When he saw Claire, Jackson stopped and gave her a look that was hard to read. It could have been an apology or an accusation; she wasn't sure which. Sergeant Barker started to approach her, but Jackson held him back.

"Why don't you come into my office; we can talk there," he said quietly, then turned and headed for his cubicle without looking to see if Claire was following. Claire got up and motioned to Meredith, and the two of them followed Jackson. Barker circled them like an eager retriever, obviously wanting say something, but constrained by Jackson.

"We were instructed to arrest Mr. Schwartz after receiving an anonymous tip regarding his involvement in Ms. DuBois's death," Jackson said wearily in what sounded like a rehearsed statement. Claire realized that he would probably say something very similar to the press when they got wind of the arrest.

"Subsequent to receiving the information, we obtained a search warrant and found incriminating evidence in Mr. Schwartz's office, at which point we arrested him," he said as though he were reciting a memorized text. Claire thought the formal speech was an attempt to keep his distance from her.

"What kind of evidence?" Meredith said. "What did you find?"

"A syringe with traces of cyanide in it," said Sergeant Barker before Jackson could stop him.

"Oh, that's ridiculous!" Meredith snorted. "He's obviously being framed."

"Whether or not he is guilty, we've been ordered by the DA's office to arrest him, and we have done so. I really shouldn't be discussing this case with you at all," he added with a sigh.

There was a pause, and then Claire said, "Do *you* think Peter is guilty?"

"What I think doesn't enter into it at this point," Jackson said, picking up a paper clip from his desk and bending it back and forth. "When the DA's office says to collar someone, we do it."

"It's political, you know," Barker added, an air of confidentiality in his tone.

"Wow, so you had no choice?" Meredith chirped.

"Not if I want to keep my job," Jackson replied.

"So what *do* you think?" said Meredith.

"Well, I can't really discuss the case in detail, but if you want my opinion—"

"Yes, I do," Meredith answered.

"No, I don't think Peter Schwartz is guilty. Even if he is, I can't believe he'd leave that syringe in his office. It's so clumsy a device that I can't believe someone would actually think we'd fall for it—but they *would* use it to keep us occupied for a while, and they've succeeded in doing that."

"So is he going to go on trial?"

"That will be up to a grand jury," said Jackson, "unless of course the DA decides to let him go before it gets to that."

"Why would the DA let him go?"

"Oh, lots of reasons—an alibi would be one reason, although this is a tricky case for an alibi, since the apples were delivered and could have presumably been treated at any time prior to the delivery, then delivered by someone who was totally innocent."

"I don't think so," said Meredith.

"Why not?"

"Because this murderer is obsessive and controlling, and wouldn't leave something like that in someone else's hands. Someone who came up with such a bizarre form of death would want to see it through to the end, even if it meant there was more risk involved."

"How do you know the murderer is obsessive and controlling?" said Sergeant Barker.

"Well, for one thing Blanche's murder was no spontaneous crime of passion. Poisoning is a premeditated act. This one was meticulously planned, and had a twisted sort of humor to it. I mean, really, a poison *apple* of all things, which indicates an obsessive personality—a bit of a perfectionist, you might say."

"Well, maybe you're right," said Jackson, "but I don't see how that helps Mr. Schwartz."

"It doesn't," said Meredith. "It just might help you."

"Oh, well, thank you," Jackson said, a little sardonically.

Peter didn't spend even one night in jail; the judge at his arraignment determined that there was not much probability of flight, and he was released on a minuscule bail. The judge evidently disagreed with the DA's office concerning the likelihood of Peter's guilt.

"Maybe there is such a thing as bad publicity," Peter commented grimly the next day, tossing the Metro Section of the *Times* onto Claire's desk. Claire looked at the headline: BOOK EDITOR ARRESTED IN MYSTERIOUS AUTHOR'S DEATH. Underneath, a headline in smaller print read, MOTIVE STILL UNCLEAR.

"Are you all right?" Claire said.

"Oh, sure; I'm fine, I've been led in handcuffs in front of all my colleagues, spent a charming afternoon at Rikers—and now I'll have to get an unlisted phone number. The press are already hounding me. I'm fine—I'm just great."

Meredith walked into Claire's office carrying two paper cups of tea and a blueberry muffin. She was taking an afternoon train to Connecticut and had come into work with Claire with her bag packed. She loved to buy tea from the office vendor.

"It's all just so *stupid*," she said, handing one cup to Claire.

"That's easy for *you* to say," Peter grumbled.

"Well, anyone can see that." Meredith carefully peeled the paper from her muffin. "They're just grasping at straws. I'll tell you one thing, though: it means the murderer is still among us, and close enough by to break into your office." She discarded the paper and broke the muffin in two, setting one half on a napkin on Claire's desk.

Peter laughed bitterly. "*That's* a comforting thought."

Meredith took a bite of muffin. "But I don't think for a minute that he—or she—thought the police would take the syringe seriously. They were just having a little fun at your expense."

"What did *I* ever do . . ."

"That's not the point. The point is that it tells us something about the psychology of the murderer: that he or she is playful—in a bizarre way, of course—and that to some extent sees this as a game."

"Well, if you think that is helpful information, I'm glad," said Peter, "but I don't see how—"

"Oh, anything is potentially helpful information," said Meredith. "It's a question of how well you use it."

"Well, that's enough sleuthing for this morning," said Claire. "We have to get you on a train."

Meredith rolled her eyes and sank back into the couch. "Oh, God, back to the Land of the Living Dead."

"Oh, come on, Connecticut's not that bad," said Peter. "After all, I've just spent some time in Rikers."

"Then you were lucky," said Meredith.

"Hardy-har-har," said Peter. "Well, if you'll excuse me, I've got to phone my lawyer." He wandered off in the direction of his office.

"Come on," said Claire, picking up Meredith's suitcase. "It's time to go."

Meredith popped the last bite of muffin into her mouth and followed Claire silently, communicating her reluctance to leave through her dragging feet and slumped shoulders.

Since Amelia's death Claire had been spending more and more time with Sarah. Claire had a sense—which she thought Sarah shared—that the two of them shared a bond as "survivors" of Blanche and Amelia's tragic deaths. Before the events of the preceding weeks, Claire would never have thought of Sarah as a close friend, but that had changed, and she now felt herself increasingly drawn to her, and to the large, airy living room on Bethune Street, where the two of them would sit having tea or sherry in the evening as the cars slid slowly by on the street outside. Claire found Sarah's presence comforting, and was pretty sure that Sarah felt the same about her.

That evening Claire went to Sarah's after work. With Meredith back in Connecticut, Claire didn't want to go straight home to an empty apartment. Claire was sitting on the couch and Sarah was in the kitchen opening a bottle of Merlot when the doorbell rang.

Claire poked her head into the kitchen. "Do you want me to get it?"

"Hmm . . . I'm not expecting anyone," Sarah replied. "I'll get it."

Sarah went out into the hallway, and Claire heard Anthony's voice in the corridor—except that it wasn't any voice she had ever heard Anthony use. She couldn't make out all of the words, but she did hear him say, "Oh, Sarah," and then the rest dissolved into a kind of muffled weeping, as though he were crying into her shoulder. Claire could only imagine how uncomfortable Sarah would be with that, and she was about to rescue her when Sarah entered the room, followed by Anthony.

Anthony was so much thinner that it was shocking. He looked like the victim of a wasting disease like cancer or AIDS or something, and Claire couldn't help staring at him. His handsome face was gaunt, and his dark eyes looked sunken and feverish. Seeing her reaction to him, he shook his head sadly.

"I know, I do not look well. Don't worry, it is only my heart which is wounded." There was still a trace of Palermo in his voice, a rise on certain consonants that suggested the sloping hillsides and baking sun of Italy. He sat heavily on Sarah's settee.

"I am sorry to bother you like this," he said. "I have been wandering around the city and I saw your building . . . well, maybe my feet led me here on purpose; who knows? I don't know anything anymore . . ." He sighed deeply and stared at the carpet, as though all of his energy had been expended in those few words. Claire thought she had never seen anyone look so . . . empty. She looked at Sarah to see how she was reacting to this.

Sarah stood in the center of her living room, eyes averted, her face serious. Claire couldn't read her expression, and didn't know if she was feeling sympathy or irritation with Anthony. Sarah always hated the way Blanche led him on, reeling him in and then letting him back out, but Claire didn't think she blamed Anthony for this. She didn't think Sarah blamed Anthony for Amelia's unrequited attachment to him either—but you could never tell with Sarah. Sometimes Claire thought that Sarah viewed other people as figures on a chessboard, to be manipulated as she saw fit. She wasn't exactly insensitive; she just had a strong idea of the way things should be and was impatient with those who couldn't see the logic of her way. Amelia and Anthony together would have been perfectly logical, whereas the idea of Blanche and Anthony was laughable; hence Sarah's utter impatience at everyone's refusal to get it right.

"Well, you're here now, so how about a drink?" Sarah said finally.

Anthony looked up at her with the eyes of a grateful dog who has just escaped a beating.

"Oh, bless you, *mia serra,*" he said. He smiled at Claire. "In Palermo they say that wine, not fire, was the gift Prometheus brought to mankind before they chained him to the rock." He looked away and his face went slack again. "Well, we are all chained to a rock of some kind or other, I think . . . what is your rock, do you think?" he said to Claire.

Caught off guard, Claire felt herself blush. "I don't know . . . I haven't really thought about it."

Anthony sighed. "Well, for me it is clear now, all too clear, and I have only myself to blame."

"What are you to blame for?" said Claire.

"Why, for Amelia's death, of course," Anthony said as though it were self-evident.

"How could you possibly be to blame for—" said Claire, but just then Sarah came in with the bottle of Merlot and three glasses.

"I thought maybe we could all use a drink," she said.

"Gracie, cara," said Anthony.

Sarah poured three glasses of wine. Claire watched it swirl into the glasses, a deep dark red. Sarah lifted her glass.

"To Amelia," she said.

"Che Dio ti accompagni," Anthony said softly.

The three glasses touched each other—a thin, hollow sound which was quickly absorbed by the silent, waiting air.

"Why do you think you're responsible for Amelia's death?" Claire asked.

Anthony looked at her tragically. "Is it not clear to everyone that she killed herself out of love for me?"

"Well, it isn't clear to *me*," Sarah answered rather brusquely.

"No, no; affanni del pensier," he replied sadly. "It is a private thing, such suffering."

"Look, Anthony, I know Amelia loved you," said Sarah, "but I don't think she killed herself because of that."

"Really?" Anthony said blankly. "Then why?"

"Because . . ." Sarah began, and looked at Claire.

"Because she may have been pushed," Claire replied.

"Pushed? Pushed?" Anthony asked, as if the meaning of the word escaped him. "But who would want to kill Amelia—poor, soft, innocent Amelia?"

"That's what I'd like to know," said Sarah, and for a moment Claire thought she sounded exactly like Meredith.

Chapter 24

On Wednesday Claire walked around the office in a kind of haze. Her mind was foggy and she felt as if she were just pretending to be present; it was as though she was doing an imitation of herself.

Around lunchtime Peter wandered into her office and sat down on the couch.

"Are you okay?"

"I'm all right," she replied, "just a little tired."

"Do you want to take the rest of the day off?"

"No, I'll be fine, really." Claire suddenly wondered whether Peter knew about the orange seeds.

"Well, let me know if you need anything," he said, and left.

After he had gone Claire realized how self-centered she had become. Peter had troubles of his own; he was facing a possible indictment by a grand jury, and yet he had time to express concern for her—but all she could think of was her own danger. She realized, too, how paranoid her thinking had become. She had a sense that no one around her could really be trusted, and that somewhere in her world there was someone who was willing to kill ... first Blanche, then Amelia, and now ... her. The phone rang, startling her.

Even the familiar sound of the telephone seemed sinister now, Claire thought as she answered it.

"Claire Rawlings."

"Hello, Claire." It was Ted Lawrence. He seemed uncomfortable using her first name. He was a man more at ease with formality, with prescribed behavior.

"Oh, hi. I just put Meredith on the train this morning."

"Yes, I know. I'm going to pick her up in a few minutes. That's not why I'm calling. I . . . I'm not sure how to ask you this, but . . . " He paused, and Claire could hear the slow intake of breath as he gathered his courage.

"What?"

"Well, have you—have either you or Meredith heard from my wife?"

"No. Why?"

"She's . . . she's sort of missing."

"Missing?"

"Yes, she never came home yesterday. She was in the city doing some shopping—"

"You mean Hartford?"

"No, New York. She didn't come home, and nobody seems to have heard from her since yesterday morning when she left here."

"Does she have any friends in the city?"

"She has a sister on the Upper East Side, but she's in Florida for the winter. I tried calling her sister's apartment, but no one is picking up, and the answering machine has been turned off. I don't know what to do."

He sounded so forlorn that Claire felt sorry for him. Emotion sat on him awkwardly, like a badly tailored suit of clothes.

"Well, if you hear from her let me know. Otherwise, I guess I'll call the police."

Claire could hear the reluctance in his voice. For a man like Ted Lawrence, involving the police in his private life would be a humiliation. He was the exact opposite of the people who crowd the talk shows day after day, eager to share the sordid details of their lives, like patients showing off ugly scars after an operation. To these people, sordid

events and pain are a badge of honor, whereas to Ted
Lawrence they were indignities to be borne patiently and
quietly. Claire promised that she would let him know if she
heard anything.

After they hung up, she remembered Meredith's wither-
ing portrayal of her stepmother as a cocaine junkie. Perhaps
Jean Lawrence had passed out somewhere—or worse.
Claire wondered if she should call Ted Lawrence back and
suggest this, but she was afraid to. She didn't think it was
her place, and she did not want to be the one to suggest to
him that his wife had a drug problem. Even if he knew in his
heart of hearts that this was true, Claire didn't think he'd
take kindly to having his face rubbed in it. She tried to imagine Meredith's response when her father told her the news.
Would she tell him what she had told Claire, and would
there be a terrible fight? Or would she be kind and sympathetic and try to help her father through this difficult time?

Claire looked out the window onto Sixth Avenue. People
scurried about the sidewalks, bent over against the November wind, intent on—what? What was so important that you
would sacrifice everything for it, even your life? Claire suddenly had a desire to leave everything, to step out of her life.
Beyond the frenetic energy of the city, up the shining Hudson River, peace awaited her . . . a quiet weekend with
Robert. She considered telling Peter about the threat she had
received, to ask him if she could drop finishing Blanche's
book, but then she remembered Wallace Jackson's words: it
was better not to mention the seeds to anyone. The subtext
of this, of course, was quite clear: you never could tell who
was just waiting for the right opportunity to kill you.

That afternoon she had an appointment with Marshall
Bassett to have an impacted wisdom tooth removed. She
didn't mind going out to New Jersey; Marshall was an excellent oral surgeon, and he sometimes gave her a special
rate. She also usually enjoyed the bus ride, although this
time she just sat and stared out the window, gazing at the
blond grasses of the Meadowlands, thinking how beautiful
the landscape must have been before it was turned into an
industrial wasteland. The smell of sulphur rose from tall

white smoke stacks, bluish clouds of chemicals billowing into the air. Claire leaned back in her seat and closed her eyes.

> *Dem Vater grauset's; er reitet gesch wind,*
> *er hält in den Armen das ächzende Kind*

Sitting in Marshall Bassett's tidy waiting room, Claire inhaled the familiar sour smell common to all dental offices. What was it, she wondered. Formaldehyde? Novocaine? Laughing gas? She looked at the inevitable *Highlights* magazine on the coffee table: *Gallant holds doors open for ladies.*

Goofus sends them death threats in the mail.

Marshall was, as usual, cheerful and impeccably professional. Once again Claire felt a comfort in his presence that she never fully understood. It was partly his self-assurance and partly his lightly ironic take on life, his utter lack of cloying earnestness. After showing her the X-ray of her tooth, he suggested intravenous Valium as an anesthetic.

"The tooth is pretty bad," he said. "The roots are really twisted. I'd go for the Valium if I were you."

Claire disliked drugs, even if they were professionally administered.

"Well . . ." she said.

"It's kind of like a twilight state," Marshall told her. "It's not at all unpleasant. Is it?" He turned to his dental assistant, who stood by ready with the injection.

"No, it's kind of fun," she said. The girl was young, barely out of college, with highlighted blond hair and perfectly applied lipstick. Her full young breasts swelled under the crisp white uniform.

"All right." Claire nodded.

"Believe me, you'll be glad you did." Marshall smiled as he bent over her with the syringe.

Claire felt the needle go into her arm and then almost immediately her head began to float. She heard voices and supposed they were in the room with her, but she couldn't be sure. She heard music, and knew that it was the classical station that Marshall always had on in his office, but the music sounded strange to her. A man was singing in German: *"Ich liebe dich, mich reizt deine schöner Gestalt"* . . . but she didn't know if the song was on the radio or in her head. She could see people moving over her and around her, but they had no faces . . . they were white, such a bright white, and yet everything was blurred, as though filtered through a sieve . . . her mind tripped and looped around itself, and then it gave up the idea of consciousness altogether, and everything went black.

When Claire woke up her jaw ached, and when her eyes were fully focused she saw Marshall standing over her, holding a tooth in his hand. The roots were twisted and deformed.

"Ugh," she said drowsily.

"The little monster put up a struggle, but we got him," Marshall announced. "How do you feel?"

"Woozy. May I use the bathroom?"

"Of course. It's all the way down the hall and to the right."

Claire walked down the hallway and opened the first door she came to on the right. She stood there for a moment before she realized it was not the bathroom. The room contained a workbench covered with fine tools for jewelry making. A pair of unfinished gold earrings lay on the bench.

"Wrong room. It's all the way down to the right," said Marshall's voice behind her.

Claire turned around, startled. "Oh, sorry," she said, and backed out of the room.

"No problem." Marshall closed the door behind her. "Happens all the time." His words were dismissive, but she thought he sounded irritated.

"I didn't know you made jewelry," she said when she emerged from the bathroom a few minutes later.

"It quiets my nerves," Marshall said. He held up a small bottle of pills. "Take two of these tonight and call me in the morning."

Chapter 25

Claire went straight to bed when she got home that evening and slept eleven hours. She awoke early on Thursday and decided to save money and take a bus instead of a cab to Grand Central. Her tooth throbbed dully, but after only one of the Tylenol with codeine Marshall had given her the throb settled down into a mere ache. She put out extra food for Ralph, packed her bag, and left the apartment. The Riverside Drive bus came almost immediately. Claire got on and sat near the back, her duffel bag in her lap, Blanche's manuscript clutched under her arm.

Sitting on the bus, watching the people with their placid, impassive faces, she wondered about the private thoughts and prejudices hidden underneath all those calm exteriors. She thought about the group of people she had seen on the news, brandishing their racism along with their Confederate flags. How could these people be so *wrong* and not know it, she wondered. The ideals they cherished were so evil, and yet they loved their children, watered their lawns, and greeted their neighbors—the white ones, at any rate. How did they treat the black ones? With icy silence? Disdain? Fire bombing? The Constitution gave them the right to wave the Confederate flag, but it was still wrong—wrong, wrong,

wrong. She thought about how the black women in her gym had leaped and shouted for joy at the Simpson verdict, while Claire and the other white women stood by in stunned disbelief.

After a few stops a disheveled man with wild eyes stepped on to the bus. He lurched down the aisle and took a seat in the back. A few of the women instinctively pulled their purses closer to them as he passed. He wore a dingy green army-surplus jacket, boots with no laces, and an old-fashioned aviator's hat.

Claire remembered a quote from Goethe which had always stuck with her: "I must have an ideal to love, but also one to hate."

Yes, Claire thought, *that's true, but why?* Why was human nature so constructed that an enemy was equally important as an ally? Claire stared out the window at the elegant townhouses on Riverside Drive. She had no doubt that ethnic hatred was at the root of man's most virulent mass evil—whether whites against blacks, Nazis against Jews, or Serbs against Croatians. Was it for everyone as it was for Goethe; was the need for an enemy hardwired into our brains, as it were, like the need for sex or companionship? Was it possible for an individual to evolve beyond this need, to achieve an enlightenment of universal goodwill?

"Why can't I work at the post office? Why can't I give orders?" the crazy man was mumbling from the back of the bus. "I'll be a postal supervisor," he said in a tone so conversational that Claire wouldn't have known he was crazy if she hadn't seen his arrival. He was the only one on the bus talking, and a couple of people glanced at him, but looked away quickly when they saw who was speaking. Claire sighed. The avoidance instinct was well developed in her fellow New Yorkers—a matter of survival. The man caught her eye and smiled, and she smiled back.

Claire worked on Blanche's manuscript on the train, line editing, rearranging material, making notes in the margins. She would show it to Peter on Monday.

When Claire got off the train, Robert was waiting to meet

her. He wore a red-and-black-checked flannel shirt, jeans and work boots. Even in these clothes, he looked neater than Detective Jackson did in his rumpled suit and tie.

"Hello," he said, taking her bag. The sun fell on his hair, with its honey-colored highlights.

"How nice of you to come meet me."

"I wasn't sure if I'd be able to, but this morning's job finished early. Want to go have an early dinner?"

"Sure."

They climbed into his Rover and drove up Warren Street, past the jumble of architectural styles and into Hudson's main square.

"So what are you working on these days?" he said as they drove along.

"I'm almost done with Blanche's book."

"Which book?"

"You know, the Klan book—the one she was writing when she died."

"Oh. You mean, you're finishing it for her?"

"Yes. Peter asked me to, and I agreed."

"Awfully nice of you. I hope you'll be getting some of the royalties."

"Well, not exactly, but he did say that he'd 'make it worth my while.'"

Robert laughed. "Good old Peter, always the pragmatist."

They celebrated Thanksgiving with a quiet dinner at Antoine's, where Robert joked about "these American holidays where you all stuff yourselves comatose," then went to bed early. Claire still felt a little woozy from her tooth extraction, so she took it easy on Friday, spending the day editing Blanche's manuscript.

By Saturday she was feeling better. After a late breakfast, Claire puttered around the house for a while, then went out to the garden where Robert was working, his long back bent over a bed of bulbs.

"I think I'll go riding," she said.

He looked up, his face smudged with dirt. "All right. Mind you don't fall off."

He always said that. *Mind you don't fall off.* Claire

thought it was a little hostile, a faintly passive-aggressive comment that supposedly demonstrated concern for her safety but that really hid a desire to spoil her fun. Every rider falls sooner or later, and it can be frightening or no big deal, depending on the circumstances, but it is the one fear that sits with you every time you climb on the saddle. Will you fall this time, and if you do, how bad will it be? Riders make light of it, they joke about it; they tell stories of falls they've had, but even before Christopher Reeve every rider had heard stories of crippling accidents, and it is the specter of such bad falls that haunts every rider, from casual hackers to Grand-Prix jumpers.

Now, as she pulled on her jodhpurs and boots, Claire tried not to think of the possibility of injury but of the beckoning woods. She had grown up in the country, and living in the city, she yearned for the wind, the leaves, the smell of the woods, the thrill of it, being in the center of this world of bark and roots and rocks. She longed for the sound of rain on leaves, the whistling of wind through bullrushes, the caw of a crow on a black tree limb. Claire put on her old red-and-green wool jacket over a turtleneck shirt; the sun was out but the air was brisk outside.

Shady Acres Farm was in Garrison, right across the river from West Point, on a dirt road off Route 9. Claire had found out about the farm three years before when she saw a hand-written poster at the Half Moon Inn in Cold Spring Harbor. TRAIL RIDING—BEAUTIFUL SCENERY, GENTLE HORSES, it read, and there was a phone number scribbled at the bottom in red Magic Marker. When Claire called the number Lena Dougan answered. When Claire asked how long the rides were, Lena said, "How long do you want to go out for? Two hours, three—five?" Claire knew then this was the place for her.

An hour later she pulled up to the farm in Robert's "second car," a battered Ford pickup. There was no sign of people. The horses stood in the paddock, dozing with their heads down, and at the sound of her car they looked up with mild curiosity in their big soft eyes. Claire thought of them as five-year-old children who happened to weigh a thousand pounds. Lena raised mostly Morgans, a smart, sturdy, sure-footed breed developed in Vermont in the nineteenth century by John Morgan. All the horses had grown their winter coats, furry and thick, and the three ponies in the paddock looked like stuffed animals, fat and fuzzy. Claire got out of the car and walked over to the corral. Her favorite horse, a chestnut mare named Cora, stood on the other side of the paddock under a scrub oak.

"Cora," she said softly, "do you want a carrot?"

Cora trotted over to her, and so did all the other horses. Cora was the dominant mare, the alpha female at Shady Acres, and she picked on the other horses constantly, asserting her status. She frequently tried to bite or kick the other mares, especially when she knew people were watching. It was mostly show; she usually ended up just biting the air, but Lena said that the important thing was that Cora was demonstrating her willingness to take anybody on. None of the other mares challenged her; they were all afraid of her, and just backed away when she got it into her head to nip at them.

Just then Lena Dougan walked down from the house, carrying a halter and a bag of apples.

"Hello there," she called.

Lena Dougan was a tiny, fierce blond woman who treated her horses as if they were her children. She had been everywhere and done everything, much of it revolving around horses. She had been a circus rider in Sweden, a carriage driver in Belgium, and a trail guide in Ireland. She had studied dressage in Germany, ridden with the Lipizzaners in Austria, and performed in shows all over Europe. Now retired to her native Putnam County, she raised Morgans and gave lessons and trail rides. She knew horses the way Claire knew books, and there was no horse she couldn't train. Lena's Morgans were well trained, schooled in dressage and jumping, and very agreeable.

"Going out on the trail today?" Lena asked as she let herself into the paddock. She had just turned seventy, but her legs were tanned and trim as a teenager's.

"Yeah, I thought I might go down to Mystery Point."

The horses in the paddock went up to Lena and sniffed at the bag of apples. The younger horses followed her everywhere. If she was in the paddock setting up jumps, they would trail along after her like obedient dogs. Claire brushed Cora, cleaned her hooves, then put on a saddle and a bridle with a simple snaffle bit.

Claire mounted Cora and started off down Manitou Road. Lena had told her that "manitou" was an Indian word for a wood spirit, a sprite who lives among the rocks and trees and likes to cause trouble and play tricks on people. The woods were still and quiet today, but across the river Claire could hear the cadets at West Point taking target practice, the crack and pop of their rifles echoing thinly through the trees. During the Revolution, West Point had remained an American stronghold in spite of Benedict Arnold's attempt to deliver it to the British. *We hold these truths to be self-evident* . . . Was there such a thing as a self-evident truth? wondered Claire, or was everything our imposition of meaning over an essentially indifferent universe? Claire felt that her nature mysticism was at bottom deeply suspect, a product of wishful thinking, the most naive kind of personification. *Pathetic fallacy.* Well, it was most probably false, and pathetic as well, she supposed, wanting to feel a bond with a tree. You might as well feel a bond with a head of lettuce, or a carrot, before you fed it to your horse.

Still, as she rode down the long dirt road toward the Hudson, Claire marveled that an animal as beautiful and graceful as a horse would let her climb onto its back and ride it. On a horse, she felt like the Greek hero whose strength derived from the earth: she felt connected, rooted, a part of the greater plan of nature, whatever that might be. Claire patted Cora's neck, feeling the warmth of her smooth long muscles underneath the soft coat. She ran her hand through Cora's chestnut mane, picking out a briar her curry comb had missed.

A gust of wind picked up some dead leaves on the road and blew them in a little whirlwind in front of her. Again Schiller's poem came to her:

Wer reitet so spät durch Nacht und Wind?
Es ist der Vater mit seine Kind

The Erl King was Death, of course, but he was more than that. He was Fate, the apparitions you see at night in the darkness behind your own eyes; he was Loss and Grief and all of the things you can't escape because they're a part of life. You can pretend they're not there, like the father does as he rides through night, but his son knows better. The boy hears the crooning voice of the Erl King, soft in his ear, beckoning him to the darkness of sleep. And in the end, of course, the father's punishment for not listening to his son is losing him: the Erl King claims his own. Maybe the father's refusal to hear the voice of the Erl King is part of what saves him from the same fate as his son, she thought. Maybe the Erl King is also madness, that slipping into a darkness of the soul from which there is no return.

The *clip-clop* of Cora's hooves along the hard-packed dirt road lulled Claire deeper into her meditative state. A lone turkey vulture circled overhead, looking for carrion. Carried by air currents, wings outspread, the bird was her only company except for the tiny brown and white chipmunks who scampered and scurried among the dead logs at the edge of the woods.

And if the Erl King exists, Claire thought, does his opposite also exist, and what is it? Love, courage, compassion; what? With what resources do we fight the forces of darkness as they close in upon us? Illness, disease, death . . . do we just ride our horse faster and faster through the woods and hope that we elude for a time the gathering darkness? Or do we turn and face it, issuing a challenge full square in the face of disaster, like a gunfighter at high noon? The opponent we all go out to face in the sun-drenched dirt and dust of a lonely Western town isn't another gunslinger, she mused; it's Death, and sooner or later it will outdraw us all.

Reaching the bottom of Manitou Road, Claire crossed Route 9D and continued down to the river, past the historical sign marking the place where the American army stretched a chain across the Hudson to keep out British ships during the Revolution. When she was only a few hundred yards from the river, she turned right, passed through a gate, onto the straight dirt path that ran parallel to the railroad tracks. At the end of this path was the place the locals referred to as Mystery Point, a slip of land jutting out into the river.

The path was straight and about a mile long, perfect for a good long canter. Claire urged Cora into a sitting trot, and then a canter. The horse's hooves resounded against the hard ground, one two *three,* one two *three.* Cora liked to run, and never needed much urging; this was one of the reasons Claire enjoyed riding her. *One two three, one two three . . .*

> *Wer reitet so spät, durch Nacht und Wind?*

Well, we can keep riding, Claire thought, *and not look over our shoulder, and see only the road ahead. One two three, one two three . . .*

Claire could see the Hudson through the trees, the water grey and choppy in the gathering wind. She cantered parallel to the railroad tracks for half a mile or so, then stopped to let Cora rest and eat grass. She dismounted and sat on the ground next to the horse, listening to the soft crunching sound the mare made as she chewed. Claire thought of all of the people who had ridden through these same woods, patriots and Tories, engaged in the struggle out of which emerged a new nation . . . *under God, indivisible, with liberty and justice for all.*

A sudden gust of wind whipped across the water and through the trees, shaking their thin, naked branches. Claire shivered and pulled her wool coat closer around her.

> *Mein Vater, mein Vater, und hörest du nicht,*
> *was Erlenkönig mich leise verspricht?*

"Come on, Cora," she said, "it's time to go home." She mounted and turned the horse back toward the barn. Cora left her grazing reluctantly, pulling up one last mouthful of yellowing grass, chewing it as she walked.

Sei ruhig, bleibe ruhig, mein Kind;
In dürren Blättern säuselt der Wind.

Claire wasn't even aware a shot had been fired until the bullet grazed a tree next to her. Even Cora didn't respond immediately; she stood completely still, and then she jumped up in the air, all of her feet leaving the ground at the same time. Thrown forward, Claire instinctively wrapped her arms around the horse's neck, burying her face in Cora's mane. She closed her eyes, waiting for the second shot, but there was none. After her initial moment of panic, Cora stood still, trembling. She was waiting for Claire to tell her what to do, how to react.

The first thing Claire did was dismount. If there was another shot, Cora would be easier to control from the ground. Claire took the reins firmly in her hand and looked around in all directions. A blackbird rose suddenly from the branches of a white birch, disturbing the air with the loud flapping of its wings, but other than that the woods were completely silent. It was then Claire realized she had not heard the shot being fired. She looked at Cora, who had already forgotten her fear and was sniffing around the ground, looking for tidbits of grass among the dead leaves.

Claire knew that these woods were full of hunters, both legal and illegal. She knew that stray bullets could travel long distances, and that the hunter who had fired this shot could be far out of sight. Was it possible he could also be out of hearing range, though? She looked at the tree that the bullet had scraped—the bark was torn and frayed. She tried to calculate the angle and direction of the approach, and decided it had come more or less from behind her.

Claire patted Cora on the neck; the horse had found a small tuft of winter grass and was pulling up the green shoots, munching contentedly. Claire considered the options. It was possible that she had not heard the shot because the hunter was far away. But why, then, could she hear the sounds of target practice from West Point, all the way across the river? Her stomach filled with ice as it dawned on her: *she had not heard the shot because the shooter had used a silencer.* If that was the case, then she was definitely in danger.

Panic growing inside her, Claire mounted Cora. All she wanted was to get back to Lena's as quickly as possible.

"Come on, Cora, let's go," she said, putting the horse into a fast canter. Cora complied eagerly; like all horses, her gait was always brighter when she was headed toward the barn. As they rode over the dry leaves scattered on the ground up the hill toward Manitou Road, Claire wondered if she was being paranoid. Why would the murderer want to kill her? She didn't have any idea of who he or she was, so what possible threat could Claire be? Then she had a thought that frightened her even more: if the murderer was after her, he or she might go after Meredith.

Once she reached Manitou Road, Claire felt safer. She was fairly certain that whoever it was would not risk trying to shoot her on a public road. She slowed Cora down to a walk to cool her down, then trotted slowly up the long hill to Shady Acres.

When Claire returned to the farm, the ponies were gone from the paddock, and she found a note from Lena. *Gone to a pony party—hope you had a nice ride.* Part of Lena's income came from pony rides she gave at children's parties. Claire occasionally helped out at these parties; she enjoyed seeing the pleasure the children got from the horses.

By the time Claire had taken off Cora's tack, given her one last apple, and put her out in the pasture to graze, she had decided that she was being paranoid, and that the bullet was a stray from a hunter's rifle. Claire cleaned the saddle and put everything away, then climbed into the car and started the drive back to Hudson.

Chapter 26

The Federal Express truck sat in front of 465 Warren Street for less than three minutes. Andrew McNair had had a long day—it seemed like there were even more deliveries than usual on this Saturday—and his day was almost over when he handed the package to the man who came to the door and signed for it. He couldn't wait to get home to a nice cold six-pack of Budweiser and the football game. A couple of his chums were coming over to watch Cleveland play Dallas. If Andrew noticed anything, it was how polite and well spoken the man at number 465 was. That and perhaps the fact that there was a trace of an accent, although whether it was Southern or English Andrew couldn't say; he never had much of an ear for dialects. Andrew climbed back into his truck and pulled away. Only one more delivery and he was free! He hummed cheerfully as he put the truck in gear and pulled onto the street. After he had gone a few yards something prompted him to look back at the house he had just left. He turned and looked behind his shoulder, but was blinded by the glare of sunlight off the rear window. He shrugged, shifted into second gear, and thought of how good that first cold beer would taste.

· · · · ·

Detective Wallace Jackson didn't think much about the promotional offering from Apple Bank addressed to Amelia Moore, and he was about to toss it aside when he was struck by the return address; it had been sent from the branch on Fourteenth Street. Wondering why Amelia would open an account at a bank so far away from where she lived, he lifted the receiver and dialed the bank.

The bank was on Saturday hours and closed for the day when Consuela Rodriguez unlocked the front door to let in the grey-haired man in the frayed trench coat. He didn't look like a detective, but when he showed his badge Consuela unlocked the glass door and let him in. The manager was there, but Consuela had volunteered to stay late too because she was curious. She remembered the small, distracted woman with the delicate features, and now that the police were interested in her safe-deposit box, Consuela wanted to know why.

"I knew there was something strange about that woman when I first saw her," she would say later that night to her husband over *pernil con arroz y frijoles*. "Something was on her mind, I could tell. And that single piece of paper—*Dios*, who would put something like that in a safe-deposit box?"

But Consuela didn't learn anything more from the policeman than she already knew. When she gave him the deposit box, the detective with the tired eyes opened it (how did he get the key? she wondered), took out the single piece of paper, glanced at it, then put it in his pocket. Thanking her politely, he left without a word of explanation. Consuela was dying to ask him what was on that paper that was so important. Disappointed, she watched him walk off into the night, his breath steaming white in the frosty November air.

Meredith Lawrence sat on Claire's bed playing with Ralph. She was back in New York, having escaped Hartford at the earliest possible moment. She knew it was wrong; she knew that she was a bad daughter, but she couldn't stand being around her father while he worried about the whereabouts of her horrible stepmother. Seeing him like this was too hard for her; it brought back memories of her mother's death which she just couldn't face right now. So she took the train to New York and let herself into Claire's apartment, where she planned to live on pizza and cookies until Claire returned from Hudson.

Now she was trying to befriend Ralph, her only company. The cat lay on his back, his tail flicking over Meredith's outstretched fingers. Suddenly he decided he had had enough and abruptly rolled away. Meredith sprang to grab him before he leaped off the bed; just missing him, her right hand struck the play button of the answering machine, which sat on the bedside table. The tape started up and began to play all the old messages. Meredith reached over to turn it off, but then she paused. She would not be able to say exactly why later, but she decided to listen to the backlog of old messages. Then she turned the tape over and listened to the ones on the other side. She sat on the corner of the bed, her eyes fixed on the carpet, elbows wrapped around her knees. Ralph, who had gone as far as the closet door, sat in front of it licking his fur.

There were a lot of messages on the tape, some of which Meredith had heard before, and then, toward the end of the tape, she heard an unfamiliar voice:

". . . but when I saw the photograph, Claire, I just had to call and tell you." Meredith had never met Blanche, but she was certain this was her voice. It was similar to Sarah's, but more feminine, more drippingly Southern. "I'm afraid, Claire," the voice went on, "afraid for you and for me. I never thought he'd show up again, after all these years, but we're both in danger now! Please call me as soon as you get this ... ." and then Meredith heard something that made her hold her breath. Moments later Ralph was sitting alone in the apartment, flicking his tail irritably at having been left alone so abruptly.

When Wallace Jackson arrived back at his building, Meredith was pacing back and forth in the lobby. When he entered she practically threw herself at him.

"We've got him!" she cried. "But we'll have to hurry!"

• • •

In Hudson, the wind began to blow the bare trees outside as Claire watched from Robert's parlor. All during dinner she had the impulse to mention the incident with the gunshot to Robert, but something had held her back—the fear of appearing foolish, probably—and she had decided that it was in all likelihood a stray bullet from a hunter's gun after all.

Robert had gone into his darkroom shortly after dinner, saying he had some developing to do, and as Claire stood looking out the window she noticed that the vision in her left eye had begun to blur. She had experienced this before; it inevitably signaled the beginning of a migraine. After about twenty minutes of blurred vision, the migraine began—a reaction to the Valium she had the day before, perhaps. Her eyes felt feverish, her shoulders ached, and her right temple throbbed gently. Her migraines were seldom severe, and there was a kind of euphoria that often accompanied the headache. It was as though the same nerves which caused the pain also caused an elevated mood, a delicate feeling of strange and fragile joy which Claire experienced only during migraines. For that reason—and also because they did not come often—she didn't dread the headaches. She wouldn't want one when she had anything very important to do, but the arrival of one tonight released her from the obligation to work.

Claire climbed the stairs and went into the back bedroom, which was quiet, protected as it was from the noises of the street. She stretched out on the bed, pulled a blanket over her legs, and put on a tape of Carl Orff's *Carmina Burana*. She listened to the opening chorus with her eyes closed, the murky harmonies perfectly matched to the Latin text, creating the mysterious sensuality of religious fervor in the Middle Ages. As she listened Claire imagined parades of brown-hooded monks, their torches held high in the blackness, the sound of their shuffling feet accompanying the low chanting voices. Lying on the quilted coverlet, she felt fatigue, gentle but insistent, pushing her down, down into a thick sleep.

•   •   •

Robert worked for about an hour, then he went to the parlor and put on a recording of Verdi's *Otello*. He lay on the couch and listened with his eyes closed, following the sweep of the melodic line and the accompanying harmonies as Desdemona and Otello, pushed onward by Iago, rush toward their doom. Anyone looking at him on the couch would have thought he was asleep.

The desk sergeant on duty in Hudson that Saturday was Sergeant Joseph Ferraro. He had just come back from his dinner break when the detective from New York City called and asked him to put a couple of cruisers out on Warren Street. He replied that since it was Saturday night there were already a couple of cars out driving around.

"How much backup do you need?" he said.

"Whatever you can spare."

"What are we lookin' for?"

There was a pause and he thought he heard a child's voice in the background at the other end of the phone line. The detective came back on the line.

"Do you have a James White listed in the Hudson directory?"

Ferraro pulled out the dog-eared copy of the Hudson phone book and looked up the name.

"Nope," he said. "There's a Ned and a William, but no James."

"It's probably an alias anyway."

"He lives in Hudson, you say?"

"Yes. We don't have an address, but we think it's—" He turned away from the receiver and Sergeant Ferraro heard him speaking to the child. "It's a green house," he said into the phone, "somewhere on Warren Street."

"Do you have any idea how *long* Warren Street *is*?" said Sergeant Ferraro, drawing his words out.

"I'm sorry—I have to go catch my train. Just put whoever you can out there and tell them to look for anything suspicious."

Sergeant Ferraro hung up and took a sip of coffee. Anything suspicious . . . as far as he was concerned, that could describe half the population of Hudson.

The Amtrak Lakeshore Line glides along the Hudson River most of the way to Albany, and the view is so spectacular that the passengers often just sit and stare out of the window. On this particular train, however, there were two passengers who did not stare out of the window but sat, heads close together, whispering. They were an odd couple: an ungainly redheaded girl and a shaggy-haired man with tired eyes.

The conductor passing through the train took their ticket stubs out of the overhead metal clips and announced, "Next stop Hudson. Hudson next stop."

The murderer looked at the clock in the kitchen. The time was ten twenty-five.

Put out the light, then put out the light.

He smiled sardonically at the lines which came to him now, so appropriate, so fitting for the occasion. He had considered other methods but had finally chosen this one. She would never have to feel a thing—not much, anyway. It was all for the best. He ascended the polished staircase, treading softly on the slippery oak steps.

Upstairs, Claire stirred in her sleep and moaned softly.

Star Taxi, across from the Hudson train station, turns off its green and red neon sign at ten-thirty sharp most nights. Tonight John Meadows had a sick child at home, so he turned the sign off at ten-twenty, turned on the answering machine, and left. He noticed the police cruiser driving slowly along Warren Street, but didn't think too much about it. The cops liked to make their presence known, especially on a Saturday night, to keep everyone on their best behavior. As John started up his '94 Chrysler the cop car made a U-turn and headed in the other direction, away from the train station and toward the center of town.

Anyone watching the ten thirty-five Amtrak coach pulling into the Hudson station would have seen a curious sight. Before the train came to a full stop, two passengers jumped out and raced up the hill that led to Warren Street. The girl, long and thin, ran with uneven, loping strides, while the man ran with quick, short steps, his trench coat flapping out behind him like a grey sail.

Upstairs, the murderer paused to look at his victim. She lay on her back, mouth slightly open, breathing hoarsely. He had an impulse to touch her hair.

Being done, there is no pause.

Slowly, so as not to awaken her, he closed his hands around her neck.

Outside on the street in front of the line of row houses, Meredith's eyes searched the buildings frantically.

"I've only been there once," she muttered. "I don't know why Claire has to take her address book with her everywhere she goes!" She suddenly stopped and pointed. "That's it—there, number 465!"

Wallace Jackson was not an especially athletic man, and the sprint up the hill from the train station had severely taxed his lungs.

"Stay out here!" he called over his shoulder to Meredith, then, gasping to catch his breath, he pulled out his revolver and flung himself at the green painted door of 465 Warren Street. To his surprise, the door was not locked, and he went tumbling down onto the Persian-carpeted floor of the foyer.

Upstairs the murderer heard the crash of a body landing in the front hallway. He let go of his victim's neck, grabbed the sharpened bronze-and-copper letter opener from the writing desk, and sprang out of the bedroom onto the upstairs landing.

Detective Jackson picked himself up off the floor and saw the tall figure at the top of the stairs. The light was behind him and Jackson could not see his face.

"James White," he said, "I arrest you for the murder of Blanche DuBois and Ame—"

At that moment the tall figure stepped forward, so that Jackson could see the face, which made him stop midsentence. Never in all his years of police work had Jackson seen such a concentrated mask of pure evil. The lips were curled into a grimace of fury and hate. The deep-set eyes locked with his.

"Ha!" said the murderer in a raspy voice. "That's very amusing, it really is. Come and get me, why don't you?"

Jackson started up the stairs but hesitated, realizing the man on the landing had the upper hand. He drew his gun and held it aimed at the man's chest.

"You have the right to remain silent," he said, trying to keep his voice steady. "You have the—"

But the man was laughing at him.

"Oh, I'm so frightened!"

Suddenly Meredith pushed her way in front of Jackson and screamed, *"What have you done with Claire?"*

At that moment, Claire appeared on the landing, disoriented and gasping for air.

"What's going on—" she began, but before she could finish, the murderer grabbed her and pressed her body to his, keeping her between Jackson and himself, holding the sharpened letter opener to her throat.

"She's right here, you stupid little brat." He laughed. "What's the matter, Detective? Why don't you go ahead and shoot me for resisting arrest?"

Jackson took a step back.

"Just take it easy and no one will get hurt," he said, immediately realizing the foolishness of his words.

"Oh, but you don't know me very well, do you, Detective?" His proper English accent had turned into a southern snarl. "You're missing the whole point. I don't think *enough* people have been hurt, actually, and I would really like to hurt some more before I go. See, I don't mind going at all, but I'd like to take some people with me when I do. Don't you think that's reasonable, sweetheart?" he said to Claire, who was crying silently now.

"You see, Detective, I'm not much for confined spaces, and now that the jig is up, as they say, I'd rather just throw in the towel, so why don't you just go ahead and shoot? You know, you could always say that she just ran in the way of the bullet at the last moment. I think that's a fair offer, don't you?"

"Now, just take it easy. If you give yourself up now, we can work something out," Jackson said.

"Oh, you *are* stupid, aren't you—but then, I already knew that. I mean, to have fallen for my little ruse with the planted syringe—that was just for fun, for God's sake, a little joke! But you actually *believed* it and arrested that poor excuse for an editor! Of course, I did use his syringe originally, and I wasn't going to plant it at all, but you were having such a hard time I thought I'd give you something to go on. Good Lord, it was hardly a challenge, deceiving you—though I must admit I did have fun with the subway caper!"

"So you did murder Amelia Moore," Jackson said, his voice steady.

"Let's just say I assisted her with a well-timed shove, and the train did the rest. She was a talker, that woman. I found that out at the Duke class reunion; I found out a lot of other interesting things, too, by the way—like what our friend Blanche was up to. Too bad she was such a busybody. I don't know how she found those photographs; my old friend Jeff assured me the negatives had been destroyed, but I guess he lied to me. I should have taken him out, too." He laughed and tightened his grip on Claire. "I should have taken you out in the woods, too; I gave up after one shot because I was afraid someone would see me.

"Your friend Blanche was stupid, though. If she had called the police instead of you that night she saw my picture at the party, she might still be alive. She was right about one thing, though: I did kill that nigger she was dating at UNC."

He ran the sharp edge of the letter opener lightly over Claire's throat. "Didn't you wonder just a little bit why things moved so fast between us, sweetheart? Not that you aren't fascinating, of course, but did it never occur to you that I was a little *too* interested in your line of work?"

"So you were just using me to get to Blanche," Claire said.

"Well, her address and number were unlisted; I had to get them somehow. And you have to admit, you kept me well posted on her career. I couldn't very well allow her to finish that book, could I? You know, it's funny; I thought that killing white people would feel different than killing niggers, but it really isn't any different."

Jackson took a step forward.

James White tightened his grip on Claire. "One more step and she goes over the railing."

Jackson looked up at Claire, who was white-faced, her eyes closed. He took a step backward and glanced behind him for Meredith, but she was gone. Maybe she had run into the street to flag down the backup cars that were patrolling the street, though Jackson wasn't sure what use they would be right now.

Actually, Meredith had left the house, but not to find the police. Closing the front door softly behind her, she ran down the side alley to the back garden, let herself in through the gate, and then in through the kitchen door, which was unlocked. She crept through the kitchen, and saw the perfectly sharpened knives in their rack. Her hand trembling, she removed one—a long, thin, carving knife—from its wooden slot, then she crept up the back staircase. She wasn't sure what she was going to do when she reached the top, but she had to try something. She tiptoed through the back bedroom and into the hallway, stopping when she caught sight of Claire and her captor.

"Go ahead, Detective—shoot. What are you waiting for?" he was saying, and did not hear Meredith as she crawled up to the door separating the bedroom from the hall. A long thin green carpet ran the length of the hall, and Meredith saw that one of his feet was on the runner, the other on the wood floor.

Claire whimpered a little as he tightened his grip around her neck. "Do you know, I was getting a little tired of this already? Well, Detective, what shall it be? What are you going to do? Do I have to make *all* the decisions around here?"

Meredith reached for the carpet. She took a deep breath, swallowed, then pulled it as hard as she could. Caught off guard, James White staggered as the foot on the carpet was pulled out from under him. Claire screamed and pulled away, and his grip on her was momentarily loosened. He recovered, though, and grabbed her again, and it was at that moment that Meredith leaped forward and plunged the carving knife into his leg. He screamed and instinctively reached for his leg, this time allowing Claire to break free.

"Run, Claire—*run!*" Meredith yelled as the murderer wheeled and saw her. He started to reach for her, and the look on his face was so horrible that Meredith screamed, so loud that the sound filled her own head completely and she did not hear the gunshot. The murderer's hand holding the letter opener shot out toward her, then suddenly jerked and twitched. His eyes widened in surprise. The look of hate that had twisted his features was suddenly transformed into one of astonishment, and he turned awkwardly back toward Jackson. It was then that Meredith saw the tiny trickle of blood that seeped from his chest just above his heart. Moving in slow motion, he grasped the banister and took one unsure step down the stairs, ignoring Claire, who had collapsed weeping in the corner. He opened his mouth as if to say something, then his legs gave way and he fell, tumbling down the stairs as if he were a rag doll, arms and legs banging against the steps all the way. When he reached the bottom he lay still, facedown. It was then that Meredith realized she was still screaming, and had been screaming nonstop since the moment when she pulled the rug. She quieted abruptly, and the sudden silence was startling.

Jackson approached the inert form warily, holding his gun with both hands out in front of him, pointing it at the man's head. Claire picked herself up slowly, shakily, using the wall for support. Slowly she began to walk down the stairs, her legs trembling with every step. Meredith followed, her throat dry and sore from screaming.

"Is he . . . ?" she said in a voice so soft that it was barely a whisper.

Jackson rolled the body over with his foot, and as soon as Meredith saw the upturned face with its open staring eyes, she knew. Meredith had never seen death before, and she realized at that moment that at some point she had lost control of her bladder.

Chapter 27

T he media circus that followed the resolution of the case centered around Meredith and Claire, and while Claire quietly yearned for it to be over, the girl enjoyed the whole thing enormously. She returned reporters' phone calls, gave interviews, and even appeared on the popular PBS children's program *Where in the World Is Carmen Sandiego?* When her father came into town to take her back to Connecticut for the Christmas holidays, she presented him with a pile of newspaper clippings.

"Of course, it was my idea for Detective Jackson to go through Amelia's mail," she said, swinging her legs under her stool as she and Claire sat with her father at the counter at Rumplemeyer's. "But when he finally came across the entry from Blanche's diary, I had already solved it."

"What was in the diary?" said Ted Lawrence.

"It said, 'He has returned—he is here to get me, if he doesn't get Claire first,'" said Meredith. "Detective Jackson showed it to me."

"So then what did you find on the answering machine?" said Ted Lawrence, stirring his pot of chocolate.

"Oh, there was a message from Blanche to Claire. The night of Amelia's party Claire showed her a picture of

Robert, and she recognized him as James White, her old boyfriend from college, the one she had always suspected of murdering Cliff, her black boyfriend—the one she threw James over for."

Ted Lawrence nodded. "I see. So Blanche tried to warn Claire that night."

"Right. She left a message saying that she was sure Robert and James were the same person, and that Claire should call her immediately."

Ted Lawrence turned to Claire. "But why didn't you ever hear the message?"

"Meredith asked me the same thing. I went over all of my actions the weekend Blanche was killed, and I finally remembered coming back from a walk and finding Ralph playing with the answering machine. The tape was lying on the floor; I must have put the tape in on the wrong side, because Meredith told me that she turned the tape over to hear Blanche's message."

The same two well-dressed old ladies who had eavesdropped on the earlier conversation at Rumplemeyer's sat at the other end of the fountain counter, resplendent in their flowered hats and white gloves. When they heard the word "killed" there was a noticeable upward adjustment in their posture. "So Robert—James—was just pretending to be English all that time?"

"Yup," said Meredith. "It was part of his cover. It's not that much of a stretch from upper-class Virginian to British."

"Did you ever find out who was calling you and hanging up?" Ted Lawrence asked.

Meredith licked whipped cream from her spoon. "I'm pretty sure it was Robert—I mean James White—checking up on Claire. I think he heard Blanche's message to Claire the night of the party, and that was how he knew he had to act quickly."

"How could he have heard it?"

Meredith turned to Claire. "You said you went out Saturday morning, right?"

"Right—and when I returned I found the cat playing with the tape on the floor."

"Right. Well, I think Robert called in from Hudson, picked up the message for you from Blanche, and that's when he decided to kill her."

The two ladies at the end of the counter stopped stirring their chocolate and leaned toward Meredith.

"But how . . . ?" said Claire.

"It's easy enough. I saw you pick up your messages from Hudson: you just call your machine and then press the '2' key on a Touch-Tone phone. Anyone could do it."

"But how did Robert know?"

"Oh, come on, Claire," Meredith said scornfully. "All he had to do was look over your shoulder once when you were checking your messages to see what key you pressed—child's play for someone like him."

"Hmm . . . I see what you mean." Claire shuddered at the thought of Robert having access to all her phone messages.

"Well, it's over now," said Ted Lawrence sympathetically. "You can go on with your life."

The ladies at the end of the counter relaxed visibly at these words, their faces expressing both disappointment and satisfaction.

If Meredith was basking in the publicity surrounding her triumph, Claire was blaming herself for Blanche and Amelia's deaths. She felt that if she had been able to see Robert for who he was, the entire tragedy would have been avoided.

"But it wasn't you, don't you see that?" said Sarah one day over a glass of Merlot. "He would have found another way in sooner or later, and maybe even more people would have died."

Claire shook her head. She appreciated Sarah's kindness—she had grown fond of Blanche's sister during the events of the past few months—but she still felt responsibility lie heavily on her shoulders. If she had only *seen* him for who he was, she might have discovered clues that could have prevented everything. The idea haunted her days and nights, until she had to talk to someone about it. When she came to this conclusion, only one person came to mind: Wallace Jackson.

It was a rainy Tuesday in December when they met, at the

same Indian restaurant where she had first stumbled upon him by accident so many weeks earlier. The garden was closed now, so they met in the main dining room, sitting within view of the rapacious devourer of goldfish, who ignored them, swimming around slowly in his tank. Claire thought that he was sinister looking, even if you weren't a goldfish.

Wallace Jackson arrived looking rumpled as usual, but she noticed that the missing button on his trench coat had been replaced. The sight of it caused a wave of disappointment to pass over her: could it be there was a woman in his life now, and if so, was it serious? Or had he finally sewn the button on himself, prompted by the glare of the publicity spotlight which had suddenly been focused on the Ninth Precinct? Jackson was a hero to some people, but he had shot a suspect, and although it was actually the fall and not the shot that had killed James White, there was a routine departmental investigation of the shooting. (Peter had been cheered up to no end by this; after his close encounter with the justice system, he dined out for weeks on the story of his arrest.)

Jackson settled into his chair with the same air of weary intelligence which had so impressed Claire on their first meeting.

"How have you been?" he said in a way that made her feel he was really interested in the answer.

"Oh, pretty good," she answered, wanting to avoid coming to the point. Now that she was actually face-to-face with him, she felt her personal anguish was silly. The murderer had been caught; it was all over, so why couldn't she just let it go?

"Where's Meredith?" he said.

"Oh, she's in Connecticut for the holidays."

"That's too bad. I mean, you must miss her."

"Yes, I do. I—" she began, and then stopped. *I what? I want you to say something to me to make me feel better, give me a reason not to hate myself over this whole thing.*

"Does she take full credit for the discovery of the murderer's identity, or does she share it with me?" he said.

"Oh, you mean the diary? Well, she likes to point out that you found it, but it was her idea that you go through Amelia's mail."

"True enough. And of course she found the message from Blanche on your machine."

Claire picked at her vegetable samosa. "Right."

"Oh, by the way, did her stepmother ever turn up after her disappearance?" he said.

"Yes, she did—the next day, actually. She had checked into a detox center and was too embarrassed to call her husband and tell him."

Jackson smiled and his hands twisted the pink linen napkin in his lap.

"Oh, well . . . maybe that will improve Meredith's home life."

"I hope so," she said, and wondered why the thought gave her so little comfort. Perhaps it was because she wanted Meredith for herself, and she wasn't sure what was going to happen after the holidays were over.

"How is Sergeant Barker?" she said, searching for something, anything, other than what was on her mind.

Jackson smiled.

"Oh, he's fine. He landed a role in a student film, playing a gangster, of all things."

"I would never buy him as a gangster."

"Me neither—but, then, you never know . . ."

There was a pause and Claire heard the rain dripping slowly from the roof onto the street outside as cars whooshed by on First Avenue.

"Do you think . . ." she began.

"What?"

"Do you think he would have tried to kill me if I hadn't discovered the photographs?"

Jackson shook his head.

"I don't know. I think they represented the main threat to him—unless the book itself revealed information which pointed to him."

"It's so odd that he escaped being charged with the murder of those marchers. I mean, other people were charged."

"It's not that odd, really. From what I read about the incident there was a lot of confusion that day. I can see how one of the shooters could have slipped away in the commotion. He was just unlucky that someone caught him on film."

Claire shook her head.

"I'll never know how Blanche tracked down those photographs."

"Well, she was a woman with a mission. When she discovered that the man she thought had murdered Cliff had probably also killed others, she must have seen her chance to bring him to justice."

"Yeah, and she did in a way, but the cost was . . ." Claire trailed off. She looked at the giant silver fish in its tank, swimming back and forth, back and forth. The little clump of goldfish hovered in the far corner of the tank, trapped in their glass prison until their jailer got hungry.

"You know, it can take a while to get over something like this," Jackson said. "How are you doing with all of that?"

"Oh, all right, I guess . . ."

He looked at her, all the weariness drained from his eyes. "You don't look all right."

"What do you mean?"

He coughed delicately and twisted his napkin.

"Excuse me if I'm prying, but I've seen this before, you know. I've been through it myself, so I guess you might say I'm an expert on it."

It. Did it have a name, this obsessive replaying of the past, this refusal to accept the outcome of events, the incessant nagging desire to turn back the clock?

"There was nothing you could have done, you know," he said simply. It was neither an excuse nor an explanation: it was just a statement of facts.

"But I keep thinking—"

"Don't," he said. "Don't keep thinking; it will only hurt you. What you have to do is stop thinking and just go on—move on with your life."

"But I can't help wondering . . ."

"Wondering what you could have done—should have done—differently? Stop wondering. The chances are that you couldn't have done anything, but even if you could have, you have to stop thinking about it or it will poison your mind."

Claire smiled ironically. *Poison.* From beginning to end, she and her friends had been poisoned.

"Like I said," Jackson continued, "you're going to have to stop thinking about it sooner or later, so why not stop now? You can't spend the rest of your life wondering what you could have done. You just have to *let it go.*"

The fervor in his tone made her look at him, and she saw his grey eyes, so full of need, so full of feelings she couldn't even begin to identify. She felt at that moment how thin the line between compassion and desire, and she was flooded with both.

"What did you do?" she said softly, not wishing to open old wounds, but needing the answer.

He studied the prongs of his fork for a moment, his long fingers tracing the lines of smooth metal, then he spoke.

"I did what I'm asking you not to do. I tormented myself with the idea that it was my fault, and that if I had only done the right thing, made the right moves, known the right spell, I might have cheated fate." He looked at her again, the same intensity in his eyes. "Don't you see?" he said. "That's *magical thinking.* It's like the belief in religious ritual; it's a belief in magic, nothing more. It's a desire to be able to control things that we actually have no control over. It has nothing to do with reality."

He leaned back in his chair and ran his hand through his shaggy grey hair.

"You see, it took me a long time to figure this all out, and I'm trying to save you the trouble." He smiled. "I suppose it sounds ridiculous to you. Maybe there's only one way to learn lessons like this—the hard way, as they say." He leaned forward again, his hands spread out on the white tablecloth. "It's just that if they are hurt too much, people can lose their grip on reality, or become bitter and angry, and I don't want to see that happen to you."

I don't want to see that happen to you. Claire played his last statement over in her mind, trying to figure out if there was any significance in it. Was it her in particular, or would he feel that way about anyone? He spoke again before she had the answer.

"You can't imagine all the scenarios I played out after Anne's death," he said softly. "I wondered what would have happened if I had been in the car with her that day, or if I had gone to the bank instead of her. Then I wondered if the boy who killed her had been stalking her, and if so, how I could have stopped it. None of this did any good, of course, but thinking about it became a compulsion for me, something I couldn't control—or thought I couldn't. It also became a way of torturing myself over what had happened. I actually think I maintained a sense of control over the situation by inflicting this mental torture on myself—at least I was the one inflicting the pain."

He stopped and looked at her. "Does this make any sense to you?"

"Yes," she said, "yes, it does. I'll try to do what you say, although you may be right that the only way to learn this lesson is the hard way. I mean, I hope that's not true, but I have my suspicions . . ."

They both looked at the untouched food in front of them, then they laughed.

"Well, that was quite an appetite stimulator," Jackson said.

Claire could not say that her desire for him had taken away her desire for food.

A short while later, as they stood outside the restaurant, holding their leftovers in plastic doggie bags, Claire said, "Which way are you headed?"

"I live just a few blocks away . . ."

Claire looked down at her shoes, holding her breath. Jackson cleared his throat.

"It's funny," he said, "people complain that most cops don't live in the city, and actually, they're right. A lot don't—except me, I guess . . ."

There was a pause, and then he said the words.

"Do you want to come up for coffee?"

"Yes," she said, trying to control the dry swelling suddenly attacking her throat, "that would be nice."

It was nice—very nice. His long hands were as gentle as his weary voice, and he was in no hurry. Claire relaxed into the rhythm that the two of them created, and she enjoyed his pleasure even more than her own. Afterward, they lay on his bed looking out the window at the trees behind his apartment. The branches swayed in the wind, thin dark strips silhouetted against the fading light.

"You know," she said, her hand resting on his chest, feeling the slow movement of his breath, "I just had a thought that made me feel very guilty."

"Oh? What's that?"

"If this all hadn't happened, I never would have met you."

There was a pause, and then he said, "That's probably true, but you don't know for certain." He rolled over on to his side and leaned up on one elbow. "See, that's what I was trying to say before. You can never know for sure, so there's no point in wondering, really."

"Right, I know. You're right, of course. Still . . ."

Claire looked out the window, the light almost gone now, and thought of Ralph, alone in the darkening apartment, lonely and hungry, waiting for her.

"Do you like cats?" she said, and then laughed at the ridiculousness of the question.

< A FELICITY GROVE MYSTERY > THE

DEAD PAST

Tom Piccirilli

Welcome to Felicity Grove...

This upstate New York village is as small as it is peaceful. But somehow Jonathan Kendrick's eccentric grandma, Anna, always manages
to find trouble. Crime, scandal, you name it...this wheelchair-bound
senior citizen is involved. So when the phone rings at 4 A.M. in
Jonathan's New York City apartment, he knows to expect some kind
of dilemma. But Anna's outdone herself this time. She's stumbled
across a dead body...in her trash can.

BERKLEY
PRIME
CRIME

❏ 0-425-16696-1/$5.99

Elizabeth Daniels Squire

Peaches Dann is "memorable!"
—Sharyn McCrumb

Is There a Dead Man in the House?

Peaches's father and his new wife, Azalea Marlowe, were in Tennessee to oversee the renovation of Azalea's family home. Peaches finds the excavation process fascinating—almost like watching the house's memory come to life.

But some of the house's memories are less than pleasant, as proven by the discovery of century-old buried bones...and Azalea's fall from a broken ladder hints that violence may visit this house again...

___ 0-425-16142-0/$5.99

Whose Death Is It, Anyway?

While promoting her book, *How to Survive Without a Memory*, a family secret comes to light: Peaches learns that her cousin's daughter Kim is missing—and presumed dead. And if there's any hope for a future family reunion, it's up to Peaches to provide it...

___ 0-425-15627-3/$5.99

Memory Can Be Murder

___ 0-425-14772-X/$5.99

BERKLEY
PRIME
CRIME

Prices slightly higher in Canada

Payable in U.S. funds only. No cash/COD accepted. Postage & handling: U.S./CAN. $2.75 for one book, $1.00 for each additional, not to exceed $6.75; Int'l $5.00 for one book, $1.00 each additional. We accept Visa, Amex, MC ($10.00 min.), checks ($15.00 fee for returned checks) and money orders. Call 800-788-6262 or 201-933-9292, fax 201-896-8569; refer to ad # 845 (8/99)

Penguin Putnam Inc.
P.O. Box 12289, Dept. B
Newark, NJ 07101-5289
Please allow 4-6 weeks for delivery.
Foreign and Canadian delivery 6-8 weeks.

Bill my: ❑ Visa ❑ MasterCard ❑ Amex _____ (expires)

Card# _____

Signature _____

Bill to:

Name _____

Address _____ City _____

State/ZIP _____ Daytime Phone # _____

Ship to:

Name _____ Book Total $ _____

Address _____ Applicable Sales Tax $ _____

City _____ Postage & Handling $ _____

State/ZIP _____ Total Amount Due $ _____

This offer subject to change without notice.

<u>Jane Waterhouse</u>

"Waterhouse has written an unusual story with plenty of plot twists. Garner Quinn is a memorable creation and the book's psychological suspense is entirely successful."

—*Chicago Tribune*

<u>GRAVEN IMAGES</u>

A murder victim is discovered, piece by piece, in the lifelike sculptures of a celebrated artist. True crime author Garner Quinn thinks she knows the killer. But the truth is stranger than fiction—when art imitates life...and death.

___0-425-15673-7/$5.99

A Choice of the Literary Guild®
A Choice of the Doubleday Book Club®
A Choice of the Mystery Guild®

PENGUIN PUTNAM INC.
Online

Your Internet gateway to a virtual environment with
hundreds of entertaining and enlightening books from
Penguin Putnam Inc.

*While you're there, get the latest buzz on
the best authors and books around—*

Tom Clancy, Patricia Cornwell, W.E.B. Griffin,
Nora Roberts, William Gibson, Robin Cook,
Brian Jacques, Catherine Coulter, Stephen King,
Jacquelyn Mitchard, and many more!

**Penguin Putnam Online is located at
http://www.penguinputnam.com**

PENGUIN PUTNAM NEWS

Every month you'll get an inside look at our upcoming
books and new features on our site. This is an ongoing
effort to provide you with the most up-to-date
information about our books and authors.

**Subscribe to Penguin Putnam News at
http://www.penguinputnam.com/ClubPPI**